D1483246

The
Web
of Fire

Also by Steve Voake:

The Dreamwalker's Child

Praise for *The Dreamwalker's Child*:

'Ingenious premise, relentless pace and a sprinkling of thought-provoking philosophy – I loved it.'
Herbie Brennan

'This elegant, intelligent book has a good sprinkling of wisdom – about what you miss, for instance, if you don't look carefully at your environment . . . It is Sam's friendship with Skipper that makes this not just an ordinary action adventure but a tale to remember.' *Sunday Times*

'Steve Voake's debut, *The Dreamwalker's Child*, is an ingenious and fast-paced thriller . . . his book buzzes and hums with ideas.' *The Times*

'It's a brisk, adventure-filled quest, complete with a gung-ho girl companion named Skipper and hordes of grisly adversaries.' *Observer*

STEVE VOAKE

The Web of Fire

ff

faber and faber

First published in 2006
by Faber and Faber Limited
3 Queen Square London WC1N 3AU

Typeset by Faber and Faber Limited
Printed in England by Mackays of Chatham plc, Chatham, Kent

All rights reserved
© Steve Voake, 2006
Illustrations © The Maltings Partnership, 2006
Chapter headings and map © Mark Watkinson, 2005

The right of Steve Voake to be identified as author of this work has
been asserted in accordance with Section 77 of the Copyright,
Designs and Patents Act 1988

A CIP record for this book
is available from the British Library

ISBN 0–571–22348–6 (HARDBACK)
ISBN 0–571–22945–X (PAPERBACK)

2 4 6 8 10 9 7 5 3 1

For my mother and father

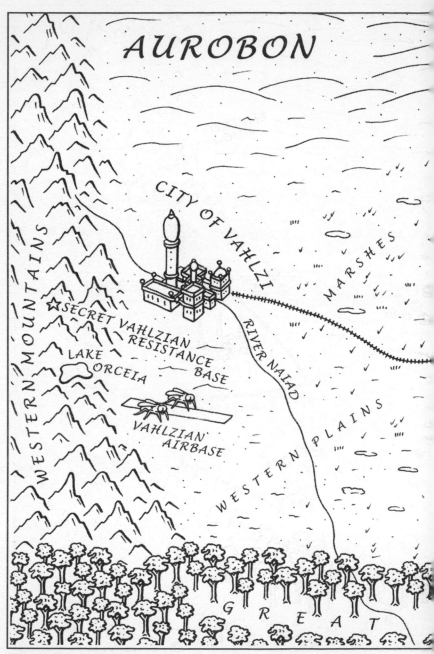

Vahlzi: A city situated west of the Great Plains of Aurobon, occupied by Vermian forces. Resistance led by General Firebrand.

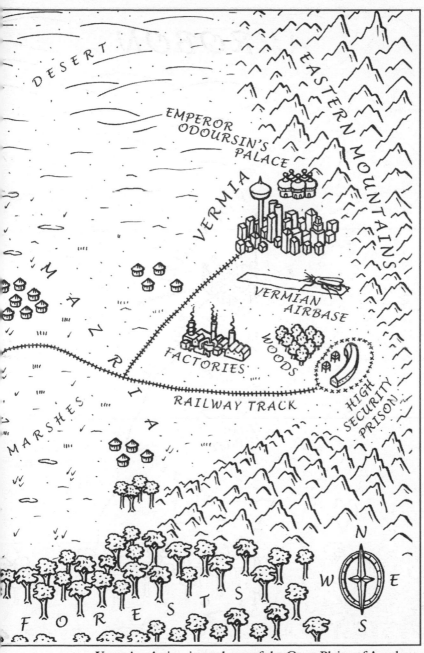

Vermia: A city situated east of the Great Plains of Aurobon,
ruled by the Emperor Odoursin.

Prologue

Prologue

The huge black fly swooped low over the mountain ridge and Commander Firebrand just had time to throw himself behind a rock before the hideous insect swept past his hiding place with a loud buzz, the wind from its wings stirring up a flurry of ice and snow in its wake.

Watching it disappear into the shadows, Firebrand shivered and knew that it wouldn't be long before they found him.

In the distance, a pall of thick black smoke hung above the city of Vahlzi and he could see the orange glow of fires raging through its streets and suburbs. The dark shapes of gigantic insects swarmed through the night sky and the thick, irregular pulse of explosions shook the ground beneath his feet.

Firebrand shut his eyes and steadied himself against a rock for a few seconds. Then, as if to place a physical barrier between himself and the horrors he had so recently witnessed, he walked the last few steps up the mountain, crossed the ridge and disappeared from view.

Later that night, as he stood before the lake that lay in the hollow palm of the mountain, he looked across its sullen, stone-black surface and heard the whisper of secrets that were hidden like pearls in its fathomless depths.

Looking up at the stars, Firebrand realised that the chill he felt inside was not only from the cold night air. It was a deeper, all-pervading chill; a dead, lifeless despair born of the knowledge that the years of hope and freedom had passed away for ever. He thought of Sam and Skipper – his beloved Skipper – and of all the other good people who had been lost in the fight. And for what?

Firebrand opened his fingers and felt the weight of the blue stone that lay bright and strange in the palm of his hand. He had discovered it yesterday in the rubble and retrieved it before the Vermian soldiers could destroy it along with everything else.

It was – without doubt – the most beautiful, exquisite stone he had ever seen. Lit only by starlight, it sparkled and shimmered a summer-sky blue and there – deep within its heart – Firebrand could see twisting, smoke-like columns of azure and aquamarine.

The Earthstone.

Firebrand shivered and looked up at the darkening sky, remembering his father's words from years before.

'I know the Earthstone is buried somewhere within it,' he had told him as they stood beneath the Foundation Stone. 'Even though I cannot see it, I know it exists. I can feel it in my heart.'

He had told Firebrand the story of how the Earth-stone had been given to the Olumnus people by Salus, the Guardian of Worlds. It was a gift to show his love for both worlds – for Earth and for Aurobon – a promise that he would always look after them. The Olumnus had made it their greatest treasure and built the Foundation Stone around it to protect it.

'Your faith must be like the Foundation Stone,' his father had said. 'It must be strong enough to shield your heart from the storms that will try and destroy it. If your faith should crumble, then your heart will be lost.'

But as Firebrand stared down at the blue shining beauty of the stone in his hand, it seemed to him in that moment that he had been deceived all of his life.

The Foundation Stone had been destroyed and Vahlzi lay in ruins. The things he had believed in, the things that had seemed so precious and valuable, all of them had fallen and shattered before his eyes. His faith had brought nothing but death and destruction to Aurobon.

And so it was that he stood alone on the empty shore and, with a bitter cry of despair, flung the Earthstone into the middle of the lake.

The stone seemed to hang in the air for a single, glittering moment before it fell with a splash and disappeared beneath the water's surface. For a heartbeat there was only darkness and silence. Then from the depths of the lake came a pulse of brilliant blue light so intense that Firebrand fell to his knees and covered his face with his hands. The earth trembled and shook, then was still.

When Firebrand finally lowered his hands, all that remained was a shimmering phosphorescence upon the water; a million tiny particles of blue light that sparkled and shone before sinking beneath the surface and fading like stars into the darkness below.

Firebrand stared out across the lake and shivered. He noticed that the night air was suddenly filled with a flurry of grey and realised, to his surprise, that it was snowing.

'What have I done?' he whispered. 'What have I done?'

But his words were taken by the wind and lost among the snowflakes and the distant thunder of water falling upon stone.

Skipping beneath the boughs of ancient beech trees, the little blonde girl watched her red shoes dance over frosted leaves and listened to the music of the wind as it sang to her from the treetops. She saw how the branches scratched at the grey clouds with their twisted fingers and as the first snowflakes began to fall she smiled and turned her face towards the sky.

Life was new and strange, and the days and years lay ahead of her like fields of fresh snow, awaiting her tiny footprints.

She left the path and squeezed through gaps in the thick, shiny green rhododendron bushes, emerging at last onto a grassy verge at the water's edge. Snow fell all around her and from the woods she could hear the sound of voices calling to her.

She smiled.

'Look!' she said, pointing happily. 'Pretty!'

Then, clapping her yellow mittens together in excitement, she stepped out onto the ice.

Up ahead of her, something fluttered and danced above the surface of the frozen lake, and she slipped over several times in her efforts to catch up with it. But in spite of her young age she was a very determined little girl, and it wasn't long before she reached the centre of the lake. There she stood all alone, a tiny figure in red shoes with the snow falling all around her.

Of course, anyone who knew anything at all about the world would have found it curious to see a small blue butterfly in the middle of winter. But the little girl was new to the world and all she knew was that it was beautiful, and that she wanted it more than anything.

She knelt down and reached out her hand. The voices were closer now, shouting to her.

She looked up and waved.

'Look!' she cried. 'See!'

Then the ice cracked and the butterfly flew away.

One

One

General Martock stood in the silence of the Outer Chamber and glanced up at the clock on the wall.

Three minutes to seven.

Walking across to the window, he stared at the snow that lay in thick drifts across the lawn of the Emperor Odoursin's Palace. A bronze statue of Odoursin gleamed in the pale morning sunshine and beyond it Martock could make out the icy fingers of a waterfall, crystallised in time above a frozen, artificial lake. In the distance, a tall, emerald-green tower stood out against the winter sky while below the streets of Vermia shivered and stirred beneath a blanket of ice and snow.

Turning away from the window, Martock glanced around at the gold lamps, the ornate chandeliers and the floors constructed from the finest marble, plundered from the tombs of Vahlzian graveyards. There had been no expense spared, and Martock had been a strong supporter of the palace's lavish construction, arguing that it was a visual symbol of the Emperor's power. But over the last few months he had begun to dread coming here.

Odoursin was becoming dangerously unpredictable.

Only last week he had ordered the execution of one of his most loyal ministers, accusing him of being a traitor. Nothing was further from the truth, but once Odoursin got an idea into his head, there was no point in arguing. Just the other day, Martock had made the mistake of disagreeing with the Emperor on some small matter of policy and he had lain awake afterwards in a cold sweat, waiting for the knock on the door in the middle of the night.

It had been four years since Vermia's failed attempt to infect the humans on Earth with a deadly virus. Vahlzian forces had foiled their plan, attacking Vermian mosquito squadrons and destroying all remaining stocks of the deadly virus, both here and on Earth.

But Odoursin had been resourceful. Together with his generals and the cream of his fighting force, he had retreated underground into an intricate network of tunnels, bunkers and laboratories that lay hidden beneath the streets of Vermia. As Vahlzian soldiers searched the alleyways above, Odoursin and his men had bided their time, listening, watching and plotting their next move. Odoursin had known that, despite this humiliating setback, his scientists were busy developing a range of deadly new weapons.

A year later, just as Vahlzian forces were beginning to relax and drop their guard, the long-awaited breakthrough came.

A new, powerful generation of insects had been created and they were ready to attack.

On a dark, moonless night when the streets of Vermia lay silent beneath a heavy snowfall, the creatures came creeping from their holes and burrows. Giant robber flies took to the skies and began hunting down Vahlzian wasp squadrons with ruthless efficiency, seizing their victims from above, piercing their bodies with a needle-sharp proboscis and sucking the life out of them. Ambush and assassin bugs moved rapidly out of the northern deserts to attack ant and wasp formations on the ground while bombardier beetles, fire ants and huge tarantula spiders swept through the streets and alley-ways to engage the enemy wherever they found them.

The Vahlzian forces were taken completely by surprise. Unprepared for an attack of such speed and ferocity, they were overwhelmed in a matter of weeks. The Vermian armies moved in to occupy the once great city of Vahlzi and began to exact a terrible revenge upon its inhabitants. Those who were not killed immediately were forced to flee into the mountains as their comfortable homes and quiet suburban neighbourhoods were torn apart around them. Thousands were either sent back east to the slave labour camps or simply never seen or heard of again.

From a military point of view, it had all been a tremendous success.

But Odoursin wasn't happy, and Martock knew why.

Odoursin had never forgiven the people of Earth for causing the wasp crash which had killed his brother and

left him with terrible burns. He saw them as selfish parasites, responsible for the desecration of their world.
Since his attempt to destroy human life on Earth had
been thwarted by the Vahlzian attack four years ago, his
rage and frustration had known no bounds. And now
that Odoursin had Vahlzi beaten, his obsession with the
destruction of humanity was total.

He wanted revenge.

All of which left Martock with a big problem.

The problem being that, with all traces of the original
virus destroyed, no one could figure out a way to do it.

'His Excellency will see you now,' said the middle-aged
woman with her hair scraped back in a tight bun, gesturing toward the double oak doors from which she had just
emerged carrying a small brown medical bag.

'Thank you,' said Martock, wondering whether she
derived any enjoyment from being nursemaid to the
most feared man in Aurobon. Looking at her sour little
face he decided, on reflection, that it was probably right
up her street.

'This will not do, General. Do you understand me?'
Odoursin's eyes flashed threateningly. 'It is not accept-
able.'

Martock peered through the gloom and saw the burned,
twisted face of his Emperor glaring back at him with a
look of determination that bordered upon madness. The
fact that the curtains were closed and the only light came

from a dull, orange wall lamp merely added to Martock's discomfort.

'I understand, Your Excellency. I am sure that we are very close to finding a solution to the problem. It can only be a matter of time before –'

'Do not patronise me, General,' hissed Odoursin, his lips flecked with foam. 'Do you take me for a fool?'

'Of course not, Your Excellency,' replied Martock hurriedly. 'It is just that the solution is proving more complex than we had imagined.'

He swallowed nervously. 'I am afraid the search for a new virus powerful enough to destroy the human inhabitants of Earth has – so far – been unsuccessful. We have been unable to find anything virulent enough to pose any real threat.'

Martock felt the intensity of Odoursin's rage as the cold eyes regarded him from their sunken, skeletal sockets. Then Odoursin rose from his seat and moved slowly and deliberately towards Martock, his voice becoming harder and angrier as he spoke.

'Have you forgotten the prophecy, General? Am I not the Great One who shall save the Earth from its human parasites? Are you trying to tell me that the prophecy is false? Is *that* what you are telling me, General?'

'No, n-no, Your Excellency,' stammered Martock nervously, suddenly afraid for his life. 'I am just saying that perhaps we need to find another way!'

At this, Odoursin stopped in his tracks, clasping his bony hands together in front of him. Focusing his gaze upon Martock he began to sway almost imperceptibly back and forth, like a praying mantis about to strike.

'*Is* there another way?' whispered Odoursin.

'I am certain that there is,' replied Martock. 'I know we can do this.'

Odoursin nodded.

'Very well,' he said at last. 'I will give you a month.'

Two

The last bubbles of oxygen trickled from the boy's mouth as he tumbled through liquid darkness, falling away from the light that was already fading behind him. As the warmth seeped out of him and the freezing water poured into his lungs he no longer knew where he stopped and the water began. And finally, when the light was gone and it was finished, he understood nothing and everything, and saw all at once how he was forever lost and it was the beginning. And then he was cold and awake, and it was morning.

He opened his eyes and saw ice crystals frozen on a pebble. He thought that he had never seen anything so beautiful. Blinking, he got unsteadily to his feet and saw the blanket of snow that covered the rocks and stones all the way to the edge of the lake. Clouds heavy with snow hung from a winter sky above him and he watched their bruised, grey reflections move silently across the face of the water.

He was surrounded on all sides by thickly wooded, mountain slopes which rose steeply from the rocky shore. The branches of trees were bent low under the weight of snow which had fallen during the night. The boy began to shiver violently in the cold wind and his teeth chattered so loudly that he failed to notice the approaching figure until he was standing right in front of him.

The man was dressed in a thick woollen robe and his long, dark hair was woven with coloured threads. He carried two more robes and as he held one out in front of him, the boy saw that his eyes were full of kindness.

'You have been cold for long enough,' he said. 'It is time that you were warm again.'

He slipped the robe over the boy's head and the boy immediately felt warmer as the soft fur lining enveloped his skin. But as he looked around at the lake and the snow-covered mountains, he felt lost, like a boat adrift in an endless sea.

'Please,' he said softly. 'I am so afraid.'

The man put a hand on his shoulder. 'It will be diffi-cult at the beginning. But there are others here who will help you, Sam. You must find them quickly.'

When the boy heard this, something stirred in his memory and his eyes widened. He looked up hopefully at the man and asked, 'Is that my name? Sam?'

The man nodded and smiled. 'Yes,' he said. 'That is your name.' He put his hand on Sam's shoulder.

'And there will be many in Aurobon who will be glad to hear it once more.'

A light snow was falling, drifting from the sky above Vahlzi and settling on the rubble that was strewn across its empty streets. The occasional crack-crack-crack of gunfire suggested groups of Vahlzian Resistance fighters were still engaging the enemy on the east side of the city, but otherwise the streets were eerily quiet.

A Vermian soldier picked his way cautiously through the debris, nervously scanning the blackened ruins for signs of life. As his boots disturbed a sheet of corrugated iron there was a flurry of brown and he swung his rifle around to see a large rat darting away across the stones. Swearing under his breath, he kicked at the rusty metal before resuming his slow progress over the bricks, nervously training his rifle upon each doorway as he passed. When he finally disappeared around the corner, there was silence for a moment, followed by a faint scraping sound and then the strip of rusty corrugated iron began – very slowly – to move. Below it, the face of a young man was just visible, his anxious expression framed by a straggle of dark, shoulder-length hair.

'We have *got* to get out of here, Mump,' said Zip, lifting the sheet of metal just enough to peer out from his hiding place at the street above. From behind him there came a loud clang, followed by a yelp of pain.

'For goodness sake keep it down!' he hissed as the air was filled with loud, angry curses. 'If anyone spots us, we're dead meat!'

'Suits me,' said Mump, rubbing his head. 'Might as

well be dead anyway, the amount of time we've been buried under this thing.'

Ignoring him, Zip turned his attention back towards the street. He knew how Mump felt. They were part of a well-organised Vahlzian Resistance movement which operated from a secret base back in the mountains. They'd been hiding in this bombed-out cellar for over a week now, observing enemy movements and carrying out attacks on supply lines in order to cause as much disruption as possible.

But Vermian forces were getting wise to them. It hadn't taken them long to work out that the attacks were coming from groups operating in the heart of Vahlzi. So Vermian soldiers had started to carry out a systematic search of the city in an attempt to hunt down and kill the people responsible. If a place looked slightly suspicious, they either torched it or – if they were especially annoyed – came with high explosives and blew it apart. So now the streets were full of hollow-eyed refugees, women, children and old men picking their way through the ruins in the hope of retrieving something of value: clothes, shoes, warm blankets or – the greatest treasure of all – food.

The Vermian attack had been so unexpected that the people of Vahlzi were completely unprepared. One moment they were tending their gardens, visiting the theatre or having friends round for dinner, the next they were huddled in bombed-out buildings, scrabbling around for food and arguing over who had eaten the last slice of rotting potato. Suddenly they had woken up to find their beautiful city torn apart and filled with ruthless men in black uniforms; men who bullied or murdered them on a whim and then went on to plunder their farms and food stocks, filling their bellies while the people of Vahlzi starved.

It was a terrible time and it seemed that things could only get worse.

Zip knew that the Vermian High Command was desperate to discover where the Vahlzian Resistance fighters were hiding out and would stop at nothing to find them.

And if they discovered the location of the Resistance base, then the war would be as good as lost.

'Maybe we should head back to the mountains for a while,' suggested Zip, keeping a watchful eye on a group of soldiers at the far end of the street. 'I reckon things are getting too dangerous here. Let's go and get cleaned up, maybe find something to eat. We can come back in a week or two when the heat's died down a bit.'

From the cellar below came the sound of Mump's boots splashing about in the puddles. Zip lowered the sheet of corrugated iron again and looked down to see Mump busily ferreting around in the dark.

'What do you reckon, mate?'

Mump stopped what he was doing and looked up, squinting into the light.

'Eh?'

'What d'you say we get out of here?'

Mump furrowed his brow, the idea gradually filtering

into his mind like water seeping through stone. Finally
he nodded his head vigorously up and down.

'Good idea, yep. Let's get out of here. Yeah. Only . . .'
Mump hesitated. His face wore the expression of someone who has had a great idea, but is worried that their
opinion of its greatness will not be shared by others.
'Only what?' said Zip. 'Come on, buddy. Those soldiers
are getting a bit close for comfort.'

'Only I think we might as well use this stuff before
we go,' said Mump. 'It would be a shame to waste it.'
He raised his eyebrows and looked hopefully in Zip's
direction.

Zip stared down into the gloom of the cellar and saw
that Mump was standing proudly with his arms folded
and a small wooden crate between his feet. Stacked up in
the crate were about half a dozen square lumps of what
looked like grey plasticine. Each lump was about the size
of a pack of sausages.

'Explosives?' Zip raised one eyebrow quizzically.
'Where did you find that little lot?'

Mump grinned. 'Remember when C troop stopped
off here on their way to blow up the ammunition dump?'

Zip nodded.

'Well they left this behind.'

'Left it behind?' echoed Zip. He looked at Mump
doubtfully. 'And I suppose they asked you to look after it
for them, did they?'

'Well, not exactly,' said Mump, staring awkwardly at
the floor. 'But I figured they had more than enough

explosives to do the job. Anyway, it was a bit unfair to expect them to carry so much.'

The corner of Zip's mouth turned up in a little half smile.

'You nicked it, didn't you?'

'No!' said Mump indignantly. 'I re-*assigned* it, that's all. It was a logistical decision.'

'A logistical decision,' repeated Zip, jumping down onto the cellar floor. 'Mump, you wouldn't know a logistical decision if it came up and whacked you in the woolahs.'

He picked up a lump of explosive and weighed it thoughtfully in his hand for a moment. Then he tossed it to Mump who smiled happily and held out his shirt to catch it.

'OK,' he said. 'But first we need a plan.'

Sam stared into the fire and watched the embers glow red against the dark stones. He tried desperately to remember something – anything – but his mind was full of wispy, insubstantial memories that floated around him like silken scarves in a breeze. Whenever he tried to catch one he would feel it slip from his grasp, spinning and whirling with all the others in a dance that he could not understand. But suddenly, as he looked at the stars and the lake and the mountains he remembered: this was Aurobon and he had been here before.

He had fought in a war against Vermia, training as a wasp pilot to stop Odoursin's mosquitoes infecting the people of Earth with a deadly virus.

As he looked at the man who sat opposite him on the shore, he recalled how the two of them had once walked together upon these stones.

'I remember you,' he said. 'Your name is Salus.'

'Good,' said the man and smiled. 'Now we both have a name.'

Sam watched in silence for a while as snowflakes fell into the fire and melted in the heat.

'Why am I here?' he asked after a while. He shook his head and stared across the dark waters of the lake. 'I went home to my family on Earth again, I know I did. Why have I come back?'

When Salus made no reply, Sam said, 'I feel as though I have lost something. Have I left something behind?'

'Now is not the moment to be looking back,' answered Salus. 'These are dangerous times in Aurobon. Your friends are in grave danger and you must go to them without delay.'

Sam was puzzled. 'My friends?' he asked. 'But how will I find them?'

'You will find them,' said Salus, 'because they are already calling to you.'

'All done,' said Zip cheerfully, rolling the last lump of grey explosive into a ball and pushing a piece of wood into it. 'Now for the sticky stuff.'

He held the wood firmly in one hand and dipped the explosive into a large pot of thick, gooey axle grease, wiping it around the inside until it was completely covered.

'Well, don't they look scrummy?' said Mump admiringly. 'Those bugs are in for a treat.'

He watched as Zip placed the finished sticky-bomb with the others on the metal lid of an old biscuit tin and wiped his hands on the front of his jacket.

'Right,' said Zip. 'The one nearest you has got the twenty-second fuse. The rest of them are about eight seconds. Now remember, we don't want to be hanging around out there. Soon as we've got one of those things after us, we leg it straight back here, do the business and then get out. OK?'

'OK,' said Mump.

He picked up the nearest sticky-bomb and smiled.

'Toffee apple, anyone?'

They edged slowly and carefully past the crumbling walls of bombed-out buildings until at last they reached the end of the street. Zip peered cautiously around the corner and immediately drew his head back again.

'We're in business,' he whispered. 'Six man patrol plus an eight-leg.'

Mump giggled nervously and put a hand over his mouth.

Zip gave him an angry stare.

'This isn't a game you know, Mump. Those things'll tear you apart.'

He took another look around the edge of the building

and saw that the soldiers were heading in their direction. But the soldiers weren't the real problem. The real problem was the massive, brown-haired tarantula spider crawling across the rubble in front of them. Zip could see its black, beady eyes staring into every building as it passed, checking for signs of movement. As it squeezed its way through the narrow street and rubbed up against the ruined houses, brickwork smashed and crumbled to the ground, filling the air with clouds of dust.

Zip shuddered and stepped back hurriedly.

'We really don't need to do this, Mump,' he said. 'There's a whole bunch of trouble waiting around that corner. Maybe we should just leave it.'

But turning around he saw that the fuse on Mump's sticky-bomb was fizzing and that leaving it was no longer an option.

'Too late,' said Mump. 'I've gone and lit me lollipop.'

Then he ran off around the corner.

'Wait!' shouted Zip. 'Come back!'

Peering around the side of the building he saw Mump standing in the middle of the street, waving his sticky bomb above his head and dancing around like an enthusiastic cheerleader.

'Cooo-eee!' Mump shouted at the top of his voice. 'Spiiiiideeeee!'

The soldiers raised their guns.

Zip watched Mump throw the sticky bomb high into the sky.

Then the air was alive with the crack and whine of

bullets and Mump sprinted past him like a whippet with its tail on fire.

'Quick!' he yelled in a hoarse, wheezy voice. 'Leg it!'

Zip turned and ran just as the sticky bomb ignited with a loud thump and a hot wind of smoke and dust came howling down the street behind him. Up ahead he saw Mump pull aside the strip of corrugated iron and disappear down into the cellar. His heart pounding in his chest, Zip reached the hole and jumped down without breaking stride. He landed heavily next to Mump and noticed that he was already holding two sticky bombs in each hand.

'You OK?' he asked.

'I'm good,' said Mump. 'Come on. Let's blast 'em!'

They scrambled back up to the entrance hole and Zip quickly pushed the cover back into place so that there was only a thin strip of light showing. As the huge spider approached, the ground began to shake and a shower of loose earth cascaded between them into the cellar below.

Zip lifted the cover slightly, peered out and then turned to Mump.

'Right, here they come,' he said, unbuttoning the top button of his jacket and taking out a box of matches. 'Remember, these are only short fuses. The moment that thing's on top of us, we light, stick and cover. Got it?'

Mump nodded and shook the sticky bombs in the air as though demonstrating how to play the maracas.

'Showtime,' he said.

Zip gingerly lifted the cover again. Adrenalin shot

through his veins as he saw that the gigantic spider was only a few metres away now, its massive body crouching low above the street as it advanced. He noticed that some of its hairs had been burned off in the explosion and pieces of dust and debris were lodged in its thick bristles. A pair of sharp, curved fangs hung from its slime-covered mouth, glinting in the winter sunlight like silver scimitars. From somewhere behind its legs a group of soldiers began to fire indiscriminately into the ruins, the flashes from their guns clearly visible as they attempted to flush out their unseen attackers.

Zip flipped over onto his back and took a match from the box.

'Ready?' he asked.

Mump nodded.

'Ready.'

'OK,' said Zip. 'Let's do it.'

He struck the match against a stone and as it flared he saw Mump's eyes blinking in the darkness. For a brief moment he wished that all the horror and killing was over and that the two of them were fishing once more, high in the mountains where salmon leapt from bright streams and the water ran clear across polished stones.

Then the fuses were lit, the cover was off and in the confusion of smoke and gunfire he thrust a sticky bomb deep into the bristles of the spider's leg, threw another one at its belly and dived back into the hole just as the bombs ignited and the world blew apart in a blistering roar of fire and flame.

Crashing down into the cellar he covered his head with his arms as lumps of rock and earth rained down on top of him. Something hard struck his arm and he cried out in pain, but he was quickly distracted from his own troubles by another cry which came from the far side of the cellar. Kicking off a slab of stone that lay across his legs, he staggered through a cloud of dust towards the shouting figure in the corner.

'Get it off me,' breathed Mump's scared, shaky voice in the darkness. 'Zip please – get it off me!'

Peering into the gloom, Zip saw Mump lying awkwardly on his back next to the wall. Something had fallen across his chest and pinned him to the rubble.

He seemed very frightened.

'Hold still, mate,' said Zip. 'I'll get you out of there.'

Coughing his way through the smoke and dust, he bent down to get a better view of the obstruction and then suddenly leapt backwards with a shout of alarm.

'Aw, *no!*' he exclaimed, recoiling in horror. For what he had thought was a piece of wood was, in fact, a fat bloodied segment of one of the spider's legs. As Zip stared at it in disgust it twitched spasmodically, like a worm caught in the heat of the midday sun.

'Take it away, Zip,' Mump pleaded. 'Please!'

'Don't worry, buddy,' said Zip as the limb continued to jerk and tremble. 'We'll soon have you out of there. Now when I say push, you push, OK?'

'OK,' wheezed Mump breathlessly. 'But hurry up, will you? I can't breathe!'

Zip braced himself against the wall of the cellar, shouted 'Push, Mump!' and kicked the spider's leg with both feet. The still squirming limb rolled off and fell with a loud crash onto the sheet of corrugated iron that lay with the rest of the debris on the cellar floor.

Zip pulled Mump to his feet and they stared at the circle of grey sky above them, listening to the sporadic rattle of gunfire.

'Time we were gone I think,' said Zip.

Slipping away through the smoke, they saw that the huge spider had crumpled over onto its left side and was now engulfed in flame. Mump stooped to pick something up from the wreckage and when they had put several streets between themselves and the trigger-happy soldiers, Zip saw that it was half a loaf of bread. It had been toasted on one side by the flames, but it smelled delicious and Zip realised how long it had been since they had enjoyed proper food. They stopped beneath the twisted metal of a lamppost and Mump broke off a piece, handing it to Zip before breaking off another chunk and stuffing it hungrily into his mouth. For a moment, the warm, yeasty taste reminded Zip of his childhood, when his mother used to feed him freshly baked bread from the oven.

He was about to tear off another piece when he noticed Mump staring at a blackened house on the other side of the road. The first-floor wall had been torn off in an explosion, revealing a room with two little beds. The interior walls were covered in a yellow, flowery wallpaper which was now ripped and peeling. A small dressing table could still be seen against one wall and items of children's clothing were strewn untidily across the floor. A tiny wooden cot lay crushed beneath a heavy timber beam.

Zip followed Mump's gaze to where two young children – a boy and a girl – stood silently in the doorway, their clothes no more than rags which hung in tatters from their tiny frames. The horrors of war had taken the shine from their eyes and they now stared blankly out at a world that had abandoned them.

Without a word, Mump crossed the street and held out the loaf of bread. The girl snatched it from his hand and the two children ran quickly away across the rubble, darting off through a sea of grey stones until they were lost from sight.

Mump stood staring after them for a long time until finally the sound of gunfire brought him back to his senses and he crossed the street again to rejoin Zip.

Zip put an arm around his shoulder.

'Come on,' he said. 'Let's go and get the bikes.'

Together they made their way to the outskirts of the city before heading out towards the mountains over fields of freshly fallen snow.

Sam stretched out his hands and felt the heat begin to warm them. He watched Salus push a piece of wood into the fire and saw how quickly the blaze engulfed it until at last the wood became the flames and there was nothing left except grey embers, crumbling away to nothing.

'It's strange,' he said, 'but I feel younger here than when I was on Earth.'

'That is because you have become the person you were the last time you walked in Aurobon,' Salus replied. 'You are here because Aurobon needs you, Sam.'

Once more, Sam tried to remember how he had got here, but instead a blackness grew inside him until he could bear it no longer and cried out in fear and loneliness. Then Salus put a hand on top of his head and Sam felt the fire and the flames, and the smoke twisting away into the sky. When he opened his eyes, the cold mountain air rushed into his lungs and he felt refreshed and clear-headed, as though he had just woken from a long sleep.

'The darkness comes again,' said Salus, picking up the other robe, 'and the people of Earth are in terrible danger. You must find the one who is true of heart. And remember: if you should ever lose your way, look for a guiding light.'

'Wait!' called Sam as Salus began to walk away across the shore toward the mountain. 'I don't understand!'

'Be patient,' answered Salus, 'and in times of trouble, listen with your heart.'

Three

The lake was as smooth as steel and the early morning sun had already begun to thaw a few patches of snow on the lower reaches of the mountain.

As Sam gazed at the circle of mountain peaks and the sweep of pale-blue sky, his eyes were irresistibly drawn toward a small gap in the trees where the shore met the base of the mountain.

Find the one who is true of heart.

Something stirred deep inside him and his mind was suddenly filled with memories of warmth and sunshine, of a small blonde-haired girl swimming in the lake's crystal waters.

'Skipper,' he whispered, remembering how the two of them had once flown wasps together in Aurobon, before something happened which returned him to his old life again.

Back on Earth, he had forgotten that this world ever existed.

But now that he was back in Aurobon, it seemed as though he had never left. Instead it was his life on Earth that felt like a distant dream, fading like sunlight on a winter's afternoon.

But what had become of Skipper? Was she still alive?

He decided to try to make his way to the airbase, which as far as he could remember, was somewhere down on the plains. If he could find Commander Firebrand and the others, they might be able to tell him what was going on . . .

The wind blew fiercely across the face of the mountain and Sam crawled behind a large rock to try and get some respite from the storm. The morning's climb through the forest had been quite pleasant. Sheltered from the cold wind and accompanied by the occasional burst of birdsong he had made good progress, following the path of the stream up through the trees with a feeling of hope in his heart. The world had become more and more familiar to him as he made his way beneath the fragrant pines. Every now and then he had stopped to stare at the sunshine filtering through the trees, watching fingers of steam rise from the icy ground to form layers that hung like gossamer above the twisted roots. As he stood alone in the woods and listened to the wind blowing high in the treetops, he had experienced a feeling of belonging, of coming home.

But now that he had climbed over the ridge onto the exposed slope of the mountain, things were very different.

Thick white snowflakes swirled all around him and it

became almost impossible to see. Afraid that if he carried on he might stumble into some deep abyss, he decided to rest in the shelter of the rock and wait out the storm.

Pulling his robe tightly around himself, he curled up into a ball in an effort to conserve some heat. As he lay there shivering, he heard a humming sound which grew louder and louder until it felt as though it were coming from inside his head.

Sam looked up and was immediately confronted by a horrific sight. Only a few metres away hovered a creature that seemed to have flown from the depths of his darkest nightmares. It was the biggest, most frightening insect that he had ever seen in his life.

Sam shrank back in terror as the grey, evil-looking fly landed in the snow with a heavy thump. It swivelled its head around and scanned the rocks as though looking for something. White bristles sprouted from its body and as it surveyed the winter landscape the snow-covered mountains were reflected in its jet-black eyes.

There was a loud click as it folded a huge pair of brown-veined wings over its back and then started to walk forward a little way, collecting crystals of ice in the stiff black hairs that covered its legs. It stopped and looked around. Then it began to grind its sharp mandibles together with a rasping, grating noise. As it did so, a dark, foul-smelling liquid spilled from its jaws and a brownish-yellow stain spread out across the snow.

Sam felt his stomach heave, but he gritted his teeth, swallowed and slowly began to edge his way back around the rock. If he could just make it to the other side, maybe the hideous creature wouldn't see him. The jagged edges of the rock pressed into his back as he cautiously moved his feet sideways and slid his body along towards the corner of the stone. Keeping his eyes fixed on the massive insect, he was about to manoeuvre his body back around the rock when the fly suddenly tensed and Sam saw that the hairs on its body were quivering. It seemed to be picking up vibrations through the air and, terrified that it might be sensing his own movements, Sam held his breath and remained perfectly still. His natural instinct was to run away as fast as he could, but he knew that to do so would be suicide.

The fly began to scuttle around in a circle until it was pointing back down the mountain. As Sam began to breathe again its head suddenly twitched around and for one dreadful moment he saw his own terrified reflection mirrored hundreds of times in the insect's compound eyes. But then it unfolded its wings and rose into the air with a loud buzz, stirring up a huge cloud of snow behind it. Sam was knocked sideways by the stinging blast of cold air that followed in its wake, but as he scrambled to his feet again he saw that the snowstorm had stopped and the sky was beginning to clear.

Watching the fly disappear across the valley, his heart leapt wildly with excitement as a break in the clouds revealed the outline of tall towers rising from the snow-covered plains below, and he realised that he was looking down upon the great city of Vahlzi.

Four

Doctor Janik Jancy was Head of InRaD (Insect Research & Development) and to say that he was having a bad week would have been something of an understatement.

Vermian government forces had started to lose a lot of their ant squadrons during reconnaissance patrols on Earth. It seemed that many of the ants were being eaten by sheep, and no one could understand why.

Jancy knew there had to be a solution, but he was damned if he could find it.

It had never been a problem before. Ant crews were well trained in safety procedures and specifically taught to avoid putting themselves or their vehicles in danger. But interviews with those who had managed to escape from their ants revealed a disturbing pattern.

It appeared that in each case, the control panels installed in the ants had ceased to function and the ants would suddenly go onto auto-pilot. They would head for fields where sheep were grazing, climb to the top of a blade of grass and then clamp their jaws onto it. No matter how hard they tried, the ant crews simply couldn't get the ants to move again.

The lucky ones managed to evacuate and get picked up by other crews. Those less fortunate were never seen again. Over a hundred ant crews had been lost in this way and now all Earth missions were cancelled until further notice.

Jancy had several teams of his best engineers working on the problem, but so far no malfunctions had been discovered.

It was proving to be a logistical nightmare and now, as if that wasn't bad enough, he had heard rumours that another major attack was being planned against the people of Earth. Not that this bothered Jancy in itself – Earth would certainly be a whole lot better off without them – but it meant that General Martock was breathing down his neck, insisting that the ant problem be rectified immediately. Martock was the Emperor Odoursin's second-in-command and he was not a man to be crossed.

Jancy shut his eyes and sighed. He knew that if he didn't sort this one out pretty quickly he would be 'relieved of duty' as the government liked to put it. He was just beginning to imagine some of the horrible things they might do to him when there was a knock at the door and he opened his eyes to see Alya, the new research assistant, standing in the doorway of his office. She was young, keen, and quite pretty, Jancy thought.

He also thought that he didn't need any interruptions right now.

'I think I know what your problem is,' Alya said, and walked into the office.

Jancy frowned, adjusted his glasses and peered over them at her in order to make a point. The point being that junior research assistants do not just barge into their superior's office whenever they feel like it.

'Young lady. Firstly, I was not aware that I had a problem. Secondly, if I *did* have a problem then I believe I would have more sense than to share it with you.'

Alya blushed and began to look uncomfortable. Jancy watched her tuck a wisp of long, black hair behind her ear and waited for her to explain herself.

'I'm sorry – I didn't mean . . .'

Satisfied that her discomfort had reached an appropriate level, Jancy gestured towards an empty chair next to his desk. He had heard that she was a good student who worked hard for the company and decided, for once, to be magnanimous.

'So tell me,' he said in the more kindly, indulgent tones of an uncle listening to a slow-witted niece, 'what is my problem and what should I do about it?'

Alya folded her hands in her lap and looked at him with serious brown eyes.

'The ants,' she said. 'I think they're infected.'

'Infected?' Jancy raised an eyebrow quizzically. 'With what, may I ask?'

'With a parasitic worm,' Alya replied.

'I see,' said Jancy. He smiled patiently. 'Perhaps you would like to explain?'

Taking Jancy's tone to be a sign of encouragement, Alya continued with renewed confidence.

'Well . . . Like a lot of parasites, the worm has to move between several different hosts before it can reproduce successfully. In this case it needs to live inside snails and ants before moving on to sheep.'

Jancy studied the young woman carefully as she spoke and decided that he was not dealing with a fool. She knew what she was talking about, and Jancy's interest stepped up a gear.

'Go on.'

'The worm starts life as an egg which is eaten by a snail. The worm hatches out inside the snail before being expelled in a ball of slime. The slime is then eaten by an ant which in turn is eaten by a sheep. The worm is then released into the bloodstream of the sheep to continue the next stage of its life cycle.'

Jancy shook his head. 'But sheep don't naturally eat ants. They eat grass. They might occasionally eat an ant by mistake, but surely there's too great an element of chance for it to be a reliable method of transmission?'

'That's just it,' said Alya, leaning forward excitedly. 'Don't you see? It isn't left to chance at all. The worm instinctively knows that, under normal circumstances, an ant is unlikely to be eaten by a sheep. So somehow, it rewires the ant's brain and suddenly, all the ant wants to do is climb to the top of a blade of grass and hang around until a sheep comes along and eats it. The worm has actually figured out a way of *controlling* the ant's behaviour.'

Jancy narrowed his eyes and looked at her.

'Prove it,' he said.

The double doors swung open and Jancy led the way through the sterile neon glare of the insect labs to an area where one of the research teams was carrying out its investigation. The head of a malfunctioning ant had been recovered from Earth and brought back for analysis. Sections of the head had been dismantled and various switches and circuit boards were laid out on workbenches. Coloured electrical wires hung like spaghetti from the remaining head section which had been hoisted onto a tall scaffolding tower to allow better access.

The engineer in charge, a thin, arrogant looking man called Frinser, clambered down from the tower clutching a screwdriver and a handful of crocodile clips.

Jancy nodded. 'How's it going?'

Frinser threw the clips and screwdriver onto a bench and shook his head.

'Can't find anything wrong,' he said. 'We've checked nearly all of the circuits and they're fine, sweet as the day we installed 'em.' He wiped his hands on his overalls and shrugged. 'I don't suppose,' he added pointedly, 'we could be talking about driver error here?'

Alya stepped forward. 'Maybe you should check the brain stem.'

Frinser threw Jancy a *Who the hell is this?* look. Then he stared back at Alya and gave her a condescending smile.

'I don't know who you are, my dear, but you obviously don't know much about bio-mechanics. You see, there is really no need to go delving down into sensitive brain tissue. All our electrical connections are made directly to neurons on the periphery of the brain. If we were to start rooting around in the central brain cortex we'd cause all kinds of damage.' His smile widened. 'Didn't they teach you that at college?'

Alya smiled back. 'I guess not,' she said. She walked across to the work bench and picked up what appeared to be a small silver torch. 'A cellular restructuring beam,' she said. 'Mind if I borrow it?'

'Hey!' Frinser protested. 'Don't mess with that!'

Jancy put a hand on his arm and quietened him. 'Let her be,' he said.

The two men watched as Alya climbed the scaffolding tower and pointed the CRB at the ant's head. There was a blue flash and a hole the size of a football appeared just below the ant's antennae.

'What's she doing?' hissed Frinser.

'I think,' said Jancy acidly, 'she may just be doing your job for you.'

With a loud squelch, Alya thrust her arm deep into the hole and cautiously began to feel around inside the ant's head.

Frinser winced and mumbled something under his breath.

Suddenly, Alya gave a shout, dropped the CRB and braced herself against the metal scaffolding poles. Plunging her other arm into the gaping hole she leaned backwards and pulled hard. There was a sucking, slurping sound like a wet flannel being dragged through a tube and then without warning a white, slimy worm as thick as a man's arm came slithering out into the light. With a final grunt Alya turned her body around, flicking her arms so that the worm flew from her hands and landed, writhing and twisting, at Frinser's feet.

Alya climbed down the scaffolding, returned the CRB to the bench and dried her hands on a towel. Then she turned to the white-faced Frinser and smiled.

'They didn't teach me that in college either,' she said.

Frinser tried to speak, but all he could do was stare into space, opening and closing his mouth like a drowning man.

Alya held up a hand. 'Please,' she told him. 'No need to thank me.' Then she turned to Jancy and saw that he was still looking down at the worm in amazement.

'What do you think, Doctor?' she asked. 'Do you want me to check the others?'

Jancy shook his head. 'No need,' he replied. 'I think that Frinser and his team should be able to manage on their own now. Don't you think so, Mr Frinser?'

Frinser blinked and came out of his shock-induced trance. 'Yes, of course,' he said hurriedly. 'We'll get on to it immediately.'

As Frinser walked off to gather his team together, Alya

turned to Jancy and said, 'What do you want me to do, Doctor Jancy? I could help them if you like. I know which part of the brain the worms will be located in.'

Jancy took her by the arm and steered her towards the double doors. 'I'm sure you do, my dear,' he said. 'But I think I'd rather you came with me.'

He smiled.

'You see, there are some people I'd like you to meet.'

Five

Sam was about halfway down the mountain when he noticed two tiny black specks moving quickly across the white plains below him. At first he thought that it was just his eyes playing tricks on him, that he had merely been dazzled by the glare of sun on snow, but after closing his eyes for a few moments and then opening them again he saw that the black specks were getting nearer. They seemed to be travelling at an incredible speed and Sam guessed that it would only be a matter of minutes before they reached the mountain.

His recent experience with the fly told him that getting caught out in the open might not be such a good idea, so he ran towards a clump of pine trees and concealed himself behind their thick trunks.

A few minutes later he heard a curious *thwump, thwump* sound, as if something was travelling rapidly up the mountain and repeatedly hitting the powdery snow. The sound became progressively louder until suddenly Sam heard a shout and a wet crunching noise. This was followed by another *thwump, thwump, thwump* and then the sound of laughter began to echo around the mountains.

Cautiously, Sam peered out from behind the trees. Crouched in the snow was a dark brown, very flat insect with a segmented body and keel-shaped head. Its body was covered in backward pointing bristles and its long hind legs were tensed as if it was ready to pounce at a moment's notice. Sam realised that he was staring at a very large flea. Sideways on, it looked like a squashed penny stood on end, but it was about the same size as a powerful sports motorbike and on either side of its head were silver handlebars with what appeared to be brake levers on the front. Its upper back had been sculpted and covered with a seat of thick, padded blue foam. Sitting on the flea with his boots just touching the snow was a young man with dark, shoulder-length hair and a week's worth of stubble on his chin. He wore a brown leather flying jacket and a pair of grubby blue trousers which were ripped above his left knee. He was laughing loudly and staring at the big snowdrift next to him.

Sam followed his gaze and saw that another flea was partially buried in the snow. A pair of boots waved languidly around in the air, as if their owner – who appeared to reside somewhere within the snowdrift – was not unduly worried by his new surroundings.

Sam looked back at the first man and suddenly remembered where he had seen him before. They had been sitting together in a big hall, listening to Commander Firebrand discuss plans for an attack against Vermia. His hair was longer now and he no longer wore the neatly pressed uniform that Sam remembered, but he felt sure that it was the same person.

Wiping the tears of laughter from his eyes, the man climbed down from his flea, kicked out its side-stand and walked across to the snowdrift.

'What y'doin' in there, Mump?' he called, still laughing. 'Building an igloo?'

Mump.

Sam smiled a sudden smile of recognition, for in that moment he clearly remembered standing at the side of a swimming pool during his training as a wasp pilot, with the dark-haired man and another thin, gawky-looking man standing next to him.

Zip and Mump.

Sam got up from his hiding place and walked over to where the man was leaning forward to grab hold of the still waving boots.

'Hi,' he said. 'Need any help?'

In less time than it takes to blink the man dropped to one knee, pulled a silver hunting knife from his jacket and leapt at Sam with such speed and force that he was knocked backward into the snow.

'Zip,' Sam gasped as he felt the cold steel of the blade press against his throat, 'it's me, Sam.'

The pressure on his throat suddenly relaxed and as he stared up he saw Zip's astonished face silhouetted against the grey winter sky. His eyes shone with amazement.

'*Sam?*' he said. '*Sam Palmer?*'

Sam grinned, which isn't easy when you've just had the wind knocked out of you.

'Yeah,' he said. 'It's me.'

The next thing he knew, Zip was pulling him to his feet and grabbing him in the biggest, roughest, most welcoming bear hug he had ever experienced.

'Sam, my *man*!' he said, lifting Sam up so that his feet were several centimetres above the snow. 'I don't believe it! You're alive!' He set Sam down on the snow again and took a step back to take a proper look at him. 'Oh boy, this is just incredible. I can't . . . I mean, this is amazing. Unbelievable. We heard you got killed in the attack.'

Sam shrugged. 'I don't really remember much about it. All I know is – here I am.'

Zip scratched at his stubble and shook his head in disbelief.

'And you look . . . oh, just you wait 'til Mump hears about this!'

He looked at Sam and then they both turned towards the snowdrift where the boots had started to flail and kick at the air with a newfound urgency.

'Uh-oh,' said Zip. 'Time we defrosted him, I reckon.'

Running across to the snowdrift, they each grabbed a boot and pulled. For a few seconds there was only the muffled sound of grunting as Sam and Zip tugged determinedly at his legs; Mump had obviously been travelling at high speed when he hit the snow and drilled himself down deep. But then, in a slither of ice, Mump emerged swearing and spluttering into the light. He tried unsuccessfully to stand up but lost his balance and fell down again, wobbling around on all fours like a baby polar bear. Finally deciding it was all too much effort, he rolled over onto his back and lay with his arms by his sides, gazing up at the sky.

Sam leaned over and looked down at him.

'Hello, Mump,' he said. 'Are you OK?'

Mump stared at him for a moment or two, shut his eyes tightly and then opened them again.

'Am I dead?' he asked.

Sam heard Zip start to chuckle behind him.

'No,' he said, smiling down at the wet, bedraggled heap of confusion that was Mump. 'But I've seen you looking better.'

Mump sat up and threw a quick glance at Zip.

'Zip,' he hissed from the corner of his mouth. 'I think I'm having a *vision*!'

Zip sighed, slapped Sam on the chest a few times and tapped his knuckles against his forehead.

'Look, you great wally. Hands do not go through chest, knuckles do not disappear through head. This boy's as real as you and me, Mump. He's as solid as a rock.'

Mump was silent for a long while, seemingly unable to move his gaze away from Sam's face. Then, without saying a word, he turned and walked away toward the trees.

'What's the matter?' Sam asked. 'Is he all right?'

Zip shrugged. 'It's been quite a day what with one thing and another. He'll get over it.'

Sam looked at the dark tracks in the snow and saw that Mump was some way off with his back to them, leaning against a tree.

'He thought you were dead, Sam,' said Zip. 'We both did.'

Sam nodded thoughtfully. 'To be honest I don't know what I was,' he replied, 'or why I'm here exactly.'

He watched Zip stamp the snow from his boots and saw that his dark hair was full of ice crystals. 'But there's one thing I do know.'

'What's that?' asked Zip.

'It's good to see you both again.'

Zip nodded.

'Yeah, you too, Sam,' he said. 'You too.'

When they had finished digging Mump's flea out of the snowdrift, Mump produced a small stove and began to brew up a pan of acorn coffee.

'So tell us,' he said, 'what happened to you and Skipper after you took the mosquito back to Earth? Last thing we heard, you were Missing In Action.'

Sam shook his head. 'That's the weird part. I remember taking off at the start of the mission. And I know I found my way back to Earth again, although my memory's a bit hazy. Last thing I remember is crawling out of the lake and meeting up with you and Mump.'

As he studied Zip's long hair and rough beard, he saw then how he had changed; how the angular features and muscular forearms had replaced the figure of the fresh-faced youth that Sam remembered from the last time he was in Aurobon. It was still the same Zip all right, but somewhere along the line he had become a man. Glancing across at Mump he saw that he too seemed older than before.

'I've been away a long time haven't I?' he said quietly. Zip nodded.

'You went missing about four years ago.'

'Four years?' replied Sam incredulously. 'But how can I have lost all that time?'

'I don't know,' said Zip. 'But you still look the same as you always did, which is weird. Maybe it's got something to do with Salus. I heard a rumour that he's been seen around these parts recently.'

'Who *is* Salus exactly?' asked Sam.

'Salus is the Guardian of Worlds,' Zip explained. 'He watches over Earth and Aurobon, making sure that everything is kept in balance.'

'Yeah right,' said Mump. 'Of course he does. That's the story they used to tell us when we were kids. But if you ask me, the guy's either nodded off or died.'

'No one *is* asking you,' said Zip. 'And anyway, you shouldn't say things like that, Mump.'

'Don't see why not,' said Mump. 'I'm only saying what everyone's thinking.'

'Well, I know this is going to sound stupid,' said Sam

quietly, 'but I think I might just have seen him myself.'

'Seen who?' asked Zip.

'Salus,' Sam replied. 'Although the way my mind is at the moment, I can't be certain – it could have been some kind of hallucination. But when I was by the lake he gave me this robe to wear, I'm sure of it. And he said that Aurobon needed my help.'

'He certainly got that right,' said Mump. 'Aurobon needs all the help it can get.'

'Why?' asked Sam. 'What happened here exactly?'

'That,' said Zip, handing Sam a mug of coffee and a hunk of bread, 'is a long story.'

As Sam warmed his hands on the hot mug and listened, Zip began to recount the events that had occurred in the years since Sam's disappearance, and told the story of how the Vermian insects had attacked and overrun Vahlzi. When he had finished, Sam shook his head in disbelief.

'That's terrible,' he said. 'So what happened to all the others?'

'Well,' said Zip. 'Skipper went missing the same time as you, Firebrand was captured a few weeks ago and the rest of us are hiding out with the Resistance movement up here in the mountains. There are still enough of us around to cause the Vermian Empire a few headaches, but without control of the skies we've got no real chance of being anything more than a nuisance. They've got total air superiority.'

'What about the wasps?' said Sam. 'Surely you've got some of those left?'

'Sure we have,' said Mump. 'In fact, we've got a whole squadron of them tucked away, for what it's worth. But you even try and take a wasp up there and those robber flies will just tear it out of the sky. Believe me, I've seen it happen.'

Sam frowned. 'What about Skipper?'

Zip shrugged. 'What about her?'

'Well, she's the best, right? When she's flying a wasp, no one can get near her.'

'She's just one person,' said Mump. 'One person against thousands. What could she do?'

'She'd think of something,' said Sam. 'I know she would. She always used to say that anything's possible.'

'You're forgetting something,' said Zip.

'What?'

Zip put a hand on Sam's arm.

'We don't even know if she's still alive,' he said gently.

Later, when they had finished their coffee, Mump wiped the seat of the flea with his jacket and slapped it a couple of times with his hand.

'Come on,' he said. 'Time for your first lesson.'

'Are you sure?' asked Sam uncertainly. 'I don't want to break it or anything.'

'Oh, I shouldn't worry about that,' said Zip. 'These things are pretty much unbreakable.' He looked across at Mump who was giving one of the handlebars a quick polish with his sleeve. 'As our friend here has so recently demonstrated.'

'Oh yeah,' said Mump. 'Remind me, who was it who smashed into the side of a bombardier beetle last week?'

'That was different,' said Zip. 'It was dark and he didn't have his lights on.'

'Course he didn't have his lights on,' retorted Mump. 'There's a war on.'

'Exactly,' said Zip with a wry smile. 'Which is why I cunningly took advantage of the conditions to carry out a surprise attack.'

'Oh I see,' replied Mump sarcastically, 'it was a *surprise* attack.'

'Yeah,' said Zip, winking at Sam. 'Surprised the hell out of me.'

He roared with laughter and Sam began to laugh too. But Mump just patted the seat of the flea and Sam saw that there was a twinkle in his eye.

'Come on, Sam,' said Mump. 'If you're going to join the Resistance, you need to be able to ride one of these.'

Sam looked at the lean, powerful-looking insect crouching on its side-stand and felt excitement hum through his blood. The world of Aurobon was opening up to him once more and for a moment he became acutely aware of all the possibilities, dangers and adventures that lay before him, like a secret pathway hidden beneath the snow.

Walking over to the flea, he threw a leg across it and plonked himself down on the seat, grabbing the handlebars and feeling the insect bounce gently up and down as the suspension in its legs took his weight. The seat was soft and comfortable and, leaning across the smooth, segmented back like a motorcyclist over a fuel tank, he peered out between the antennae and saw Mump grinning back at him.

'How's it feel?' asked Mump. 'Reckon you could handle it?'

'Not sure,' said Sam. 'How does it work?'

'I'll show you,' said Mump. 'Slide off a minute.'

Sam jumped down as Mump slung his leg over and pulled the insect off its side-stand, balancing it with his toes on the ground.

Sam leant over and saw that a bright green light was shining from a small instrument panel behind the creature's head.

'What are the other lights for?' asked Sam. He saw that a blue one was winking slowly on and off and another was glowing a dull yellow. A red light remained unlit.

'The red one means you're low on fuel and it's time to fill up.'

'Where's the fuel tank?' Sam looked towards the back of the insect to see if he could spot a filler cap anywhere.

Zip smiled. 'Doesn't work quite like that,' he said. 'Remember, these things are biological, not mechanical, so food is the fuel.' He pointed to a sharp tube which protruded from the flea's mouth. 'See that thing?'

Sam nodded.

'Well, this insect works on a dual fuel system. It can function using either the sugary juices from plants or the blood of mammals. Show him how it works, Mump.'

'OK,' said Mump. He pressed a button and Sam jumped as the tube in the creature's mouth suddenly flew forward and drove deep into the snow.

'If we were on Earth now and that was a dog, a cat, or a human, then that thing would pierce the skin and suck up a nice warm gutful of the red stuff.'

Sam grimaced. 'Yuck,' he said. He looked at the long tube and imagined what it would be like to be impaled on the end of it. 'So how do you keep them alive here on Aurobon? Surely if this thing tried to suck the blood of any animal here it would kill it?'

'True,' agreed Zip. 'That's why we generally feed 'em on tree sap when they're not taking part in Earth missions. Those tubes can cut through bark like butter and the sap has enough nutrients to keep them functioning for weeks.'

'Mm,' said Mump. 'Trouble is, these things actually *prefer* blood. So you have to be a bit careful. Always make absolutely sure that the tracker system is disabled when you're not using it.'

'Tracker system?' asked Sam. 'What's that?'

'Watch,' said Mump. He flipped a switch and Sam noticed that the blue light immediately began blinking quickly on and off while the other light glowed bright yellow. The flea twitched a couple of times and then suddenly jumped round so that its little black eyes were staring straight at Sam. Its back legs tensed and it quivered all over. Then Mump flipped the switch off again and immediately the tension seemed to drain out of the creature as it sank down on its legs once more.

'Jeepers,' said Sam. 'What happened there?'

'Fleas bite animals, right? Animals are warm, they breathe and they move. So in order to track them down, fleas are very sensitive to nearby vibrations, to heat sources and to concentrations of carbon dioxide in the air. This blue light indicates the presence of carbon dioxide; the more there is of it, the faster it blinks. The yellow light indicates a heat source and it glows more brightly the nearer you get to it. When I switched the tracking system on, the flea sensed the warmth of your body and the carbon dioxide in your breath. It was getting ready to bite you when I turned it off. Do you want me to show you how it works again?'

'No thanks,' said Sam hurriedly, turning rather pale. 'I think I get the idea now.'

'You'll probably never need to use it,' said Zip. 'But it's handy if you ever need to find someone in a hurry.'

'All right,' said Mump. 'Now for the really good bit. You see this?' He tapped his fingers against the lever on the right handlebar. 'That's the jump lever. All you do is make sure your harness is done up good and tight, squeeze the lever and then hang on for dear life. I'm telling you, this baby'll do nought to a hundred metres in less than half a second. Want a try?'

'Whoa there,' said Zip, holding up his hand. 'Don't you think you'd better talk him through the vision goggles first?'

'Oh yeah,' said Mump. 'Nearly forgot. Hop on a sec, Sam. It's easier to show you if you're sitting on it.'

Sam made himself comfortable on the seat again and saw that Mump was holding out a pair of black rubber goggles which were linked to the flea's head by a curly, blue plastic lead.

'Here, put these on.'

'What are they for?' asked Sam, pulling the goggles down over his eyes. He stared through the lenses and saw that there was now a bright red cross in the centre of his vision.

'Head-up visual display,' said Zip. 'It's linked electronically to the flea's optical nerve, so that whatever you look at is exactly what the flea's brain sees. It's also got a zoom function so you can check out what nasty things are waiting for you in the distance. But basically it makes steering the thing a whole lot easier. You just look in the direction of where you want to go and the flea goes there. Clever, eh?'

'Amazing,' said Sam. He looked at Mump dubiously. 'Do you think it's safe for me to have a go then?'

'Yeah why not,' said Mump. 'As long as you hold on tight and don't let go, you'll be fine. Don't you think, Zip?'

Zip nodded. 'Should be. Experienced pilot like you, shouldn't have a problem. Only thing is, if you've never been on a flea before you might find your first jump a bit of a shock. Just be prepared for that, OK?'

Sam buckled the straps of the leather harness tightly across his shoulders and swallowed nervously.

'OK,' he said. 'If you're sure. How do I stop it?'

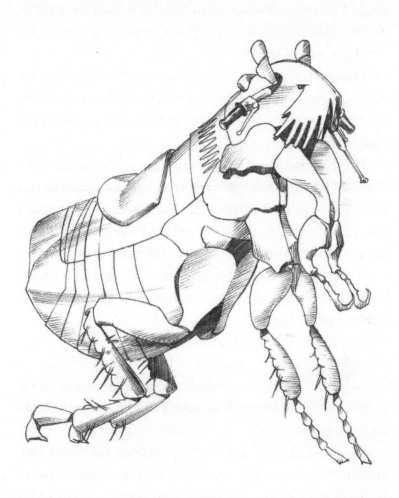

Flea motorbike

'Easy,' said Mump. 'Just release the jump lever.'

'Or alternatively,' said Zip with a wry smile, 'you could just crash it into a snowdrift.'

Pretending not to have heard this last comment, Mump reached over and turned the ignition key.

'OK, Sam,' he said. 'She's all primed and ready to go.'

'Right,' said Sam.

He took a deep breath and looked at the dark green pine trees that stood tall against the cold winter sky.

Then he squeezed the lever.

With a loud click, all the compressed energy in the flea's legs was suddenly released and Sam found himself flung high into the air with such extraordinary, breath-taking acceleration that he felt as though his insides had been ripped out and left behind in the snow. As he rocketed up into the sky at an incredible speed he looked down and noticed the two tiny black dots below him. One of the dots appeared to be waving.

Hanging on desperately to the handlebars, Sam released the lever. He immediately felt the speed of his ascent begin to slow until, just for a moment, he seemed to be hanging perfectly still above the frozen winter landscape. Looking down he saw that he was high above the trees.

Seconds later he dropped through the air like a stone, his stomach flipping as the treetops rushed toward him at a frightening rate. He was just wondering if he would be killed quickly and whether it would hurt a lot when there was a snapping of branches, a prickling of pine needles and he found himself sitting at the top of a very tall pine tree, watching two small black dots run across the snow towards him.

'Help!' he shouted as the tree began to sway slightly in the wind. 'I'm stuck!'

He looked down and saw Zip cupping his hands around his mouth.

'Pull the jump lever again!' he shouted. 'Look towards us and pull the lever!'

'Oh no,' muttered Sam queasily, looking at the long drop to the ground and feeling the soles of his feet tingle at the prospect of falling. But he moved his head around until the centre of the red cross in the goggle display was positioned directly between Zip and Mump, then squeezed the jump lever again. There was another loud click, a rush of cold air and suddenly the flea had landed neatly (and surprisingly softly) on the snow and Sam was staring at the figures of Zip and Mump who were lying sprawled out on either side of him.

'Hi, fellas,' he said, smiling happily now that he was safely back on the ground again. 'What are you doing down there?'

Zip sat up and brushed snow from his hair.

'I said look towards us,' he said, 'not *at* us.'

Sam looked puzzled for a moment until it dawned on him that he had very nearly squashed his two friends beneath the flea.

'Oh,' he said. 'Sorry about that.'

'That's OK,' said Mump cheerfully, dusting himself

down. 'I was afraid for a minute there that life might be getting a bit dull. You know, a bit ordinary. But then – Bam! – it all just kicks off again.' He grinned and held his hand out to Zip who grabbed hold of it and pulled himself to his feet. 'Wouldn't have it any other way now, would we, Zip?'

Zip looked doubtful. 'Maybe not,' he said. 'It'd be nice to have the choice, though.'

Mump stared up into the darkening sky where thick snow clouds were piling up over the mountain peaks all around them. 'There's another storm brewing,' he said.

Zip nodded. 'I say we make our way back to base and meet up with the others. I can give Mump a backer on my flea and you can have a bit of practice on the other one, Sam. What do you think?'

But Sam was staring back up the mountain again, his thoughts drawn once more to the silver waters of the lake. Although he could not have said why, a shiver of excitement ran through his veins and his heart began to beat a little faster.

'Sam? What is it? What's up?'

'Oh it's nothing,' said Sam. 'It's just . . .'

He paused, unable to explain the feelings that troubled him.

Listen with your heart . . .

'I don't suppose,' he said awkwardly, 'I could borrow this flea for a few hours, could I?'

Zip frowned.

'What for, buddy?'

Sam shook his head.

'It's just . . . I've got this strong feeling about something, that's all. It feels really important. I can't explain it any other way.'

Zip stared at him. 'That's it? Just a really strong feeling?'

Sam shrugged. 'That's it.'

'Do you want us to come with you?' asked Mump.

Sam shook his head again. 'No, I don't think so.'

Zip chewed his lip thoughtfully for a moment and then looked at Mump.

'Well, I reckon that's good enough for me, Mump. How 'bout you?'

Mump nodded. 'Can't argue with strong feelings, I say.'

Zip looked back at Sam and raised his eyebrows.

'OK, mystery man,' he said. 'Guess we'll pitch camp over in the trees until you get back. But if you're not here by morning, we'll come looking for you, OK?'

'OK,' said Sam. 'Thank you.'

Zip gestured toward the steep mountain slope with his hand.

'She's all yours, buddy,' he said. 'But be careful.'

Sam took a deep breath.

'I will,' he said.

Then he squeezed the lever and disappeared into the sky.

Six

Doctor Janik Jancy glanced over at the young research assistant standing next to him and secretly felt rather proud of her.

'Try not to be nervous, Miss Blin,' he said gently. 'Just tell them what you know.'

He knocked twice on the thick, oak-panelled door and waited for an answer. It was – as Alya had been told on several occasions – a great honour to receive an invitation to General Martock's private residence, and Jancy was obviously rather nervous himself.

Alya heard the sound of footsteps echoing across a wooden floor and then the door was opened by a soldier dressed in the ubiquitous black uniform of the Vermian Guard. Obviously expecting them, the soldier stood back to let them pass and they found themselves standing in the middle of a huge circular library, surrounded on all sides by bookshelves that stretched from floor to ceiling. The room had an old, musty smell to it and Alya could see a hundred years of dust dancing in the shafts of winter sunlight that streamed through the leaded windows.

At the opposite end of the room was a small, crescent-shaped table at which an officious looking woman sat studying a catalogue of some sort. Behind her was a large pair of doors with a guard posted on either side.

The woman continued to study the pages of her book as the two of them crossed the floor although she could not have failed to notice the sound of their approaching footsteps.

They stood in front of the desk for several seconds until it became obvious that the woman had no intention of acknowledging their presence, whereupon Doctor Jancy coughed politely and waited.

The woman slowly raised her head and regarded Jancy with practised disdain through a pair of wire-rimmed spectacles.

'Yes?' she said. 'Can I help you?'

Alya looked at the grey hair scraped back into a tight little bun and decided that helping others was probably not one of this woman's strengths.

'Yes, I believe you can,' replied Jancy patiently. 'I have an appointment to see General Martock at three o'clock.'

One of the things Jancy had always prided himself on was his ability to be punctual. The fact that the minute hand of the clock on the wall clicked round onto the hour at the very moment that he had finished speaking gave him an inordinate amount of pleasure and he allowed himself a rare smile.

'Ah yes, Doctor Jancy.' The woman adjusted her glasses a little further down her nose in order to peer over them at Alya. 'And you are . . .?'

'I am what?' said Alya.

The woman frowned. Either this girl was very stupid, or she was being extremely rude. Judging by the twinkle in her eye, it was probably the latter. She glared at her.

'What is your name, girl?'

'Alya Blin,' said Alya. 'What's yours?'

Flustered, the woman hurriedly checked the entries in the appointments book and waved the pair of them in with a grunt. Then she took her glasses off and rubbed her eyes. That was the problem with young people today: they had no respect. Such *attitude*.

She replaced her glasses and turned back to her catalogue to look at some more pictures of books, safe in the knowledge that they would never talk back to her.

'Ah, Doctor Jancy.'

With some difficulty, General Martock got up from his chair next to the fire and motioned to the pair of them to come in.

'And who, may I ask, is the lovely young lady?'

'This is Miss Blin,' said Jancy. 'She has been assisting me in my research.'

'Indeed,' said Martock. 'Well perhaps one day she will assist me in mine.' He laughed unpleasantly and, taking it as their cue, the three other men sitting around the fireplace laughed too.

'That all depends,' said Alya, looking him right in the eye.

General Martock smiled indulgently and looked around at his companions as if to check that they shared his amusement. 'On what, my dear?'

'On whether or not you are infected with parasites,' replied Alya. She smiled sweetly and noticed out of the corner of her eye that Doctor Jancy was looking horrified.

The smile vanished from General Martock's face.

'What do you mean?' he asked.

'Oh she means nothing by it,' Jancy interjected hurriedly. 'She is a specialist in parasitic studies, that is all. That is why I have brought her along here, you see. To explain the problem with the ants.'

Martock regarded Jancy suspiciously for a moment, then seemed to relax a little.

'Yes, well. In that case, let us proceed. Please, come and join us.'

He gestured towards the others and Alya sat down next to Jancy on a faded green sofa near the fire. Jancy shot her a stern warning look and she realised with a sinking feeling that she just been rude to one of the most powerful men in Vermia. It was not the most auspicious start to her scientific career. She silently determined that from now on she would try to keep her thoughts to herself. But as she watched General Martock heave his bulky frame back into the chair and saw his hard little eyes staring at her, she felt strangely alone, like a flower that has pushed its way up through a crack in the earth only to find itself surrounded by concrete.

'First, some introductions,' said Martock. 'This is Lieutenant Reisner, Leader of our Earth-Based Ant Squadrons.' A fit, hard-muscled man in his late twenties nodded curtly at them and Alya imagined him standing on some freezing cold parade ground, shouting at his men as they ran around in tracksuits.

A slightly older, more distinguished-looking man was standing up and bowing in their direction, exuding the quiet self-confidence that comes with power and success. 'Field Marshal Stanzun,' said Martock, 'is a veteran of our successful Vahlzian campaign and Overall Commander of our forces both here and on Earth.'

Alya noticed that his short black hair was greying at the sides and that the breast pocket of his uniform was decorated with lines of coloured medal ribbons.

'And Major Krazni here is Head of Intelligence and Security.'

Looking across at the thin, blond-haired man in the black leather coat standing next to the fire, Alya felt the hairs prickle on the back of her neck. There was something about the way he looked at her through his small round spectacles, the way his cold green eyes seemed to bore into her own that made her feel extremely uncomfortable.

'And I think you all know Doctor Janik Jancy, Head of InRaD, at least by reputation.'

General Martock turned to face Jancy and the others looked at him expectantly.

'So, Doctor. I understand you have some important information for us.'

Jancy nodded.

'I believe so, yes.'

'Then, please, keep us in suspense no longer.'

Jancy folded his hands in his lap and sat up straight. For some reason he made Alya think of a small boy on his first day at school.

'The cause of the malfunction in the ants is a parasitic worm which begins its life in snails. The ants are attracted to the snail's slime and when they feed on it, they swallow the worms. The worms know that they need to live in a sheep for the final stage of their life cycle. So they have learned how to change the ant's natural behaviour in order to achieve their goal.'

Alya noticed that General Martock was suddenly leaning forward in his chair with great interest.

'Are you saying that this small, insignificant creature is actually able to affect the behaviour of other creatures?'

'Well, I don't know about other creatures, but it can certainly influence the behaviour of ants, yes.'

Field Marshal Stanzun was looking puzzled.

'Can you please explain to us, Doctor Jancy, the method in which the worm can influence the behaviour of ants?'

'Certainly,' said Jancy. 'Although perhaps in this instance I will defer to my research assistant, Miss Blin, who has a particular specialism in this field.'

All eyes were now on Alya. She suddenly became acutely aware of the importance of her task, but her nervousness was tempered by the fact that she had a secure grasp of her subject. She knew what she was talking about.

'By following a series of chemical signposts, the worm makes its way through the ant's bloodstream until it reaches the brain. It is here that it begins to weave its biological magic.'

Alya looked around the room and saw the men exchanging the kind of glances that suggested they were rather more excited by all of this than she had expected. She had always found the life cycles of parasites fascinating, of course, but she hadn't presumed that her enthusiasm would be shared to such an extent by this particular group.

It was all very pleasing.

'The worm then begins to carry out selective neurological damage' – here she noticed Reisner looking confused and suddenly remembered she was not dealing with scientists – 'sorry, it alters the brain cells in such a way that it makes the ant begin to behave in ways which one would not normally expect.'

Martock stared at her.

'And tell us, Miss Blin. What ways might they be?'

'When evening comes, the infected ants climb to the top of a blade of grass and stay there until the following morning. When the sun comes up again, the ant releases its grip on the grass and returns to the ground whereupon it resumes its normal behaviour until the next evening. This process continues indefinitely until either the ant dies or it is eaten by a sheep.'

'Why doesn't the ant just stay there?' asked Reisner.

'Because the worm needs the ant to stay alive. If the ant remains motionless in the heat of the sun without food or water, then it will die and the parasite will die along with it. Simple as that.'

Alya glanced across at Martock and saw that he had a strange glint in his eye.

'Would I be right in thinking then, Miss Blin, that these parasites of which you speak are able to act as puppet masters, controlling the actions of other creatures purely for their own ends?'

'Yes,' replied Alya. 'That is a good way of putting it.'

She noticed that Lieutenant Reisner's brow – which was furrowed for much of the preceding conversation – had now been smoothed over by the warm iron of understanding.

'Well, I must say that is a great relief,' he said. 'I presume that now we are in possession of this knowledge, we will be able to carry out a programme which will rid our squadrons of these parasites and return them to full strength as soon as possible.'

'You have my assurance that the programme to eliminate these parasites will start immediately,' said Doctor Jancy. 'The technology department has already written some new software, which will regulate the feeding habits of the piloted ants so that they are no longer attracted to slime deposits. This should prevent any incidents of re-infection.'

He smiled happily at the assembled company and felt deeply satisfied by the way things had gone. Admittedly the girl had got things off to a bad start – he would have to have a word with her about that later – but she had redeemed herself with her confident presentation of the facts, so there was no real harm done. The cream of the Vermian Empire had seen that Doctor Jancy's team could fix problems quickly and efficiently – which would certainly be useful when applying for any future government funding.

'I think we can safely say that this unfortunate chapter is now closed,' said Jancy. 'I am sure you will be pleased to learn that this is the last time you will have to hear anything about parasites.'

Major Krazni, who had so far contributed nothing to the conversation, now stepped forward from his place by the mantelpiece and shook his head.

'On the contrary, Doctor Jancy,' he said. 'That is exactly what we wish to hear about.'

He turned to Alya.

'Tell us, Miss Blin, do you know anything about toxoplasma?'

'*Toxoplasma gondii*?' asked Alya, surprised.

Krazni nodded.

'It's a parasite that lives in cats. Its life cycle means that it normally moves between cats and rats.'

'Very good,' said Krazni. 'Please. Continue.'

'The cat releases the eggs of the toxoplasma parasite in its droppings and these are eaten by rats. The parasites live hidden away in the rat's brain until a cat comes along and eats it. Then they all burst out into the cat and the whole process starts again. Incredible, really.'

'Indeed,' said Krazni. 'But that's not the most incredible part, is it, Miss Blin?'

Alya looked at the green, snake-like eyes watching her so attentively and began to feel slightly anxious. But at the same time, she felt pleased to be able to demonstrate her knowledge in front of these very important people. Maybe it was the first step toward a research fellowship of her own.

'I suppose not,' she said.

'So enlighten us, Miss Blin. What is the most incredible part of all?'

Alya stared right back into Krazni's eyes, determined not to be intimidated.

'I presume you're referring to its ability to control the mind of its host.'

Krazni nodded. 'Suppose you tell us about that,' he said.

'A rat that is infected with the toxoplasma parasite,' replied Alya, 'loses all its natural fear of cats. In fact, sometimes it will even seek them out. You might say that the parasite forces its rat host to commit suicide in order to make sure that it ends up inside a cat.'

Krazni smiled.

'All very interesting,' he said. 'Yet another example of

a parasite which can influence the behaviour of another creature. I wonder, does the toxoplasma have any other natural host? Besides rats and cats I mean?'

All of a sudden, Alya saw what he was driving at. She had heard of Odoursin's hatred for the people of Earth. Could this be part of a new plan to destroy them?

'Miss Blin?'

'I–I don't know. I'm not sure.'

Alya was flustered now. Staring at the patterns on the carpet, she heard Krazni walk forwards and then the black leather coat was right in front of her.

'I will ask you again, Miss Blin. Does the toxoplasma parasite have any other natural host?'

Alya's throat was so tight that she could hardly swallow. But she guessed he knew anyway. There was nothing to be gained from keeping quiet.

'About a third of all humans living on Earth are infected by it,' she replied. 'Maybe even more.'

Krazni inclined his head and smiled.

'Thank you, Miss Blin,' he said. 'Thank you very much.'

Alya made no reply. But as Krazni walked back to his place next to the mantelpiece and the murmurs of excitement began to spread around the room, she stared silently into the flames of the fire and wondered what she had done.

Seven

At first, Sam was understandably cautious about sitting on the back of an insect that could shoot him up into the sky at such incredible speed. But once he got the hang of the controls, it was nothing short of fantastic. He discovered that if you kept the lever pulled back against the handlebars, the flea would automatically jump every six seconds. You could tell when it was about to take off because a series of illuminated red bars would gradually stack up on the display panel until they reached the end of the little glass window. Then the red bars would flash once and bam! You were up among the clouds again. Zip reckoned that each flea had enough stored energy to jump continuously for three days non-stop.

The acceleration was simply extraordinary. One second Sam would be staring at a large rock in front of him, the next he was catapulted high into the air and the rock would be a tiny speck, hundreds of metres below.

The hardest part was getting used to the landing. Once the flea had reached the highest point of its jump it would start to fall again, plummeting out of the sky at such a terrifying rate that it seemed he would be smashed to pieces on the ground that rushed up to meet him. The first few times it happened, Sam shut his eyes and pressed his face against the flea's bristly back, expecting it to crash violently into the ice and rocks below. But instead – to his relief – the landing was as soft as jumping off a sofa onto a huge pile of cushions. The suspension in the flea's legs was so efficient that it absorbed all of the impact by compressing its muscles, ready for the next spectacular burst of energy.

Sam landed with a gentle bump and stared ahead through the display goggles.

He was high above the lake on an outcrop of rock, looking down at the shining waters from which he had earlier emerged. His stomach flipped as he peered down over the precipice, but he was already becoming more used to the fact that the flea could jump from a great height and still land quite safely.

Squeezing the lever once more he rocketed over the edge at great speed, soaring through freezing air as the wind whistled around his ears and blew ice crystals into his hair.

Seconds later, the flea crunched down on the cold lake shore and Sam swung himself off, kicking out the side-stand to leave the flea parked at a jaunty angle on the stones.

Now that he was here, he wasn't sure exactly why he had come.

But as grey flakes of snow began to fall thickly from the lead-coloured sky, he felt a strange longing which grew stronger with every second that passed.

Find the one who is true of heart.

He found himself drawn towards the waterfall which tumbled down the side of the mountain before plunging into a pool of foam and glitter at the base of the cliff. Approaching along the shoreline he noticed that the air was filled with a fine, cool mist which carried upon the wind to form small, delicate clouds against the grey winter sky.

As he listened to the roar of the falls and watched a rainbow arc bright colours across the water, something in the centre of the pool caught his eye. The light was failing and at first he thought his eyes were playing tricks upon him. But as he looked more closely, he saw the body of a young girl floating beneath the surface, her arms wide open and her face tilted up toward the sky. Hidden currents dragged her downwards and strands of blonde hair waved gently around her pale, expressionless face as she drifted in the watery breeze.

'Oh no,' whispered Sam. 'Oh please, no . . .'

Running across the stones he launched himself headlong into the pool, gasping as the icy waters closed around him. Sucking cold air deep into his lungs, he dived beneath the surface and swam frantically toward the girl as she sank lower into the pool's murky depths.

The freezing water enveloped him and as he groped desperately around in the gloom he could feel the thud of his heart and the roaring of blood in his ears. With a final effort, he grabbed the girl by the arm and swam for the shore, dragging her cold, limp body onto the stones before collapsing in an exhausted heap next to her. Resting his face wearily on the pebbles, he listened to the thunder of the waterfall behind him and then, as his breath returned, he lifted himself up onto his elbows and turned to face the girl who lay so still and silent beside him.

Her face was grey and her eyes were closed. She looked peaceful, as though she were asleep.

'No,' he said quietly. 'No . . .'

Gathering her up in his arms, he carried her to a small cave at the base of the cliff where he laid her gently down upon the stones. As he did so, he noticed another robe lying in the shadows at the side of the cave and, still shivering, he carried it across to her and tenderly covered her with it. But as his fingers touched her face he felt how desperately cold she was.

And then he realised that he was crying, and that it was too late.

Hours passed, slipping away like ghosts into the grey afternoon.

Alone on the cold lake shore, Sam stared silently into the water's black depths. As the day grew dark and the setting sun rimmed the mountains with crimson, he felt empty, as though he had come to the end of everything.

'Please,' he whispered. 'How shall I save her?'

But as evening spread itself across the sky and the wheel of stars turned slowly above him, the only reply was the roar of the waterfall, splashing and tumbling over ancient stones.

Overcome by exhaustion and despair, Sam slid into a cold and dreamless sleep.

He woke early to the sound of birdsong; a single, warbling call that floated through the trees and into his consciousness. Confused, he stood up and stretched his cold, aching muscles. Then the grief rose in his throat as he remembered, and he ran quickly across the deserted shoreline towards the cave.

Reaching the entrance, his heart fluttered wildly and for a few moments he stood motionless at the threshold, unsure of what to do. He pressed his forehead against the cool rock and felt its smoothness against his skin.

Then, taking a deep breath, he stepped inside, steeling himself for what he knew he must find there.

But the cave was empty.

There was no one there.

With a cry of anguish, Sam fell to his knees and began to scrabble furiously at the stones with his bare hands, searching frantically for any sign of the body he had placed there so carefully the night before.

But there was no sign of her; nothing to suggest that she had ever been more than the cruel invention of another wretched dream.

In his anger and frustration, Sam picked up a rock and threw it at the side of the cave where it smashed into a thousand fragments, clattering away into the shadows.

'Let me wake up!' he cried. 'I don't want to dream any more – I want to know what's *real*!'

As his cries died away, fading into the dark recesses of the cave, the hairs prickled on the back of his neck and he sensed that he was no longer alone.

Slowly, he turned to face the entrance of the cave and there, silhouetted against the light, stood the figure of a young girl. Her hair was blonde and straggly, and she wore a robe like his own.

'Sam,' she said softly. 'Is that you?'

Hardly daring to hope, he got unsteadily to his feet and shielded his eyes against the light. Then, with a little squeak, the girl sprang forward and ran barefoot across the stones towards him.

'It can't be,' he whispered. 'It *can't* be . . .'

But as she launched herself at him and threw her arms around his neck, he staggered backwards, shouting her name until it echoed and sang through the shadows of the dark and lonely cave.

'Skipper,' he cried, 'Skipper – you're *alive*!'

Eight

It was late. Through the laboratory window, Alya could see the three coloured moons rising high above Vermia. She thought of a night in summer long ago, a night when she was four years old and the light of magic had yet to fade from the things around her. Her mother and father had walked with her to the edge of their village and pointed up at the sky.

'Look, Alya,' her father had said. 'There is one for each of us. The green one – that's your mother. The red one is me. And you see that pale blue one, shining in the darkness between them? That's you, Alya. The most beautiful one of all.'

And that was it; the last time she ever saw them.

That night, her village was caught up in the war between Vahlzian troops and Odoursin's renegade army. The soldiers had come and destroyed everything. Nothing had been the same since and nothing ever could be.

Oh, there had been kindnesses along the way; the

women at the Vermian orphanage for instance – saving
her from the work camps by pretending that she was
pulled from the rubble of a bombed-out air-raid shelter.
That small act of compassion in itself had been enough
to give her the chance she needed – her own natural
intelligence had done the rest. She had excelled at school
in Vermia from where she had gone on to win a scholar-
ship to the Government Academy of Life Sciences. Her
work on parasites had attracted the attention of the
people at InRaD who had quickly recognised her talent
and recruited her into their research team.

And now, it seemed, even Vermia's highest officials
were interested in her work.

But the truth was, none of this really helped to remove
the dull ache she felt inside whenever she remembered
how much she had once been loved.

She would work sixteen hour days and return exhausted to her empty flat, too tired to do anything but fall into
bed and sleep until the sound of the alarm clock woke
her again the following morning. She secretly hoped that
each new accomplishment, each new scientific discovery
or accolade would go some way towards filling the empty
void.

But somehow, it never did.

Perhaps, she thought, it would be different this time.
If she could only find a way to manipulate the genetic
code of these toxoplasma worms, then she would be the
toast of the scientific community. Finally, she would
have her proper place in this world.

Switching on the anglepoise lamp, Alya pulled it down so that a bright pool of light spilled onto the stainless steel worktop. She snapped open the catch on the temperature-controlled storage unit, pulled out a test tube and, with the help of a pair of tweezers, removed a tangled white slab of living tissue. It made little squelching noises as she placed it firmly on the shiny surface and using a sharp scalpel she carefully removed a cross-section from the centre. Leaving the rest of it glistening wetly on the worktop, she picked up the small sample and took it over to the powerful electron microscope in the corner of the lab.

The microscope hummed softly as she switched it on and Alya was pleased to note that the twin eyepiece was still set at the correct height for her; she had adjusted it for her own use earlier in the day and it seemed that no one else had used it. She wasn't really surprised. Most of the team were more concerned with macro-sized engineering developments, so she tended to have the use of the microscope to herself these days.

Placing the sample on a glass slide, she positioned it beneath the lens and then, using a dial on the side of the microscope, adjusted the focal length until the complex structure of the tissue came sharply into focus.

She smiled to herself with quiet satisfaction.

The years that she had spent studying similar creatures had enabled her to find quickly, and with unerring accuracy, whichever part of them she chose to analyse. And as the microscopic landscape of small ridges, peaks and valleys emerged from the darkness – illuminated by the glare of a billion electrons – she knew she had entered a world that few others would ever see.

She was staring deep into the mind of a parasitic worm.

Commander Firebrand lay on the cold stone floor of his cell and wondered – as he had taken to doing lately – how long it would be before they finally decided to kill him. He knew from the small scratches he had made on the wall with his fingernail that it had been nearly a month since his capture. During that time they had starved him, threatened him and beaten him to within an inch of his life.

But he hadn't told them anything.

Not a single thing.

'You are a foolish man,' they would say, tightening his blindfold and spinning him around so that their voices seemed to come from every corner of the cell. 'Why be so hard on yourself? Just tell us where the Resistance base is. Tell us where your people are hiding and we can put a stop to all this unpleasantness once and for all.'

But Firebrand would just shake his head and say nothing. And then the whole shameful business would start all over again.

Sometimes, in the lonely, tar-black hours, he would find himself wondering if the next blow might be the one that broke his spirit, the one that left him pleading for mercy in exchange for the information that they required.

It was this, perhaps, which he feared the most, for he knew that such a betrayal would dissolve the last shaky foundations of his faith and consign him to an even greater darkness; a darkness where even the light of hope would finally be extinguished. But just when it seemed that he could hold out no longer, the pain would unexpectedly unlock a place in his heart where something precious still shone, bright and strange, untainted by the corrosive horrors that closed in from all sides.

Firebrand shut his eyes and remembered it once more.

He was walking through a meadow in high summer, a soft breeze stirring the treetops as the scent of dry earth and pollen hung heavy beneath an empty sky. Next to him skipped a little blonde girl with a wild rose in her hair.

'I can't let you do it,' he was saying. 'I won't let you.'

'But why not?' she cried. 'I'm perfectly capable. You know I am!'

'That's not the point,' he said. 'That's not the point at all.'

'Then what is?' replied the girl. 'What is the point? You can't think of a single reason why I shouldn't fly this mission, but still you won't let me go.'

Firebrand had sighed and taken her by the hand.

'There is a reason,' he said, 'but I am afraid it is a selfish one.'

He had looked at the girl then, seen how much she wanted to do this and known in his heart that he would not be able to stop her.

'I don't want to let you go,' he said, 'because I do not want to lose you.'

And the girl – whose name was Skipper – had looked at him and said, 'We always lose the things that we love. That is part of what love is.'

Here in the darkness, Firebrand thought about how his fears had been justified; for he had let her go and now she would never come back.

All that remained were these vague, electrical pulses in his head, memories that tricked him into thinking the past was something that still mattered.

But there was something else that she had said right at the end, something that still allowed him to hope – *oh he knew how foolish it was* – to hope that there was something beyond the despair that he felt.

'We always lose the things that we love,' she said.

And then, seeing the sadness in his eyes, she had turned to him and smiled.

'But that does not mean,' she added, putting a small hand on top of his own, 'that we shall not find them again one day.'

Typing some numbers into a computer linked to the microscope, Alya programmed the small motor-driven belt beneath the glass slide to move a tiny fraction to the left. The beauty of working with creatures from Earth was the difference in scale; on Earth the toxoplasma

worm was so small that it would need a powerful microscope even to see the whole of it. Here on Aurobon, the
fact that it was the size of a snake meant that you could
delve much deeper into the tiniest twists of its DNA,
peer at its structural secrets and stare at the shape and
form of the very building blocks that had made it.

For several months now, Alya had been convinced that
if she could just drill far enough down into the brains of
the parasites she studied, she would eventually find the
material home of their subconscious mind, the home of
every thought and desire that drove them. She knew that
somewhere, hidden deep within the microscopic folds of
the brain, lay a code which would enable her to unlock
the secret language of their minds, the language which
told these creatures where they should go, what they
should do and even what they should wish for. If she
could somehow discover this language and learn how to
read it, then maybe – just maybe – she could learn how
to write it too . . .

Squinting through the lens, Alya increased the magnification and was pleased to see that – as she had hoped –
the familiar undulating landscapes of the worm's brain
tissue had been replaced by something entirely different.
The hills and valleys had given way to a regular series of
hexagonal rings, each one linked to its neighbours by
strands of yellow and red nerve tissue. There was no doubt
about it; here was a very orderly, very definite system of
patterns which Alya recognised instinctively as having
their own logic. She was filled with a sudden exhilaration

as she realised that she was now sailing into uncharted waters. But as remarkable as this was, there was something else even more remarkable that quickly drew Alya's attention. Up in the very top right hand corner of the slide was a jagged, blue line with numerous small spikes along its length, sticking out like thorns upon the stem of a bramble.

Alya let out a small cry of astonishment and sat back in her chair, blinking with quiet amazement under the white glare of the laboratory lights. All at once, the facts and figures gleaned from years of study and long, lonely nights of research began to gather together in her mind like a thousand chattering birds, transforming themselves into an organised flock that soared high into the clear skies of her understanding. Alya gazed after them in wonder as if seeing them for the very first time, and was filled with a strange and terrible excitement.

The blue, bramble-shaped line was, in itself, nothing new to Alya. She had come across it several times before in her biological textbooks. Studies had shown that it was almost certainly the neurological link between thought and action, the physical bridge across which a creature's desires walked in order to make themselves known in the outside world.

It was well known, of course, that all living things contained a similar structure which allowed their behaviour in the 'real' world to reflect the ideas in their minds. But studies so far had shown that these structures were each as different as the organisms of which they were a part.

Alya certainly hadn't expected to find one that looked anything like this in the brain of a parasitic worm.

In fact, Alya knew there was only one place where you would expect to see a structure with the same shape and colour as this one. She thought back to the lecture in college three years ago where she'd stared for the first time in fascination at the jagged blue image projected on the screen. She could still remember the professor's words exactly:

'Ladies and gentlemen,' he had said. 'Can anyone here tell me what we are looking at?'

There had been a long, somewhat uncomfortable silence and a shuffling of feet before the professor had spoken again.

'No? Well perhaps I should not be surprised, for it is in truth a rather recent discovery. But it is one which you should mark well, for it may contain within it the secrets of the universe – secrets which – one day – some of you may yet begin to unravel.'

A hush had fallen across the auditorium, and the professor had let it hang in the air for several moments before finally gazing out at the serious faces of his young students and telling them:

'Ladies and gentlemen, you are looking at a doorway into the human brain.'

Nine

'So you've really got no memory at all of how you got here then?' asked Sam as they sat huddled together, chattering excitedly about the turn of events that had led to their reunion.

'No, not really,' replied Skipper. 'I remember having a sort of dream that I was being carried, and I was very cold, and then someone dressed me in this warm robe. The next thing I knew I was waking up here in this cave. Before all of that, the last thing I remember is you and me flying in a mosquito, trying to get you back to Earth again.'

'Well that's the weird part,' said Sam. 'I *did* get back to Earth.'

'What?' said Skipper, puzzled.

'I know,' said Sam, 'and it gets weirder. I met up with Zip and Mump yesterday, and they told me that you and I both went missing from Aurobon four years ago.'

'Four *years*?' exclaimed Skipper. 'But that's impossible.'

'That's what I thought,' said Sam, 'and I wouldn't have believed it except for the fact that they both look so much older.'

Skipper looked at him doubtfully. 'Are you sure about this?'

Sam sighed. 'Look, I know it's hard to believe,' he said, 'although it's easier for me because I can still vaguely remember my time back on Earth. Do you really not remember anything?'

Skipper shook her head and Sam saw that she looked quite frightened. 'No,' she said, 'nothing at all. None of this makes any sense to me, Sam.'

At that moment there was a loud *thwump* outside the cave and they looked up to see that Zip and Mump had landed their flea in the snow outside. Sam ran across to the entrance and waved.

'Hey, buddy,' Zip called. 'Are you OK? We were worried about you, so we followed your tracks.'

'I'm fine!' Sam shouted back. 'But come and see who I've found!'

There followed several minutes of loud whooping and laughter, with Mump and Zip doing a little celebratory dance around Skipper while she stood amused and bewildered in the middle of the cave. Later, after the excitement and emotion of their meeting had died down a little, Mump managed to get a fire going while Zip told Skipper about all the things that had happened during her absence.

'That's absolutely awful,' said Skipper, her eyes flashing angrily as she learned of all the death and destruction that had come to Aurobon. 'We *have* to hit back at them somehow.'

'We're trying,' said Zip, 'but the fact that they control the skies makes life very difficult for us.'

'What about the wasps?' said Skipper. 'There must still be some left, surely.'

'There's one squadron of about twenty wasps,' said Zip. 'Hidden away in a secret production factory in the mountains, which is where the Resistance are based. Brindle's been in charge of them since Firebrand got captured, but he's grounded the lot of them. Refuses to let them fly.'

'What?' exclaimed Skipper in amazement. 'Why?'

'Robber flies,' said Mump. 'Meanest, nastiest things you ever saw. Soon as you get a wasp up in the air, those things just tear 'em out of the sky.'

Skipper looked incredulous.

'Surely their pilots are no match for ours?'

'It's not their pilots that are the problem,' said Zip. 'It's the flies. Our wasps have got no chance against them. They're bigger, faster, more powerful, and with a sharp proboscis that can suck the life out of any wasp in mid-air. Our dragonfly squadrons could probably have matched them, but Odoursin was well aware of that. So the first wave of robber flies descended on our dragonfly base and destroyed every single one of them before they could even take off. After that we had no chance. Their air superiority was total.'

Sam was thoughtful for a few moments, then clicked his fingers and pointed at Zip as an idea suddenly came to him.

'This factory that you mentioned up in the mountains – is it still capable of producing more wasps?'

'Well, yes,' said Zip, 'but I don't see what good it would do. Even if we sent up a thousand wasps, the robber flies would soon destroy them. It might take them a bit longer, but they'd still win in the end. The wasps just can't compete against them.'

'No, wait,' said Skipper. 'I think I know what Sam's getting at.' She leaned forward excitedly. 'Go on, Sam.'

'You said that Odoursin harvested the eggs of robber flies,' Sam continued. 'Where did he get them from?'

Zip shrugged. 'Earth I suppose. Same way as we got the wasp eggs.'

'Well, then,' said Sam. 'Why don't we go and get some too?'

Zip pursed his lips. 'We've already thought of that I'm afraid.'

'So what's the problem?' asked Skipper. 'We've got wasps haven't we? All we need to do is find the right fabric gap, fly through it and find out where these robber flies hang out. Then we steal some of their eggs, take them back to the production factory and get the development team to convert them into aircraft. The engineering can't be that different from what they've already done on wasps and dragonflies. Besides, if Odoursin's lot can do it, then so can we.'

'Yeah, but that's not the hard part,' said Zip. 'The difficulty is actually getting to the fabric gap without a robber fly spotting you and ripping you to pieces. Believe me, we've tried many times. That's why we're down to our last wasp squadron. Those flies have got such sensitive tracking systems, they can detect a wasp from miles away. Brindle decided we just can't risk any more wasps.'

'But what's the alternative?' asked Sam. 'Either we try and get these eggs, or we just wait around here until Odoursin's men track us down and kill us. If I'm going to die, I'd rather do it trying to stop him. I say we risk it and go. There's always a chance that we'll get there before they see us. What do you think, Skipper?'

Sam looked at Skipper for support and was surprised to see that she was shaking her head.

'I don't think we'd make it, Sam,' she said. 'From what Zip says about these robber flies, the chances of us getting past them in a wasp are virtually nil.'

Sam couldn't believe what he was hearing. Surely Skipper wasn't just going to give up without a fight?

'So what are you saying then?' he asked, unable to keep the anger and disappointment from his voice. 'Are you saying that we should just sit here and do nothing?'

Skipper looked at him reproachfully. 'Sam,' she said, 'I think you know me better than that.'

She turned to face Zip.

'I'm saying we don't even try to avoid them. I say we just fly out there and let them attack us.'

Zip stared at her as if she was mad.

'What on earth for?' he asked.

'Because,' said Skipper, 'then we can turn the situation to our advantage.'

Sam remembered the hideous fly he had seen on the mountainside and swallowed hard.

'Are you serious?' he asked.

Skipper looked back at him and smiled.

'Trust me,' she said. 'Zip – how far is it from here?'

'Not far,' said Zip. 'Maybe a couple of hours if you take the fleas. As a matter of fact, that's where we were headed when we bumped into Sam. But he insisted on coming here first.'

'Yeah,' said Mump. 'For some reason he thought we might find something of value.' He looked across at Skipper and grinned. 'Can't think why.'

As Zip and Mump led the way toward the mouth of the cave, Skipper bumped gently against Sam with her shoulder.

'Hey, you,' she said. 'Thanks for coming to find me.'

'That's OK,' said Sam. 'I thought I'd lost you there for a while.'

'Well, I guess you did,' said Skipper. 'In fact, it sounds as though I've been lost for a long time.' She shook her head sadly. 'I just wish I could remember where.'

Sam nodded.

'These are strange times,' he said. 'But maybe things will become clearer when all of this is over.'

'We have to *make* it over, first, don't we?' said Skipper.

'We have to find some way of getting back at Vermia. And something tells me that's not going to be easy.'

'We'll do it though, right?' said Sam.

Skipper looked at him and her eyes hardened like diamonds.

'Oh yeah,' she said. 'Count on it.'

They walked on a little way and then Sam turned to Skipper with a wry smile.

'Hey,' he said. 'D'you fancy a ride on my flea?'

'Well now,' said Skipper, her smile returning as she twirled around in a perfect circle. 'And there was me thinking the day couldn't get any better.'

Sam saw how her blue eyes sparkled and remembered the words that Salus had spoken:

Find the one who is true of heart.

He had found her, and now there was work to be done.

Ten

As the flea thumped gently down onto the tightly packed snow, Zip and Mump flew past them at great speed and Sam noticed that Mump was pointing at something up ahead. Sam released the jump-lever and flicked a switch which activated the zoom on his vision goggles. Immediately the evergreen forest in the distance seemed to rush towards him and he found himself looking at the delicate pine needles and cones of a single branch.

Locating a small serrated wheel on the side of the goggles with his finger, he gradually adjusted the zoom so that he could see a slightly wider picture. He adjusted the zoom again and saw that Zip and Mump had stopped about half a mile away next to a slab of rock, half-hidden in the trees.

'Do you think that's it?' said Sam. 'I can't see any sign of the factory.'

'I suppose that's the idea,' said Skipper. 'If it was that easy to find, then Odoursin would have found it by now.'

'Good point,' said Sam. He squeezed the jump-lever again and seconds later they landed with a soft thump next to the others.

'Hello, my children,' said Mump. 'Welcome to Wasp World.'

'I can't see any wasps,' said Sam.

'Oh wait,' said Mump, pretending to look around. 'You're right. Maybe I should just call it "World".'

'Come on, Mump,' said Skipper. 'Stop pratting about. I'm freezing.'

'All right,' said Mump. 'Sorry. OK, watch. You'll like this.'

He put his hand against the rock and moved it around. Nothing happened.

Zip grinned at Sam and Skipper. 'Pretty impressive, eh?' he said sarcastically.

'I'll get it in a minute,' said Mump.

'Not like that you won't,' said Zip. 'Try it over to your left a bit. Just above that little dark patch.'

'I *know*,' said Mump in a slightly whiny voice. 'Quit hassling me.'

Zip raised his eyebrows. 'See what I have to put up with?'

Mump moved his hand across to the left and suddenly a line of bright blue light appeared around the outline of his fingers.

'Wow,' said Sam. 'What's that?'

'Told you you'd like it,' said Mump. 'It's a recognition device.'

'At the moment it's reading his fingerprints,' explained Zip. 'Next it'll check out his eyes. As long as he continues to look as gormless as he normally does, we should be OK.'

'Hey,' said Mump. 'I heard that.'

Sam watched another blue light flicker across Mump's face, and then suddenly the wall was gone. To Sam's considerable surprise, it didn't slide away, or wobble and then dissolve. It simply disappeared, revealing a long and brightly lit tunnel stretching away into the heart of the mountain.

'Quick,' said Zip as Mump cheerfully put his thumbs up. 'Inside before it closes up again.' He jumped the flea through the entrance and Sam followed, putting one foot down and stylishly slewing the back end around as he came to a halt. Zip smiled approvingly.

'I see you're getting the hang of it, then,' he said.

As Skipper slipped off the back, Sam leant the creature onto its side-stand and turned the ignition off, whereupon the light went out of the creature's eyes and it sank down upon its suspension.

'I love these things,' said Skipper, patting the foam seat. 'Where did you get them from?'

'Let's just say we borrowed them,' said Mump. 'From a couple of Vermian soldiers.' He grinned. 'I can hotwire 'em easy. Next time we're in Vahlzi, I'll nick you one if you like.'

'Thanks, Mump,' said Skipper. 'That's sweet of you.'

Sam looked back and saw that the entrance they had

come through only moments ago was now completely sealed again. Where there had been space, there was now only solid stone.

He whistled.

'How does that work, then?'

'Coffee,' said Mump. 'Amazing what a couple of cups can do.'

'Take no notice,' said Zip. 'It's Chromotographic Optical Force Field Energy Emissions. Fairly new technology, actually. They analyse the colour and density of the original rock and then use a high concentration of light and energy to replace it. It means they can have something that looks and feels like the original rock, but it can be removed in a second simply by turning the power off.'

'Why didn't we have it at the airbase?' asked Skipper.

'Too new. This whole facility was developed before the war to test and develop new insect technologies. But when Vahlzi was overrun, Firebrand decided to pull out and organise the Resistance movement from here. As far as we know, Vermia isn't even aware that the COFFEE technology exists. So this place is pretty secure. Unless you've got clearance, there's no way you're coming in. That's why they keep the last of the wasps here, out of harm's way. Beyond the reach of robber flies.'

'Hey!' shouted a voice suddenly. Sam turned to see five men in black boots and blue combat gear walking menacingly towards them. Each carried a machine gun.

'Aww, nuts,' said Mump. 'Security cameras must've registered you as a threat.'

'Get on your knees and put your hands on your head,' barked one of them. 'Do it NOW!'

Sam dropped quickly to his knees and saw that the others were doing the same.

'Gee, take a pill, guys,' said Zip, waving his hands in the air. 'Calm down, eh?'

'Hands on your head!'

His heart thudding in his chest, Sam smacked his hands on the top of his head and swallowed hard. He saw the men raise their guns and take aim, saw their hard, angry faces and thought more than anything what a waste it all was. Now they would never get a chance to make things better, to see how things turned out.

And then, just as it seemed that the men were about to shoot, he heard a voice he recognised, echoing through the underground chamber.

'Hold your fire!' shouted the voice. Sam raised his head to see a stocky, powerfully built man in blue uniform striding towards them. He had short, close-cropped ginger hair and carried a silver topped cane in his right hand. Sam recognised him as Sergeant Brindle, a fierce training instructor who had once been in charge of aircrew training at the Vahlzian airbase. As he approached, the soldiers looked at one another and lowered their guns.

Brindle stared at Sam and Skipper for a few seconds as if unable to quite believe his eyes. 'Where in the hell,' he asked, 'did you two spring from?'

They followed Brindle and the soldiers down a gently
sloping tunnel lit by long twists of white tubing that
glowed from the roof like some sort of strange, radioac-
tive spaghetti.

'Ooh I say,' whispered Skipper. 'Very modern.'

Up ahead the tunnel curved around to the left and
Sam decided that whatever lay around the corner must
be rather important; beams of white light spilled out on
the surrounding rock and lit up the darkness as if it were
a summer's day.

Blinking and screwing up their eyes, Sam and Skipper
hurried along the last hundred metres or so of tunnel. As
they turned the corner they found themselves standing
at the entrance of a huge, egg-shaped cavern. Beneath
the glare of powerful arc lights set into the curved stone
ceiling, Sam could see the unmistakable black and yellow
stripes of a dozen huge wasps, crouching on the floor of
what was obviously part of the secret underground
hangar. Sam was struck by what excellent condition the
wasps were in. Their heads and bodies were highly
polished and Sam could see the reflection of the lights
shining from the black, inscrutable eyes that stared out
of their smooth yellow faces.

'Wow,' said Skipper voicing Sam's thoughts, 'they're
in better nick than the ones we used to fly. Showroom
condition.'

Sam nodded, feeling a pang of nostalgia as he remembered the battered leather seats and the scratched, dented
exoskeletons of the wasps he had once piloted.

'That's because these are straight from the egg,' said Brindle. 'They've never been flown.'

Sam looked at all the people busily scurrying about beneath the bright lights, some carrying spanners and screwdrivers, some holding bits of circuit board and others pushing wheeled steps against the thick, stripy bodies of the wasps.

'I don't get it,' he said. 'What's the point keeping them here in perfect condition if they're never going to be used?'

Brindle shrugged.

'Maybe a day will come when the tide turns in this war and it's safe to fly them again. But right now it would be suicide. Those robber flies have complete control of the skies.'

'Well, pardon me for stating the obvious,' said Skipper, 'but the tide isn't going to turn by itself, is it? I mean, if you're just waiting around for things to get better then you're still going to be here in twenty years with grey hair and slippers, looking at your nice shiny wasps and wondering where your life went.'

She put her hands on her hips and looked Brindle straight in the eye.

'If you want something done about all this then you've got to go out and make it happen. And – if you ask me – the sooner the better.'

'Funny – I don't remember anyone actually asking your opinion,' snapped Brindle.

'Is that funny ha-ha, or funny peculiar?'

Brindle's face reddened and he stared angrily at Skipper.

'What are you doing here anyway? I thought you had gone and got yourself killed.'

Skipper stared right back.

'Well, it would seem not, now, wouldn't it?'

Brindle's face grew redder still.

'It's obvious to me that you haven't grown up any,' he said. ' In more ways than one.'

He glanced pointedly at Zip and Mump. 'I think perhaps we should discuss this in private.'

Zip coughed awkwardly.

'Come on, Mump. Let's go and get a shower – get cleaned up.'

'I'm OK,' said Mump. 'I don't need a shower.'

Zip dug him in the ribs and he squeaked.

'Maybe I'll just take one anyway,' he said.

Sam and Skipper followed Brindle across the hangar floor, threading their way past small groups of engineers and ground crew until they reached the door of an office in the far corner. There was a glass window running the length of the room and through it Sam could see several wooden chairs and a desk. On the wall behind the desk there was a large coloured map of Aurobon. Brindle opened the door and ushered them through it before closing it firmly behind him again. Sam was surprised at how silent the room suddenly became and realised that it must be soundproofed.

'Sit down,' said Brindle, gesturing towards two wooden

chairs before taking a seat behind the desk. He formed his hands into a steeple shape and bumped the tips of his fingers against his chin, flicking his eyes between the new arrivals. Finally he allowed his gaze to settle on Skipper.

'I heard what you said out there,' he said. 'But I don't think you fully understand the situation.'

'I think I understand it perfectly,' replied Skipper. 'I understand that everyone looks terribly busy and that all your wasps are in great shape. I also understand that none of them are actually flying, in which case, they might as well be stink bugs for all the good they're doing.'

Brindle glared at her.

'Now you listen to me,' he said angrily, 'do you have even the slightest idea how many wasps we lost in the month before we finally grounded them?'

Skipper stared out of the window at a man carrying a pair of replacement antennae.

'No,' she said quietly. 'How many?'

'Four hundred. And you know how many pilots we lost?'

Skipper shook her head and said nothing.

'Two hundred and thirty-seven. Two hundred and thirty-seven young pilots who never came home again. That's an average of around eight a day, every day for a month, killed in action. Those kids never even had a half chance. So don't come in here telling me what I should be doing, OK? You ask me, we're doing fine as it is. Only last week we blew up a huge arms dump and derailed a train bringing supplies in from Vermia. In the last few days alone we've taken out four spiders and a dozen ants.'

There was an awkward silence for a few moments. Brindle glared angrily at Skipper as she continued to stare out through the window. Finally she turned back to face him and Sam saw sadness in her eyes.

'But it isn't enough, is it?' she said quietly. 'It isn't enough to win this war.'

Sam looked doubtfully at Brindle, half expecting him to explode with rage. But to Sam's surprise, he simply looked at Skipper and shook his head.

'No,' he replied. 'Nothing we do is enough.'

'Look,' said Skipper. 'If I could change things, I would. Of course I would. But I can't, can I? I can't bring those pilots back and neither can you. No one can. But they knew what they were doing, didn't they? They died fighting for what they thought was right. If we give up now, then the sacrifices they made will have all been for nothing. Don't you see? If we just sit around here playing it safe, then Odoursin wins. Is that really what you want?'

When he heard this, Brindle's anger returned and he thumped his fist down so hard on the table that the pencils bounced around and a sheet of paper slid off onto the floor.

'Of course it isn't what I want! But too many people have been killed already. I will *not* put any more pilots' lives at risk by sending them to certain death!'

Skipper picked up the piece of paper and slid it back on the desk.

'Sergeant Brindle, I'm not asking you to. All I'm asking for is one wasp, that's all. Just give us one wasp and you can forget that you ever saw us. Come on. What do you say?'

Brindle passed a hand across his eyes and when he looked up again it seemed that most of his anger had drained away, leaving only weariness behind. He turned to Sam.

'What about you, son? What do you think?'

'I'm with Skipper on this,' said Sam. 'I think the least we can do is try. If we can just get through a fabric gap and bring back a few robber fly eggs from Earth, then we can develop them back here at the lab and have them up and flying inside a month. That way, at least we're back in with a fighting chance.'

Brindle looked at him and then back at Skipper.

'You realise this is suicide don't you?'

Sam shrugged. 'The way I look at it, sitting down here polishing wasps every day is pretty much suicide. It just takes longer, that's all. And to be honest, if it comes down to a choice between dying sooner fighting for something I believe in, or dying later without ever having tried, then I'm going for the first option every time.'

Brindle folded his arms and leaned his chair back against the wall so that his head rested against the map of Aurobon.

'You know, I thought you two were dead anyway,' he

said, staring up at a patch on the ceiling where the plaster was cracked. 'So maybe I should just pretend I never saw you. That way it makes no difference does it?'

Sam looked at Skipper to see if he had understood Brindle's meaning correctly. From the uncertain smile that was hovering around her lips, he guessed that he had.

'You mean we can have the wasp?' Skipper asked, unable to keep the excitement from her voice.

Brindle returned his chair to its four legs and folded his large, rough hands together on the table top.

'On one condition,' he said.

'What's that?' asked Skipper.

Sam looked at Brindle and saw that, for the first time since they had met, there was warmth in his eyes.

'You take me with you,' he said.

Eleven

Sam zipped up the warm, fur-lined flying jacket, strapped himself into the seat next to Brindle and looked out through the screen at the front of the wasp. He could see half a dozen ground crew rushing around below, making some final safety checks and last minute alterations to the external sensors.

'You don't have to do this you know,' said Sam. 'You don't have to come with us.'

Brindle reached above his head and flicked a couple of switches. The cockpit lights dimmed and the dials on the control panel glowed red.

'Listen. I've seen those things and I've heard your plan. You want my opinion? You two are going to need all the help you can get.'

'We appreciate it,' said Skipper, leaning through the space between the seats. 'Although personally I think it's a great plan.'

'Yeah, well,' said Brindle gruffly, 'we'll find out soon

enough.'

'Now, are you sure we've got everything?' asked Sam.

Skipper patted the bulky rucksack strapped on her shoulders. 'It's all in here. Everything a girl could need: CRB, grenades, gun, rope ladder, moisturiser . . .'

Brindle pushed a red button and Sam felt a slight lift as the wings hummed into life outside the cockpit.

'Just kidding about the moisturiser by the way,' Skipper added, pulling out a small silver flask and unscrewing the lid.

'All right, we're just about ready for take-off,' Brindle announced. 'Remember, soon as that rock opens up we're going to hit full throttle, fire up the after-burners and accelerate out of here on maximum power. That way we avoid any robber flies pinpointing our exact location, at least until we're clear of the base.'

He turned round to find Skipper calmly humming to herself and drinking coffee from a small metal cup. When she saw that Brindle was watching her, she took another swig and then held the cup out towards him.

'Want some?'

'Thank you, no,' he said testily. 'And I suggest you hold on tight back there. We're going to be pulling some serious G in a minute.'

'OK,' said Skipper. 'Maybe I'll finish this later, then.'

She took a last swig, poured the rest of the coffee back into the flask and screwed the top back on. Then she leaned back on her rucksack, wedged the flask between her feet and braced herself in the small space between some wooden boxes that were stacked up in the rear of the wasp.

'Take me to the moon, Sergeant Brindle!' she called. 'Fly me to the stars!'

Brindle looked at Sam.

'Is she always like this?'

'No,' replied Sam. 'Usually worse.'

Skipper cuffed him around the back of the head just as the rock in front of them disappeared in a blue flash to reveal a vista of grey sky and ice-covered rock. Snow swirled around them as the down draught from the wings grew steadily stronger. Then with a loud roar the wasp leapt forward and Sam was thrown violently back against his seat. As they climbed rapidly up towards the dark storm clouds, Sam watched a flurry of grey flakes beat endlessly against the windscreen and wondered when – if ever – he would see blue sky again.

'Lovely weather for the time of year,' said Skipper, hanging on the back of Sam's seat as they levelled off in the heart of the snowstorm. The wasp pitched violently up and down in the turbulent air currents and Sam felt his seatbelt cut into his chest.

'How much further?' he asked, easing his hand beneath his belt in order to relieve the pressure.

'Maybe another twenty miles,' said Brindle. 'This storm might be dangerous, but it's actually quite good news for us. There won't be many robber flies up in this weather, and those that are will have their tracking systems seriously impaired.'

'So it's true what they say then,' said Skipper. 'Every cloud has a silver lining.'

'Well if it has,' said Brindle, peering through the screen. 'then it's well hidden. In fact, this one's lined with so many air currents that it's almost impossible to maintain a steady flight path. Those robber fly pilots are staying grounded for a good reason.'

'What's that?' asked Skipper.

'Self-preservation,' said Brindle. 'They don't want to die.'

'Cowards,' said Skipper. 'Don't know what they're missing.'

As the storm intensified, visibility was reduced to virtually nil. The world beyond the screen became an impenetrable blizzard of white and although the heaters were on full blast the temperature inside the cockpit dropped sharply. Sam's teeth began to chatter and he zipped his flying jacket all the way up to his chin.

'How long now?' he asked, shouting to be heard above the clattering heaters and the howling wind outside.

Brindle glanced at the air speed indicator and did a quick calculation.

'In these conditions? I'd say about twenty minutes. That's if we don't crash first.'

'What's that?' shouted Skipper from the rear of the wasp.

'I said, "That's if we don't crash first",' yelled Brindle.

'No,' said Skipper. 'What's *that*?' She reached between

the seats and pointed at a small dial near the top of the control panel.

'That's the radar,' replied Brindle. He leaned forward and took a closer look. Sam saw that a red dot was blinking furiously in the centre of the dial.

Brindle's face turned the colour of snow.

'It's them,' he said. 'They've found us.'

Then the cockpit exploded in a fury of glass and snow.

For a moment or two, Sam didn't know whether he was alive or dead. As his seatbelt mechanism disintegrated, something flew past him and he briefly experienced a floating sensation before slamming violently into the ceiling which had suddenly become the floor. With a sickening crack his knees smashed against his face and he groaned, tasting blood in his mouth. Then a hand grabbed him by the hair, yanking him back over the seats and suddenly he was lying on the floor as the wasp spun around like some crazy, out-of-control fairground ride.

Skipper's face was inches from his own, shouting something at him. He watched her lips moving, but couldn't hear a thing.

Nothing made any sense.

Everything was frozen, caught in some strange moment out of time.

Sam blinked and tried to shout.

Gradually, the world began to move again.

He saw Skipper raise her hand, watched it swing slowly through the air and felt a sharp pain as it struck him hard across the face.

There was a buzz, a whine and then the world came back again with a fast and furious roar.

'Sam, you have *got* to listen!' Skipper screamed.

Sam shook his head in an effort to clear it and concentrated hard on Skipper's lips.

'Follow me – OK?' she shouted.

'OK!' he shouted back through the confusion.

The noise was deafening. From somewhere above the shrieking of the wind and the roar of the wing motors there came a tearing sound, like someone ripping a sheet of canvas in two. Sam turned and saw that the top of the wasp had been torn open like a tin can and a huge pair of jaws was thrusting and snapping at the packing cases, splintering them like matchwood. Two shining black eyes stared down into the broken wasp, searching them out. Sam remembered the hideous creature he had seen on the mountain side and realised that he was looking straight into the eyes of a robber fly.

Skipper quickly pulled out a small silver torch which Sam recognised as a cellular restructuring beam and pointed it at the side of the wasp.

'Let's go!' she screamed.

There was a blue flash, a fizz as the side wall dissolved and then Skipper scrambled out through the hole and disappeared from view. Sam threw himself after her and found himself in the middle of a howling storm. He realised that the robber fly must have attacked them from above, clamping its legs around the wasp's body and using its powerful jaws to rip it apart. As they spun giddily through the air, Sam briefly caught sight of the ground whirling beneath them before the blizzard closed in once more.

'Quickly, Sam! Grab a leg!'

Skipper was hanging from one of the fly's legs and Sam quickly grabbed at the thick bristles, swinging himself up and away from the wasp.

It was not a moment too soon. As he pulled himself clear, the fly released its grip on the wasp and it fell away, spiralling uselessly down towards the ground. The fly accelerated away into the sky and Sam knew he wouldn't be able to hold on much longer. But he also knew that if he let go, a painful death awaited him on the rocks a thousand feet below. So with muscles aching and hands numb with cold, he grabbed hold of the coarse cable-like hairs and pulled himself upwards, inch by painful inch.

An icy wind howled in his face and he wrapped his arms around the leg, feeling the wiry hairs scratch against his cheek. Ice particles crystallised on his eyelashes like frozen sugar. Looking up, he saw that Skipper had reached the top of the leg and there was a blue flash as she made an opening in the fly's abdomen with the CRB. Seconds later, a rope ladder dropped from the hole and snaked past him. He tentatively stretched out a hand, but it hung several feet beyond his reach.

'I can't get to it!' he shouted, only to hear his words disappear on the wind.

He pressed his face against the rough hairs and felt his muscles weaken.

Glancing up again, he saw that Skipper was climbing back down the rope ladder towards him. After a little way she stopped and kicked her legs backwards so that she was just hanging by her hands. Arching her back, she began to move her body back and forth, setting up a momentum that made the whole rope ladder swing.

Come on, he told himself. *You either stay here until you fall off, or you move. No one's going to do it for you.*

Taking a deep breath he slowly unfolded his fingers from their grip on the hairs. As he stretched out an arm towards the ladder he felt the clunk of a wooden rung against his fingertips and by leaning out a little further he was able to grab it and pull it towards him. Still holding tightly with his right hand and with the heel of his right foot hooked firmly around the fly's leg, he managed to slide his left foot onto one of the rungs.

This was it.

It was now or never.

Shifting his weight slightly, he stepped out into space and with a rush of freezing wind the ladder swung away from the leg like a pendulum.

As he swept through the air he could see the mountains circling the plain below him and far away to his left he could just make out the distant city of Vahlzi. With his heart pounding in his chest, he grasped the rung above his head and began to climb.

'Well done,' said Skipper, rubbing snow from her hair as Sam fell gasping into the fly's underbelly. 'You should have been in the circus.' Pulling up the rope ladder, she pointed the CRB at the hole in the floor and it closed up again in a flash of brilliant blue light.

Sam struggled onto his hands and knees and stared at the brown, spongy floor. 'Promise me we won't do that again,' he wheezed. 'Ever.'

He sat up and looked around. Most of the insect's internal organs had been moved or re-engineered to enable it to carry more equipment, but he noticed to his disgust that a large, yellowy brown heart was pumping away in the corner.

Skipper grinned mischievously. 'I think she likes you.'

'Oh, ha ha,' said Sam. 'Very funny.'

He sat back heavily against the curved wall of the fly's abdomen. 'I don't remember anyone mentioning anything about rope ladders,' he said. 'I thought the plan was to go straight up through the fly's belly when it latched onto us.'

'Well that *was* the plan,' admitted Skipper. 'But it all happened a bit fast. Poor old Brindle nearly wet himself.'

'Brindle!' exclaimed Sam. 'He must have gone down with the wasp!'

'Don't worry,' said Skipper. 'I saw him eject just before the wasp hit the ground.'

'He must have stayed in until he knew we were out safely,' said Sam. 'He's a brave guy.'

Skipper nodded. 'He's got a bit of a hike ahead of him, that's for sure. It's a long way back to the base.'

Sam remembered that Brindle had always been notorious as a hard nut and survival expert who loved nothing more than a difficult challenge. He imagined him trekking through the blizzard with a big smile on his face.

'I don't s'pose he'll mind too much,' he said.

'Are you kidding?' replied Skipper. 'He probably thinks it's his birthday.'

She swung the rucksack on her back and pointed upwards. 'OK, Sam. Time for a change of aircrew, I think.'

Flypilot Grinx was still smiling about the way they'd busted that damn wasp right out of the sky. Most of the other pilots had stayed on the ground, but there was no way Grinx was going to let a little bit of snow keep him from doing what he loved best. And what Grinx loved doing best was killing things.

At weekends he took his rifle out and went hunting. His friends went hunting for rabbits, deer, anything they could bring home and put on the dinner table. But Grinx wasn't bothered about the eating part; he just shot anything that moved. Nothing beat the thrill of playing God, deciding whether another soul should live or die. Nothing else came close.

Not that there was ever much of a decision to make, of course.

If something wandered into his rifle sites, Grinx blew it away.

For the past year now, Grinx had been flying robber

flies. And there was no doubt about it: if you liked killing things, it was the best job ever.

He grinned at Mersh, his co-pilot, who grinned back.

'You got the old bloodlust going on there, Grinx?'

'Oh yeah,' said Grinx. 'You'd better believe it. Come on, Mershy boy. Let's go kill something else. That last one was real sweet, wasn't it?'

'*Real* sweet,' agreed Mersh. 'That sucker never even saw us coming.'

A sound from the rear of the aircraft made Grinx turn around. To his amazement, a small blonde-haired girl was sitting on the floor with her face in her hands. Her shoulders were shaking and she sounded as though she was crying.

'Hey!' shouted Grinx. 'Who the hell are you?'

The girl looked up and Grinx saw that her lower lip was quivering. She seemed very upset. It was then that he noticed the flying jacket and the blue jumpsuit.

'Well, I'll be . . .' said Grinx. He dug Mersh in the ribs. 'Hey, Mersh. We gone and got ourselves a Vahlzian kid!' He undid his seatbelt and leaned over the back of the seat.

'I don't know how you got in here, little girl,' he said in a low, threatening voice, 'but whatever you're crying about now – well, it ain't nothing compared to what Grinxy's going to give you to cry about. See, the thing is, there ain't no big strong Vahlzian boys to protect you here. How's that feel?'

He leered at her and slowly climbed over the seat into the back.

Robber fly

'Is that a flying suit you're wearing?' he asked.

The girl sniffed and nodded.

'Hey, Mersh,' sneered Grinx. 'The kid likes to fly.'

Mersh laughed unpleasantly.

'Reckon we can arrange that for you,' he said. 'You reckon we can arrange that, Grinxy?'

'No doubt about it,' said Grinx. 'You listening, little girl? Here's what we're gonna do. We're gonna open up the side of this thing and then we're gonna let you be a li'l birdy. That's right, honey. You gonna fly! You gonna fly all the way down to them rocks down there. How do you like that, hmm? You like the sound of that?'

The girl began to cry more loudly.

'Aww, I think she's frightened, Mersh,' said Grinx. 'Ain't that right, sweetheart?' He was up close, now, the stench of his stale breath in her ear. 'Are you crying 'cos you're scared?'

'No,' sobbed a little voice. 'I'm crying 'cos it's b-b-broken.'

Grinx smiled. He loved it when they got scared. He was really going to enjoy this.

'There ain't nothing broken,' he said, grinning and running his tongue across the front of his yellow, decaying teeth. 'Not yet, anyway.'

'The s-s-safety,' stammered the girl. 'The s-s-safety catch is broken!'

Grinx was getting annoyed now. Maybe he'd slap her about a bit before he killed her. Make it more fun.

'What the hell are you talking about?' he snarled, seizing

her roughly by the shoulder. 'There ain't no broken safety catch!'

'Oh, but there is,' said the girl, and as she stared up at him with her baby-blue eyes he noticed two things: firstly, that she wasn't crying at all, and secondly, that she was pointing a gun straight between his eyes.

'Mersh!' he squealed. 'She's got a gun!'

'Yes, I have,' said Skipper calmly. 'It's a big one, too.'

There was a click as she pulled back the firing mechanism.

'And here's the thing, Mersh – *nice* name by the way – the safety catch on this gun is well and truly broken. So I guess you'd better fly pretty straight and smooth from now on, or your friend here might just get his brains splashed all over the cockpit.'

Grinx cowered in the corner with his arms draped over his head.

Skipper winked at him. 'What's up, Grinxy? Not *scared* are we?'

She turned and pointed the gun at the pilot.

'OK, Mersh. I've seen how you like to whack wasps with this thing. Now let's see if you can land it.'

'How about if I refuse?' Mersh sneered.

Skipper pointed the gun back at Grinx and tightened her finger around the trigger.

'How about I redecorate your cockpit?'

'Just do it!' screamed Grinx. 'Do what she says!'

Mersh swore and pushed the joystick forward so that the fly began to lose height. Sam emerged from a hole in the floor at the back of the fly and gave Grinx a friendly wave.

'Hello,' he said. 'Enjoying your flight?'

Grinx curled his lip as if to say something, then changed his mind and spat on the floor instead.

'I'll take that as a no, then.'

'Oh, take no notice of Mr Grumpy here,' said Skipper. 'He's just worried about the cold.'

Grinx gave her a surly look.

'I ain't cold.'

'Well, that's good, Grinxy,' said Skipper. 'That's very good. You want my advice? Make the most of it.'

'Why?'

'Because,' replied Skipper, 'you're sure going to be.'

As he looked through the screen at the two men, standing alone in the middle of an ice field a hundred miles from anywhere, Sam realised that he didn't feel even the slightest bit sorry for them. He'd heard what Grinx had threatened to do to Skipper. Now the thought that him and his nasty little co-pilot had a long, miserable walk back to Vermia made him feel really rather pleased.

Sam put his left hand on the throttle and felt the potent wing motors hum with power. Suddenly, all the skills he had learned as a wasp pilot quickly came flooding back to him and he realised how much he was looking forward to flying this beast of an insect.

'Ready, Skipper?' he called.

He turned his head and saw that she was hanging out

of the doorway, shouting at the two men and unzipping the top of her jacket.

'Think I'll just turn the heating down a bit,' she called. 'I'm *boiling*!'

'Skipper, stop it,' said Sam, unable to stop himself from smiling. 'You'll only upset them.'

'Good,' said Skipper.

As the fly lifted off towards the clouds, Sam could see the two men arguing and pushing one another. Chuckling to himself, he pulled the joystick back and the powerful fly climbed steeply up into the clouds. As he watched the bleak, snow-covered landscape fall away beneath them, Sam thought about his vague, dream-like memories of life back on Earth and thought how far away it all seemed to him now. He thought about the dangers that they had recently experienced and the dangers that almost certainly lay ahead of them.

And at that moment he realised – to his considerable surprise – that he had never felt happier in his life.

Twelve

Alya pulled the sheet of paper from the printer and laid it flat on the desk. On it was a picture of a jagged blue line; an image she had photographed through the lens of the electron microscope. Her eyes flicked across to the open textbook where the words *neurological impulse translator: human* were printed beneath a picture showing an identical, jagged blue line. Typing the words *impulse translator: ratticus norvicus* into the computer, she held her breath as the powerful search engine flicked its way through a million data files in less than a heartbeat.

With a barely audible click, the screen was split down the middle by a single, bright image of a jagged blue line.

Alya gasped and put a hand over her mouth as her earlier suspicions were confirmed and the enormity of her discovery began to dawn upon her. If the evidence in front of her was to be believed then the part of the worm's brain that told it how to behave was the same as that found in rats – its natural host – and also in humans

— its accidental one. She reached for a pad and pencil and began to write:

Rats swallow worm eggs (toxoplasma gondii) from the soil. The worms hatch out inside them.

The worms need their natural hosts (rats) to be eaten by cats so that they can complete their life cycle.

SO

The worms travel to the rat's brain.

The worms replace the rat's impulse translator with their own.

The rat now begins to think like the worm and the worm's desires become its own.

SO

The rat starts to think that it wants its body to be eaten by a cat so that the worm can continue its life cycle.

SO

The rat loses all fear of death. It actively seeks out cats and allows itself to be attacked and eaten.

The rat commits suicide, the worm is also eaten by the cat and thus is able to complete the final phase of its life cycle.

Alya sat back in her chair and chewed on the end of her pencil. So far so good. But what about the human connection? She carefully ripped the first sheet of paper from the pad, put it to one side and began to write again on a fresh sheet.

Parasitic worms (toxoplasma gondii) often end up inside a human host. (more by accident than by design?) Corresponding structure of impulse translators suggests worm's desires can also be communicated to human subject.

Alya read through what she had written and tapped the pencil rhythmically on the tabletop as she considered all the facts. Then she wrote underneath in capital letters:

1. WORMS CAN ALTER HUMAN BEHAVIOUR BY SUBSTITUTING THEIR OWN THOUGHT PATTERNS

2. THE VERMIAN EMPIRE DESIRES FOR ALL HUMAN LIFE ON EARTH TO BE EXTINGUISHED

THEREFORE

3. IF WORM'S THOUGHT PATTERNS CAN BE REPLACED WITH THOUGHT PATTERNS OF VERMIAN EMPIRE, THESE WILL THEN BECOME THOUGHT PATTERNS OF INFECTED HUMANS

SO

4. INFECTED HUMANS CAN BE MADE TO EXTINGUISH ALL HUMAN LIFE ON EARTH

Alya sat and stared, unblinking, at the piece of paper in front of her for a long, long time. Krazni had hinted at a possible connection, but she was still stunned both by the speed with which she had been able to reach her conclusions and the consequences that would surely follow from their discovery.

Minutes ticked past as she read and reread her notes, trying to find some flaw in her logic.

But there was none. The science itself might in many ways be complex, but the facts themselves were simple and stark.

All it would take would be a slight reprogramming of the impulse translators and these tiny, seemingly insignificant worms could be used to turn a human being into a potential destroyer of its own race.

Gathering her papers together, Alya pushed them into the smart leather briefcase bought with the money saved from her first pay cheque and – taking care to lock the door behind her – walked quickly along the corridor towards Doctor Jancy's office, her black shoes clacking loudly on the polished white tiles and her heart fluttering like a moth that has found a flame.

It was difficult not to feel nervous in such exalted company, despite the fact that – with one exception – she had met these people before.

But this was the first time Alya had been invited to the Emperor's palace.

As she looked around the room at the crystal chandeliers and the paintings depicting scenes from the Vahlzian war, she felt her stomach flip as though she were standing on the edge of a very high cliff. Tucking her hair behind her ears, she sat up straight and felt the cold, smooth leather of the high-backed chair pressing against the thin material of her laboratory coat. A quick glance around the room confirmed that the meeting was mostly made up of the same people who had quizzed her about the ants last month.

There was General Martock at one end of the table – still rather red in the face from the effort of walking from the lift to the chamber. Doctor Jancy was seated on her left, fidgeting with his papers and Lieutenant Reisner – Leader of Earth-Based Ant Squadrons – sat opposite him, looking as though he had just been unpacked from his box. His white teeth gleamed and each little button on his perfectly creased uniform shone like a tiny golden sun.

Next to him was Field Marshal Stanzun – Overall Commander of Land and Air Forces – impatiently drumming the tips of his weathered brown fingers on the table top.

And then there was Krazni, Head of Intelligence and Security.

Alya knew, without needing to look, that Krazni was watching her right now, just as he had done when she had first entered the room. She could feel his hard green eyes staring into her soul, peering at the secret places she kept locked inside of herself.

Her throat tightened, but she forced herself to remain calm. What was the *matter* with her? She had nothing to hide. She was here to give these people what they had been looking for. There was nothing to be afraid of. She was on the verge of the biggest triumph of her young life!

And yet, as she glanced up and saw the thin, joyless smile below the eyes that persistently studied her, she found herself unable to hold Krazni's gaze.

Looking quickly away towards the head of the table, she found herself staring instead at the one person who had not been present at the previous meeting.

The Emperor Odoursin.

Alya felt her unease swell and burst into a thousand electrically charged butterflies which flew trembling to the tips of her fingers and toes. But woven into her discomfort was something else too; a brighter, richer feeling which hummed through her like honeybees on a hot afternoon. And as she looked across at the Emperor of her adopted country sitting only metres away from her, she remembered how she had once been an orphan, a faceless nonperson, abandoned in the ruins of another life.

And now here she was, sharing a table with the most powerful man in Aurobon.

She realised then that what she felt was something she had never experienced before in her life.

It was pride.

'Welcome, everyone,' said Odoursin. 'Welcome to this Extraordinary Session of the Security Council.' He squeezed his hands tightly together and Alya could see the knuckles straining against the skin, like small white maggots poised to break out of their pupae. As he turned his blanched, drum-tight face towards Martock, Alya could hear the laboured rattle of air as he sucked it down into his fire-damaged lungs.

'Perhaps, General Martock, you would like to start proceedings?'

Martock inclined his head deferentially towards Odoursin and then raised it again to look at the other members seated around the table.

'The reason we are all gathered together,' he said in slow, dramatic tones, 'is to listen to some remarkable developments that will assist us in our campaign to destroy the human inhabitants of Earth.'

His eyes swept around the assembled company, gratified by the unguarded looks of surprise that suddenly appeared upon several faces.

'Yes, indeed,' he went on. 'As you know, a few years ago we discovered a virus with the potential to eliminate human life on Earth. Unfortunately, Vahlzian forces destroyed all stocks of it. Since then, the search for a new virus has proved fruitless. However, it seems that we may have come up with a new and altogether more effective solution. But that is enough from me. Let me hand over to the expert in these matters, who will fill you in on the details.'

He smiled and raised his bushy eyebrows expectantly. 'Miss Blin, if you would be so kind?'

Alya felt her face flush as the attention of the group turned upon her, but all the years of work and her passion for the subject began to calm her nervousness and she felt the desire to share her knowledge begin to override her natural disquiet.

Wiping the moisture from her palms on the sides of her coat, she pushed her chair back, stood up and looked around at the expectant faces that had now turned towards her in anticipation of what was to come.

'Thank you,' she said. 'I am honoured by Your Excellency's kind invitation to come and speak here today.'

Odoursin acknowledged her thanks with a wave of his bony hand and then signalled for her to continue.

'As I am sure you are all aware,' she went on, 'there are many parasitic creatures which are capable of influencing the behaviour of the animals in which they live.'

There were nods from around the table; a sign, thought Alya, that Council members had actually read their briefing notes before the start of the meeting.

'We have known for some time that many of Earth's human population are infected by the *toxoplasma gondii* parasite – the same worm which causes rats to alter their behaviour and be eaten by cats. We know that this worm already affects human behaviour to some extent, making them more reckless and more likely to die in road accidents, for example. But what we didn't know was how the worm does it. How does this tiny worm make rats and humans do the things it wants them to do?'

Alya paused for a few moments to give everyone a chance to voice any questions that might have arisen from her explanation, but when the room remained silent she decided to press on.

'The process has always remained a mystery to us. At least, that is, until now. But while I was investigating some of the worm's brain tissue in the laboratory, I discovered that it shares a crucial piece of neurological equipment with both rats and humans. The *impulse translator* – the part of the brain that turns thought into action – is exactly the same in all three creatures.'

Alya waited for some kind of positive reaction to this new information, but apart from Martock – who was nodding approvingly – she saw only blank stares.

'Miss Blin,' said Odoursin coldly, 'I am sure that in scientific circles this is all very exciting, but I am not sure how it advances our particular cause.'

'I'm sorry,' Alya said. 'I'm not explaining this very well. Perhaps we can look at it in another way.' There followed a brief, uncomfortable silence punctuated by the occasional awkward cough and a shuffling of papers as she thought for a moment or two. Then she pressed her hands together and smiled.

'All right. Let's try this. Imagine that the impulse translators are like play scripts which tell the characters how to behave. The worm carries a script which contains instructions for the way its host should act. When the worm arrives at its destination, it simply substitutes its own script – the impulse translator – for that of its host – and the host's behaviour changes, directed by what is written in the new script. To put it simply, this microscopic worm has the ability to find its way into the human brain and alter the way it thinks.'

Odoursin, who up until this point had elected to listen to proceedings in silence, now stared at Alya and she noticed with some trepidation how fiercely his eyes burned.

'Miss Blin,' he said gravely.

'Yes, Your Excellency?'

'Are you suggesting that we are able to rewrite this script in any way we choose? That we can make humans see whatever we want them to see?'

Alya nodded. 'I am certain of it,' she said.

A sudden hush fell over the room as, slowly and deliberately, Odoursin got to his feet.

'In that case,' he said, 'let us begin.'

Thirteen

'I think that must be it,' said Skipper, pointing to a reddish-pink clump of cloud up ahead of them. Sam could see that the cloud was moving, rotating slowly in an anti-clockwise direction while seeming to fold in upon itself; lying there among the other clouds it appeared beautiful and strange, like a rose in winter.

'Are you sure?' Sam asked, throttling back on the engines and leaning forward to get a better view.

'No,' Skipper replied, 'but we're in the right area and I can't see another one, can you?'

Sam peered through the screen and scanned the surrounding clouds.

'I guess not,' he said.

Nudging the joystick forward slightly, he flew underneath the coloured clouds and then banked the insect around to get a better view. It certainly *looked* like a fabric gap. He remembered from his previous experience in this world that there were several gaps in the fabric of the universe which allowed travellers to pass quickly between Earth and Aurobon. Although these main gaps were now closely guarded by Vermian robber flies, Sam knew that beyond them were thousands more, each one a passageway to a different location on the Earth's surface.

According to Brindle, Vermian robber flies had been seen operating in this area on several occasions, disappearing into the characteristic swirl of clouds over a period of several weeks. Upon their return, they always flew more slowly and closer to the ground. The observers had concluded two things from this: 1) that they were probably laden with eggs harvested from robber flies on Earth and 2) that they were using a fabric gap which led to an area of North America where robber flies were plentiful.

'What I don't understand,' said Sam, 'is why they are still harvesting the robber fly eggs from Earth. Can't they produce their own now that they've got the adult insects?'

'Probably,' said Skipper. 'But I guess that at the start of their campaign they were doing both to ensure maximum production. Their factories would have been at full stretch because they wanted to saturate the skies over Vahlzi with robber flies. And unfortunately for us, those tactics proved extremely successful.'

As they began their final approach towards the fabric gap, the intercom suddenly crackled into life.

'Hey, Grinx you old dog – how did I know I'd find you

up here when the rest of the damn world is grounded? The rest of 'em ain't got no backbone. But you and me, buddy – we don't let a bit of snow keep us from doing what we do best now, do we?'

Sam looked at Skipper and saw that she was wearing an 'Oh *no*' kind of expression.

'Who was *that*?' he asked, easing off on the throttle so that they slowed their approach toward the darkening red cloud.

'Sounds like Grinxy's got a little friend,' said Skipper. 'Who'd have thought?' She suddenly pointed through the screen at a small black dot in the sky up ahead. 'And look – there he is.'

Sam watched as the dot grew bigger and realised that it was a robber fly just as the intercom came alive again.

'Hey, Grinx,' said the voice. 'Ain't ya talkin' to me today, buddy? It's me, Norzun.'

'*Norzun*?' mouthed Skipper, who, despite the danger, seemed to find this quite amusing.

Sam flipped the switch on the intercom and, deepening his voice into quite a passable impression of Grinx, said, 'Hey, buddy. How ya doin'?'

Skipper put her hand up to her mouth to suppress a laugh and Sam saw that she was clearly delighted by this turn of events. She was obviously not going to let the fact that this guy Norzun was piloting a fearsome killing machine interfere with her enjoyment of the situation.

'I'm doin' fine,' came the reply. 'Listen, what do you say we make a detour over Vahlzi and kill a few of the scumbags on our way home?'

'Love to,' said Sam, 'but the thing is I'm a bit low on fuel. I probably should be getting back.'

He flipped the intercom off again and turned to Skipper.

'What do you reckon? Shall we try and take him?'

Skipper looked doubtful. 'Up to you, but remember you're not familiar with all the weapon systems on this thing. It pains me to say it, but I think we might do better to cut and run.'

'You OK, Grinx?' came the voice again. It sounded more guarded this time. Uncertain.

'Yeah, no worries,' said Sam. He could see that Norzun's robber fly was looming large up ahead now, approaching them at considerable speed.

'You sound different,' said Norzun.

'Just tired I guess,' said Sam. 'It's been a long day.'

There was a long pause. When Norzun's voice finally came back on air there was a hard, suspicious edge to it.

'Who the hell am I talking to?' he hissed. 'You ain't Grinx.'

Sam looked at Skipper and gestured towards the intercom switch with an open hand.

'Your turn, I think.'

Skipper pulled her restraint buckle tight and leaned in toward the intercom. She gave Sam a wry smile and then flipped the switch.

'Hello, Norzun,' she said. 'This is the tooth fairy speaking. I'm afraid I'm a bit short on my quota this week, so I've decided to come and collect all yours at once. Hope that's OK with you.'

Sam slammed the stick back and pulled full throttle just as Norzun's voice came back on the intercom, swearing and screaming threats at them across the airwaves. Skipper gave a friendly little wave as they flew within a few metres of Norzun's cockpit, his hard, pale face glaring angrily at them through the screen, and then with engines howling they scorched up through the crimson clouds and into the heart of the fabric gap.

'He didn't look too happy about that,' said Sam, gripping the joystick firmly as the insect began to bump and shake in the turbulent atmosphere. 'Do you think we lost him?'

'Dunno,' said Skipper. 'Let's find out.' She flicked a switch marked 'Rear View' and immediately a coloured projection lit up in the top centre of the cockpit canopy. In the middle of it, and growing larger every second, were the grotesque features of a robber fly in hot pursuit.

'I think that's a "no",' said Skipper.

'Dammit!'

Sam's fingers tightened on the throttle so that his knuckles strained white beneath his skin and the engines protested loudly over the sound of the wind. In the distance he could see the tunnel of red cloud funnelling them down through strings of scarlet vapour towards two further spinning masses of cloud, each coloured a deep orange, spiralling in towards a central vortex like the eyes of small hurricanes.

'Which one?' Sam shouted above the noise from the engines. 'Left or right?'

Skipper looked up at the screen and saw that it was starting to fill up with robber fly.

'Left!' she shouted. 'Go left!'

Sam felt the drag on the motors as powerful forces from the spinning clouds began to act upon the insect, pulling it downwards.

'Left it is,' he said. Then he thrust the joystick forward and sent them hurtling into the dark vortex like a speck of dust in a tornado.

When he thought about it later, all Sam could remember was that it was rather like falling through a dark tunnel with trains roaring past on either side of you, except that at the same time the tunnel was spinning around so fast that you couldn't tell which way was up and which way was down. Small specks of light – which at first Sam thought must be stars – blurred into silver lines as they accelerated at fantastic speed, spinning themselves into glittering threads before suddenly disappearing again as the world returned to black once more.

And then with a whoosh of air and a flash of bright light, Sam found himself flying beneath the cool green leaves of a maple tree in the heat of a summer afternoon.

Fourteen

Realising that they were flying dangerously fast between the branches, Sam quickly put the wings into reverse and landed neatly on an emerald-green leaf.

'Where are we?' he asked. 'Have we come through to the right place?' He looked out of the cockpit window and saw to his surprise that the tree was growing from the middle of a concrete pavement. Surrounding it on all sides were busy roads jammed with traffic. Shops and skyscrapers towered above them and the streets were crammed with thousands of huge, jostling pedestrians. The roar of the fabric gap had been replaced by complex layers of sound typical of a large city: people shouting, car horns blaring, engines revving and, from somewhere above them, the incongruous music of birdsong.

'What do you want,' asked Skipper, 'the good news or the bad?'

Sam turned to her and raised an eyebrow.

'Go on. Put me out of my misery.'

'Well, the good news is I think we lost Norzun some-where on the way through.'

'And the bad news?'

Skipper looked sheepish.

'The bad news is I think maybe we should have taken a right.'

Sam watched as a bus opened its doors below them with a hiss, spilling its chattering passengers out onto the warm pavement.

'Oh,' he said.

' "Oh" is right,' said Skipper, watching the bus drive off again. 'Not quite what I was expecting, to be honest.'

'Where *should* we be, then?'

'Ideally, a field somewhere in the middle of Kansas.'

Sam shrugged. 'Well that's OK isn't it?' He pointed to the display. 'We've got plenty of fuel.'

'I admire your optimism, Sam,' said Skipper, 'but however much fuel we've got, something tells me it's not going to be enough.'

'What makes you so sure?' asked Sam.

'That,' said Skipper.

Sam followed her gaze to a large poster on the side of a shop, where a young girl was smiling and holding up a can of fizzy drink. Above it, in large, black letters were a string of words that he could not read. But there was definitely something about them that he recognised.

'Oh brilliant,' he said. 'Nice one, Skipper.'

Skipper turned to him and put her hands together in

front of her chest. Then she smiled and bowed graciously.
'Welcome to Japan,' she said.

They flew high above green parks where trees foamed
pink and white with cherry blossom, across the Sumida
River lined with its boatyards and homeless shelters and
across the Rainbow Bridge into the older part of the city
where the streets were crowded and narrow. On every
corner, *bento* stands were piled high with boxed lunches
of sushi and pickles while behind the noodle stalls the
women stood with their arms folded, smiling encouragement at the passing shoppers who stared hungrily into
the saucepans full of fat, white noodles.

'So what do we do now?' Sam asked as they skimmed
low above the heads of the people, all of whom were far
too absorbed in their own lives to notice the small insect
zipping through the air above them.

'Well, I don't know about you,' said Skipper, 'but I'm
starving. Do you fancy getting something to eat?'

Sam felt the fly lift suddenly as they caught a warm air
current rising up from the sun-baked pavements and he
pushed the joystick forward a fraction to compensate.

'What did you have in mind? A drive-thru, perhaps?'

'No, but seriously,' said Skipper, 'we don't need to
order do we? We're tiny, right? Even the smallest leftovers will keep us going for a month. So come on. Pick a
venue and we'll get stuck in to whatever's on offer.' She
patted his arm. 'It'll be my treat.'

Sam flew down a side street where unlit neon signs

advertised an assortment of small restaurants. Plastic replicas of items on the menu were displayed neatly in the windows.

'You spoil me,' he said. 'You really do.'

They sat high on a shelf in a corner of the sushi bar, listening with amused interest to the deep, booming voices of the lunchtime customers. 'Do you suppose we could understand them if they were speaking English?' Sam asked.

'I think the range is a bit low for our small ears,' said Skipper. 'We can't really get the bass notes. Girls are probably the easiest to understand.'

'That,' said Sam, 'is a matter of opinion.'

Skipper flicked a chunk of bread at his head.

'Cheeky.'

Sam absently brushed the crumbs from his hair and looked across at Skipper. They had used the fly's powerful jaws to scoop up some leftovers before parking up on the shelf and now she was leaning back against a chunk of fish with her feet dangling over the edge.

'I'd forgotten about all that,' he said. 'I'd forgotten you used to fly all those missions on Earth before I ever came to Aurobon.'

'I know,' said Skipper. 'It's funny isn't it? It all seems so long ago. Like another life.'

Sam sat down next to her and watched the customers collecting their neat, colourful little packages of fish from the counter down below.

'Do you wonder what happened to you?' Sam asked. 'In those four years, I mean?'

Skipper nodded. 'Uh–huh.'

She stared at the picture of blue mountains and silver waterfalls which hung on the wall by the door.

'I keep thinking that I must have somehow left Aurobon when you did. But whenever I try and picture what happened to me in that time, it just fades away. It's impossible for me to remember anything about it. All I've got is this feeling that I've lost something. Do you feel that?'

'All the time,' said Sam. 'And although I know I went back to my life on Earth, it already feels like someone else's life. I'm not sure I even know the difference between what's real and what's a dream any more.'

'Perhaps,' said Skipper, 'there is less difference than we think.'

Sam chewed at a piece of hard skin on the side of his fingernail and watched a smartly dressed Japanese businessman shake some soy sauce over his sushi. Sure, it all seemed real enough. But piloting a robber fly into a sushi bar and watching giant Japanese people eat their lunch from the edge of a shelf was rather a strange reality.

'I wish I could remember,' said Skipper, and there was sadness in her eyes, like clouds reflected in the ocean. 'I wish I could remember what it is that I have lost.'

Sam shrugged. 'Maybe we all lose something somewhere along the way,' he said. 'And maybe forgetting about it is the only way that we manage to keep going.'

'Want some more?' asked Skipper. 'I've got heaps of the stuff.'

Sam swallowed another piece of fish and looked across at the piles of orange sushi stacked up on either side of her. Skipper puffed her stomach out and folded her hands across it like a walrus with a weight problem.

'Go on,' she said. 'You *know* you want to.'

'No thanks,' replied Sam queasily. 'I'd probably explode.'

'Really?' said Skipper, sitting up. 'That could be a handy trick in a tight spot.' She held up a big chunk of fish. 'I'll take some with us just in case.'

'OK,' said Sam. 'You do that.' He glanced at the robber fly parked at the back of the shelf. 'I suppose we ought to make a move. If we can get back through the fabric gap, we might be able to find the other one that'll take us to Kansas.' He grinned. 'It'll be like the *Wizard of Oz. Aunt Em! Aunt Em!*'

Skipper sank back against the fish again, sighed loudly and stuck her stomach out even further.

'I have no idea what you're talking about, Sam, but right now I can't move anywhere. I am *completely* stuffed.' She belched, covered her mouth apologetically with one hand and then smiled. 'Thank you, waiter. Maybe just a little dessert, then.'

Suddenly, Sam became aware of a loud, low humming noise. Skipper frowned and looked at him.

'Do you hear that?' she asked.

Sam nodded. 'What is it?'

'Don't know.'

The sound of raised voices floated up from the restaurant below and as the two of them looked down they saw that a huge, orange-coloured wasp had flown through the shop doorway and was now hovering above a plate of food. Sam stared at it in amazement. It was at least twice the size of any wasp he had ever flown.

A young man sitting at the table hurriedly pushed back his chair and flapped ineffectually at the enormous wasp which, seemingly untroubled by his efforts, landed on his plate and began tearing off a lump of fish. A waiter stepped forward and nervously flicked a cloth at the wasp which rose angrily into the air and flew straight towards him. This time the waiter's aim was more accurate; as the cloth snapped through the air with a loud crack, the wasp banged against the plate glass window and fell to the floor. But when the waiter moved towards it, it shook itself, took off again and with a loud buzz, flew out through the open door.

'Did you *see* that!' whispered Skipper breathlessly. 'That has to be the biggest, baddest wasp I ever saw!'

Sam shook his head. 'That was no wasp,' he said, his eyes bright with excitement.

Skipper looked at him quizzically.

'What was it then?'

'That,' replied Sam, 'was a Japanese hornet. I can remember reading about them. They're the fiercest killers in the whole of the insect kingdom. Believe me, they don't come any nastier than that.'

Skipper turned towards him and he saw that a smile was slowly beginning to spread across her face.

'Sam,' she said after a moment's thought. 'Are you thinking what I'm thinking?'

Sam nodded.

'Yes,' he said. 'I'm afraid I probably am.'

Fifteen

'The thing is,' said Sam as they flew out of the shop and up over the rooftops, 'the nest has got to be somewhere close. Hornets don't catch a bus into town, do they?'

'No,' said Skipper, 'and I bet they don't take kindly to people stealing their eggs, either.'

'Really?' said Sam. 'Well, you *do* surprise me.'

Skipper smiled.

'Reckon we can pull it off?'

'No,' said Sam as they skimmed across an alleyway full of dustbins overflowing with rubbish. 'Actually I don't.'

'Look, Sam,' said Skipper, 'if we can get ourselves a few of those things, then Odoursin's robber flies are total *history*! So we are going to try, right?'

'I think we've got to,' said Sam. 'I can't see any other option, personally. I wish I could, but I can't.'

He lifted his finger and pointed ahead through the screen.

'Look,' he said. 'Talk of the devil.'

And when Skipper looked she saw that they were heading towards a wood on the outskirts of the city and there, flying not more than twenty metres in front of them, was a giant Japanese hornet.

'It's *massive!*' exclaimed Skipper excitedly as they followed the huge insect into the dappled green shade of the wood. 'Stick a few of those up in the sky over Vermia and things could turn around nicely again for us. Those robber flies wouldn't stand a chance.'

'No,' said Sam. 'Which is a bit worrying really, when you consider what we're flying in at the moment.'

'Look,' said Skipper, pointing over to the left. 'We've got company.'

Out of the corner of his eye Sam saw another huge hornet flying low over a trail of fallen branches and tree roots, hugging the contours of the ground as it manoeuvred effortlessly between the natural obstacles in its path. Swinging the fly right to avoid a low hanging branch, he spotted another one up ahead in the distance.

'We must be getting near the nest,' he said. 'We should probably land fairly soon – park up around the back and use ropes for the last bit.'

'Good idea,' said Skipper as two more hornets shot past on their left. 'They're getting a bit close for comfort.'

'Look,' said Sam, throttling back so that their speed slowed to a virtual standstill. 'Over there.'

Ahead of them, three huge hornets hovered above the forest floor. Every few seconds they swivelled through the air, constantly checking the surrounding area for signs of possible danger.

'Sentinels,' said Skipper. 'They must be protecting the nest.'

Below the guards, Sam could see an old, moss-covered tree-stump filled with rainwater. Above it, a steady stream of hornets flew in and out of a large, oval-shaped ball which hung from one of the branches.

'Bingo,' he said. 'There's the nest.'

Skipper nodded.

'Hurry up then, Sammy. Let's land this thing before they turn us into meatballs.'

They turned sharply left and flew in a wide circle before making their final approach from the far side of the tree, out of sight of the watching hornets. Sam pulled back on the joystick so that the front of the fly came up before easing off the throttle and landing neatly on the flat green surface of a beech leaf, just below where the nest was situated.

'Ladies and gentlemen,' he said, holding his nose for effect. 'I would like to take this opportunity to thank you for flying with Norzun Airlines and wish you all a very pleasant stay at the Hornet Hotel.'

'Why thank you, Captain,' said Skipper, climbing over the seats into the back. 'I'm sure it will be a once in a lifetime experience.'

'Let's hope so,' said Sam, watching her throw down the rope ladder. He handed her a rucksack that was bulging with more ropes and she swung it on her back before setting off down the ladder. Taking the other rucksack he followed her down. The rope vibrated in tune with the buzzing of the hornets and the whole forest seemed to hum like a power station. Sam's heart beat faster as he thought about the task ahead. In a few short minutes they would be trying to enter a nest of vicious hornets which would attack at the slightest provocation. If the hornets discovered them –which, given the circumstances, seemed very likely – they would be ripped apart or – even worse –stung to death.

It was not a happy thought.

'You're looking a bit pale there,' said Skipper as Sam stepped back off the rope onto the leaf. 'Not having second thoughts, are we?'

Sam smiled wanly.

'Nah,' he said. He lay on his stomach and peered down over the side of the leaf, which undulated slightly beneath him. It felt like lying on a big green water bed. 'Probably just the sushi.'

'Oh,' said Skipper. She gave him a knowing smile. 'That's all right then.'

A ray of light shone through the branches onto the leaf, making it suddenly translucent. Sam felt the sun warm upon his back and watched as wisps of steam rose from tiny holes in the leaf's surface. His whole body tingled with nervous anticipation at the thought of what was to come, but underneath he felt strangely calm. He couldn't explain it but it was as if, for a brief moment, everything in the world seemed just as it should be.

'I think,' said Skipper, 'perhaps we should go over the plan one more time, just to make sure.'

Sam looked at the thick tree trunk and listened to the humming of the hornets. 'OK,' he said. 'And then let's go for it.'

Firebrand heard the sound of footsteps coming down the corridor and his muscles tensed. He was a brave man – of that there was no doubt – but these people knew that even the bravest man has his limits. And they knew that, eventually, they would find a way to push him beyond them.

But they hadn't succeeded yet. And, although he was tired and afraid, Firebrand was determined that they wouldn't succeed tonight either.

The door swung open and three men walked in. Firebrand recognised two of them immediately; the steel toe-capped boots and wooden batons being the standard equipment of his usual tormentors. But the third man was new to him. He wore a long black leather coat of the sort favoured by top-ranking officials in the Vermian Empire and his blond hair was close cropped beneath his cap. As he stood in the middle of the cell and stared at Firebrand through a pair of round, gold-rimmed glasses, Firebrand looked back into the hard green eyes and saw that they were empty of all emotion. They contained neither hate nor pity; not anger nor love; simply a cold, ruthless determination to win.

'Good afternoon, Commander,' the man said. 'It is an honour to meet you at last, although unfortunate that it should be under such circumstances. Allow me to introduce myself. My name is Major Krazni, Head of Intelligence.' He smiled. 'Perhaps you have heard of me?'

Krazni. Firebrand had heard the name all right. Krazni had been responsible for some of the worst atrocities during the battle for Vahlzi – mass executions in the capital and the destruction of the city hospital among them. But Firebrand had also heard that Krazni was a vain man, and wasn't about to give him the satisfaction he was looking for.

'No,' he lied. 'I've never heard of you.'

He was rewarded by the tiniest flicker of anger in Krazni's eyes, but it quickly vanished again, leaving only a cold stare in its place.

'Well,' said Krazni, 'no matter. The important thing is, I know all about you, Commander. Or, perhaps I should say, ex-Commander.'

Firebrand made no reply, choosing instead to watch a small brown cockroach scuttle beneath his tattered grey blanket.

'They tell me you are a well-educated man, Commander. Is that true?'

'I know the difference between right and wrong,' replied Firebrand. 'Which is more than some.'

Krazni smiled. 'How very interesting, Commander. An attempt to seize the moral high ground. I wonder, do you know how many civilians were killed when your soldiers invaded Vermia four years ago?'

'We didn't start this war,' said Firebrand bitterly.

'No,' replied Krazni. 'And neither will you finish it. But to return to my original question – do you consider yourself well educated?'

Firebrand stared at the cold stone floor and said nothing. Oh, he was well educated all right. He had read a thousand books on history, politics, science and religion. But what good had it done him? In the end, he had lost everything.

'Oh, I'm sorry,' Krazni continued. 'I had forgotten that you are a modest man. You couldn't possibly answer such a question without recourse to vanity. But then perhaps only a well-educated man would be so self-effacing.'

He paused for a moment, apparently pleased with his own summing up of the situation.

'Let me ask another question, then. Have you ever read the Book of Incantations?'

Firebrand nodded, recalling the book of prophecies which Odoursin had stolen from the Olumnus tribe.

'You know I have.'

'Yes. Well. In that case perhaps you are familiar with the passage about a certain Dreamwalker's Child.'

Firebrand's heart leapt as he remembered how the book had foretold of Sam's arrival in Aurobon, but he forced himself to remain impassive.

'What of it?'

'Well, let me see. According to my research, I understand that this person was someone you had rather a lot to do with. Am I right, Commander?'

Firebrand shrugged.

'Listen, why don't we just cut to the part where you beat me up or shoot me or whatever else you have planned? Because whatever was written in that book is in the past now. None of it made any difference and it no longer matters to me. Nothing matters any more.'

'On the contrary,' said Krazni. 'I think it matters to you a great deal. But at the moment you consider yourself a man without hope. And curiously, that puts you in rather a strong position.'

Firebrand stared at the floor.

'I have no idea what you are talking about.'

'You believe everything you ever cared about is lost. So there is nothing left that we can take from you except your life which – I suspect – no longer means as much to you as it once did. From our point of view, such a situation is . . . how shall I put it . . . rather inconvenient.'

'At last,' said Firebrand. 'Some good news.'

'Oh no,' continued Krazni. 'The good news is still to come.' He moved several steps closer to Firebrand and when he spoke again it was almost in a whisper.

'You see, you are such an *obstinate* man, Commander. So very stubborn. So I said to myself, what does this man value? What remains in this world for him to care about? And the more I thought about it, the more it seemed that there was nothing. The war had taken away your treasures, severed the last of your foolish attachments. That, at least, was the conclusion I reached.'

He paused for a moment, letting his words dissolve in the cell's stagnant air.

'But I was wrong. You see, this afternoon I received a very strange and interesting piece of news which I believe may be of interest to you.'

Firebrand glared contemptuously at Krazni.

'There is nothing of interest that you can tell me now.'

'Oh, but I think there is,' said Krazni with a smile. 'You see, we have found your Sam Palmer, and he is still alive. The girl too – let me think now, what was her name – ah yes, Skipper, that was it.' He paused to let this latest piece of information sink in. 'Don't you think that's amazing, Commander?'

Firebrand stared at Krazni as though he had seen a ghost.

'You're lying,' he said. 'You know as well as I do that they were both killed.'

'Yes, that's what we all thought at first. Then, when we found the boy had returned to his Earth body we decided we'd all be better off if he stayed there. But surprise, surprise, he seems to have found his way back into Aurobon again. So who knows – if things go according to plan, we might all be having a little reunion. Won't that be fun, Commander?'

As the heavy metal door slammed shut, Krazni knew that he had him.

He had found the chink in Firebrand's armour.

However hard they appeared, Krazni knew he could always crack them in the end. They were all the same underneath. He would have Firebrand begging to tell him where the enemy base was by the end of the week.

And once that was destroyed, there would be no one left to challenge their supremacy.

The Vermian Empire would reign for ever.

Sixteen

Sam was just helping Skipper to untangle the ropes from his backpack when she nudged him and pointed over his shoulder.

'Hey,' she said. 'Look.'

Just beyond the leaf, where the stalk met new wood, a large green caterpillar was shuffling along the branch towards the tree trunk.

'Perhaps we won't be needing these ropes after all.'

Sam watched the emerald-coloured grub as it negotiated its way unhurriedly around the base of a twig. Tiny ripples of movement undulated like waves along the length of its ribbed, rubbery back.

'Why's that, then?' he asked.

'Simple,' replied Skipper. 'The caterpillar wants to go higher up the tree, right? Just like we do. Only difference is, he's looking for fresh leaves and we're looking for hornet eggs. And whereas we've only got slippy-soled boots on, he's got a whole bunch of grippy little feet tucked underneath there – feet which'll carry him up that tree trunk faster than a rat on roller skates.'

Sam frowned.

'Skipper, anything would be faster than a rat on roller skates. He'd just be slipping around at the bottom. Swearing, probably.'

'OK, bad example. But anyway, listen – we just climb on board, sit back and enjoy the ride, then jump off when we reach our stop.'

'Hornet City,' said Sam.

'Exactly. The city that never sleeps.'

'More's the pity.'

'What do you think? Beats climbing, doesn't it?'

'Yeah, I guess. We'd better take these with us though.' He picked up the tangle of ropes and began stuffing them back into his backpack. When that was done he peered uncertainly over the side of the leaf at the long drop down to the forest floor. Then he looked at Skipper, glanced over at the caterpillar in the middle of the branch and gestured towards it with his hand.

'After you, dear,' he said.

Skipper closed one eye and squinted up at him in the bright sunlight.

'Always the gentleman.'

She pushed him lightly aside with the tips of her fingers, walked past a little way and then looked back at him with a little smile.

'Watch and learn,' she said.

Then she did a handstand on the edge of the leaf,

arched her back and curved her legs gracefully over onto the leaf-stem behind her. As she continued to move across the surface of the stem in this way, Sam was reminded of the toy springs that walked down stairs on their own. The way she seemed almost to pour herself from one place into the next made the whole thing appear smooth and effortless.

Sam knew, however, that it wasn't so easy. At least, not for him. The stem was reasonably thick and under normal circumstances, he would have happily sauntered, skipped or even somersaulted across it with barely even a thought for what he was doing.

But it was very different when you were this far above the ground.

His pulse racing, Sam edged slowly towards the end of the leaf and took his first, tentative steps on the stem. A breeze rustled the leaves and he felt the air gently buffeting him. Swaying unsteadily, he dropped onto his hands and knees and felt his heart thump against his ribs like a clenched fist.

'Come on, Grandma,' Skipper called. 'We don't want to miss the bus.'

'OK,' said Sam, shutting his eyes. 'Be with you in a minute.'

Above the humming of hornets he could hear the sound of birdsong floating down through the forest canopy and the notes calmed him a little. With a sudden feeling of lightness he stood up again and walked quickly over to where Skipper was standing. He half expected her to make a joke, but she just looked at him with serious blue eyes and gave him a small, reassuring smile.

'Come on,' she said, and she held out her hand. 'Let's go.'

It really was the strangest feeling, like sitting on a lilo with a constant stream of water being pumped through it. When they had first climbed onto its back, the caterpillar had reared up, twisting its head from side to side. But after a while it settled down again, resuming its slow, shuffling progress along the branch. Now it reached the main trunk of the tree and began to move upwards.

'Hold tight,' shouted Skipper, 'we're going vertical!'

Sam squeezed his knees against the caterpillar's rubbery sides and leaned forward, pressing his face against its rippling back and gripping the fleshy ridges tightly in both hands. As the caterpillar moved up the trunk he felt gravity pulling him backwards and was quite relieved to hear the buzzing of the hornets grow louder above their heads. Soon, one way or another, it would be over.

Lifting his head from the caterpillar's back he was puzzled to see Skipper lean over and plunge a long silver knife into the tree trunk. Grasping the handle firmly, she slid sideways off the caterpillar until the only thing preventing her from tumbling to her death was her tenuous grip on the knife. She swung back and forth like a tiny pendulum before pulling another knife from her belt and stabbing it into the tree next to the first one.

Suspended between the two handles, she twisted her head round to look at Sam.

As the caterpillar shuffled forward and drew level with Skipper, Sam could see the look of urgency on her face and decided that she must have slipped. Grasping the caterpillar's skin tightly in his left hand, he leaned over as far as he dared and stretched out his arm.

'Quickly, Skipper!' he shouted. 'Grab hold!'

To his surprise, Skipper took hold of his arm and pulled so hard that he was wrenched violently from the caterpillar's back. With a shout he found himself scrabbling frantically for something to stop him from falling. Then he hit the side of the tree trunk with such force that it knocked the wind out of him. He just had time to feel Skipper's arm grip him firmly round the waist and notice that the knife she clutched at with her free hand was bending under their weight before there was a loud buzz, a snap of metal and he was falling like a stone. He slammed into something green and spongy and as he grabbed hold of it, he realised it was the caterpillar which was now, incredibly, flying through the air. The buzzing grew louder and the world spun into a whirl of sound and colour until suddenly he landed with a smack and everything around him was bathed in a dim, grey light.

He sat up and rubbed his forehead, feeling a big egg-shaped lump where he had whammed into the side of the tree.

'Ouch,' he said. 'What happened there?'

A hand grabbed him by the scruff of the neck and

dragged him backwards just as something very large scuttled past.

'Sam, are you all right?'

'Skipper!' breathed Sam, the relief apparent in his voice. 'Is that you?'

'I think so,' came the reply. 'It's a bit hard to tell in this light.'

Sam squeezed his eyes shut and rested his head on his knees for a few moments in an attempt to get his breath back.

'What happened there?' he asked. 'Why did you jump off?'

'Didn't you see it?'

'See what?'

'The hornet. It came round the back of the tree and I figured it wouldn't be long before it spotted the caterpillar and took it back to the nest to feed to its grubs. So I jumped off and grabbed you just before it hit. Then as the hornet took off again, I made sure we jumped back on and hitched a ride. It was a perfect way in, really. The guards never even noticed us.'

'Perfect way in?' said Sam. 'Perfect way in where?' But as he listened to the powerful humming that reverberated through the gloom and felt the scratch of the curved, papery wall behind his head, he realised that it was a question he didn't need to ask.

'Oh,' he said quietly. 'Oh, wow.'

'We've done it, Sam,' said Skipper excitedly. 'We're sitting inside a hornets' nest!'

Seventeen

Sam held out his hand and touched the smooth, papery sides of the nest. He noticed the stripy pattern and realised that each different coloured stripe represented the pulp from a different tree, fence, or telegraph pole.

'This is beautiful,' he said. 'It's like a work of art isn't it?'

'I guess so,' said Skipper. 'Wouldn't want it hanging on my wall, though.'

They crouched behind a raised layer of waxy cells and felt the breeze from a thousand hornet wings, blowing through the nest and cooling it.

'Where do you think they keep their eggs, then?' asked Skipper.

Sam thought for a moment.

'Wherever the queen is I suppose. She's one big egg-laying machine. If we find her, we find the eggs.'

They were interrupted by a ripping, squelching sound away to their left and as Sam peered through the dimly lit nest he could just make out the face of a giant hornet. It was the same one that had carried them into the nest and now it was using its powerful jaws to tear the still writhing caterpillar apart. As Sam watched in horror, it pulled off little pieces of the caterpillar and began to feed them to the larvae which twitched and squirmed in the hexagonal cells beneath it.

'Oh lovely,' said Skipper.

As his eyes became more used to the gloom, Sam saw that there were several other large hornets moving across the tops of the cells, stopping every now and then to distribute another chunk of unfortunate grub or insect to the hungry larvae.

'You know what I think?' said Sam.

'No,' said Skipper. 'Oh *gross*!' She grimaced as the first hornet proceeded to snip off the caterpillar's head. 'I think I might become vegetarian.' She glanced at Sam and noticed that he was looking slightly exasperated. 'Sorry Sam. I *am* listening. Tell me what you think.'

'I think,' Sam continued in a low voice, 'that all the eggs must be down on the next layer.'

'Like chocolates,' said Skipper, looking back at the hornet.

'Eh?' said Sam.

'You know. The horrible ones are always left at the top and the ones you want are always down on the next layer.'

She paused.

'Mind you, it'd be one hell of a shock if you got given a box of these for your birthday.'

'Skipper,' said Sam. 'Can we just forget about the chocolates for a minute?'

'Sorry.'

'Now the way I see it, these hornets are going to finish feeding their larvae pretty soon. When they do, we can make a move.'

'What about the other hornets? There must be hundreds of them.'

'Yes, but listen,' said Sam. 'Can you hear that noise?'

Skipper put her head on one side and listened. A faint scratching sound was coming from the cells beneath the hornets.

'What is it?' Skipper asked.

'That's the sound the larvae make when they're hungry – bit like baby birds when they squawk at their mothers. It's a signal that they want to be fed. But if you listen carefully, you can tell that the noise is getting fainter all the time. Soon they'll be so busy digesting their bits of caterpillar that they'll stop scratching for a while. And when they do, the hornets will deliver their food to larvae in other parts of the nest.'

Skipper gave Sam an amused look.

'You certainly know your hornets,' she said.

Sam pointed to a gap between where the layer of cells stopped and the outer walls of the nest curved down past it.

'See that gap? That's our route down to the next layer. If we're lucky, we can climb down without being spotted and make our way to the egg-laying chamber.'

Skipper held up her hand. 'Listen,' she said. 'I think that's it.'

Sam listened and nodded. The scratching had stopped.

'That's it all right,' he said.

They watched from their hiding place as, one by one, the hornets moved across the tops of the cells before disappearing with a loud buzz.

'OK,' said Sam. 'Soon as the last one goes, we make a run for it. Straight over the cells, down the gap and into the egg chamber. Then we grab one egg each, and come back for the ropes.'

'So what's our exit strategy?' asked Skipper. 'Still drop and swing?'

Sam thought about a discussion they'd had back in the restaurant where they had agreed the best way out of the nest would be to fasten the ropes somewhere near the base and swing out onto the nearest branch.

'Yes,' he said. 'Let's stick with that.'

It was certainly risky, but it had the advantage of being quick which – where angry hornets were concerned – was a definite bonus.

'Ready?' asked Skipper as the last of the hornets flew off through the gap.

Sam took a deep breath.

'Ready,' he said.

He held out his fist and Skipper bumped it with her knuckles.

'Let's go!'

Then they were off, running hard across the hexagonal ridges that surrounded the edges of the larva cells. Sam could feel the tiny vibrations of the larvae as they squirmed beneath his feet, but within seconds he found himself at the edge of the cell layer, staring all the way down to the hole at the base of the nest. In between the stream of hornets arriving and departing, he could just make out the forest floor far below.

There was a sudden scream behind him.

'Sam! Help me!'

Turning, he saw that a maggoty white larva had thrust its head up, caught hold of Skipper's foot and was attempting to drag her back into its cell. Another of the larvae had latched onto her arms and was pulling her back the other way.

'Hang on!' Sam shouted. He raced frantically back towards her and like a football player executing a dropkick in the closing seconds of a match, he booted the nearest maggot as hard as he could. There was a loud, soggy *thwack* as the creature's head flapped backwards and a gobbet of yellow slime flew out of its mouth, splattering the front of his jacket. Immediately, Skipper pushed herself up with her free leg and swung her fist around so hard that it smacked the other larva sideways, sending it wriggling back to the safety of its cell.

'You want lunch, maggot?' she asked icily, pulling a grenade from her pocket. 'I'll give you some lunch.'

Sam grabbed her firmly by the arm and steered her back towards the edge of the nest. He gently took the grenade from her hand and returned it to her pocket.

'Save it,' he said. 'We've got work to do.'

Peering cautiously over the edge he saw that, besides the outer wall of the nest which was on the far side of a five- or six-metre gap there was only an internal wall of smooth paper below them. This extended downwards for several metres until the next layer of combs was reached but, as far as he could see, there were no handholds anywhere.

'I think we're going to need the ropes,' he said.

'No we're not,' replied Skipper. She crouched down, gripped the side of the comb and then, to Sam's surprise, began to lower herself over the edge.

'Careful!' he warned as her knuckles whitened under the strain.

'Don't worry,' said Skipper. 'It's made of paper, remember?'

Swinging her leg back, she kicked at the wall with the toe of her boot. There was a muffled thud and leaning over the edge Sam saw that her foot had practically disappeared into its soft, pulpy structure. Fragments of paper floated down like confetti towards the base of the nest.

'See?' said Skipper. 'Easy-peasy.' She punched a couple of handholds into the wall and began her slow descent toward the next layer.

'All right!' said Sam. He smiled and swung himself neatly over the edge.

It was really quite simple when you got the hang of it,

like climbing down the side of a steep, snowy hill. If you needed a hand- or foothold, you just punched or kicked a new one out for yourself. And although the paper structure was quite soft, it was also amazingly strong. In no time at all, Skipper had reached the opening to the next layer. But as Sam joined her, several hornets flew past and buzzed loudly out of the entrance, the wind from their wings sweeping upwards with such force that it nearly blew them off the wall.

'Jeepers,' said Sam. 'Didn't see that coming.'

'That was close,' said Skipper, lifting her face back off the wall again. 'I thought we were goners that time. Hang on a sec while I take a peek.'

She swung her legs around like the hands of a clock so that she appeared to be doing a handstand up the side of the wall. When her feet were above her head she kicked out two fresh holes and slotted her feet in. Then, hanging by the tips of her boots, she put her hands on the edge of the chamber below and peered in. As Sam watched, she gave a little squeak and quickly pulled her head back again.

'How's it looking?' asked Sam.

'Not good,' said Skipper, climbing back up the wall again. 'The queen's in there so it's definitely the egg-laying chamber. Problem is, the place is absolutely swarming with worker hornets.'

'Are you sure it was the queen?' asked Sam. 'Was she twice the size of the others?'

'And then some,' said Skipper. 'Listen, we've got big

Hornets' nest

problems. Those worker hornets are doing nothing else but guarding her. If we go in there now and try to steal her eggs, they'll rip us apart.'

Sam felt his mouth go dry at the thought of being attacked by giant hornets. He imagined the inscrutable stare of their robot-like faces and the crunch of their jaws as they plunged their sharp, agonising stings into him like hot swords.

Closing his eyes and pressing his face into the soft paper wall, he heard himself say, 'We can't give up now, Skipper. We have *got* to get those eggs.'

'I know,' said Skipper. 'But I'm beginning to run out of ideas.'

Sam let out a heavy sigh and opened his eyes again. But what he saw next sent a sudden sparkle of excitement through his veins. The patch where he had pushed his face into the papery wall and breathed upon it had become strangely translucent, like a misted-up window. And there, on the other side of it, was a white, oval object the size of a rugby ball.

'Skipper!' he hissed. 'Over here! I think I've found one!'

Skipper quickly traversed hand over fist across the wall towards him.

'What have you got?' she asked breathlessly.

'Look,' he whispered. 'In there.'

Skipper pressed her face against the wall for a second or two and then turned to him with a smile.

'Ker-*ching*! Sammy boy, I think you've hit the jackpot.'

'All right,' said Sam. 'Let's nick it and get out of here.'

'There must be a third chamber between the other two,' said Skipper. 'Perhaps they seal it off while the eggs are developing and open it up again when the larvae hatch.'

'Maybe,' said Sam. 'To be honest, I don't give a stuff as long as it keeps me away from those hornets. Pass me your knife a minute.'

Skipper pulled the knife from her belt and held it out towards Sam, handle first.

'There you go, doctor.'

Sam pushed the knife into the wall and, using a sawing motion, cut out a thick, circular slab of paper before carefully removing it and passing it to Skipper.

'Cool,' she said. With a flick of her wrist, she sent it spinning into space like a frisbee. It glanced off the far wall of the nest before tumbling towards the bottom like a coin falling down a well.

'Skipper, don't!' Sam hissed in alarm. 'You'll have them all up here in a minute.'

'Hornet frisbee,' mused Skipper. 'Now there's an idea . . .'

Ignoring her, Sam stuck his head into the hole and found himself looking into a waxy, hexagonal cell. The egg was in the middle, some way beyond the grasp of his outstretched hand.

'How's it looking?' asked Skipper.

Sam popped his head out of the hole again.

'I can't quite reach it. I think I'm going to have to crawl in and get it.'

'Do you want me to go?' asked Skipper enthusiastically. 'I'm smaller than you.'

'No, don't worry. I think I can fit. Tell you what – if you can just hold open your rucksack, I'll pass the egg back to you.'

'OK,' said Skipper. 'But be careful.'

Using his forearms to grip the floor of the cell, Sam pulled himself over to the egg and touched its surface with the palm of his hand. The thin white membrane felt smooth to the touch, like the skin of a ping-pong ball. Gripping it firmly with both hands, he tried to pick it up, but it was stuck fast.

'Come on,' he muttered and pulled harder, but the egg wouldn't budge. Examining the base, he found that it was anchored in place by some sort of yellow glue.

Using the knife to saw away at the base of the egg, he was relieved to see that it cut through the material quite easily. After a minute or two, the egg began to wobble and he wrapped an arm around it to stop it falling over. A few moments later he was wriggling back to Skipper with it safely in his arms.

'Good work, Sam,' said Skipper.

'Do you think one's enough?'

'Should be. Once we get back, the engineers will use pheromones to make it develop into a queen. Then we can get all the eggs we want.'

'Maybe we'd better get another one – just to be on the safe side,' suggested Sam as Skipper rolled the egg carefully into her rucksack, coiling the ropes around it to provide some protection.

'One more then,' she agreed. 'But that'll have to be it.'

'Right,' said Sam. 'Won't be a minute.' He twisted around inside the cell and began to cut his way through to the next one.

'Don't be long,' said Skipper, listening to the faint scratching sound floating down from the layer above. 'I think the larvae are getting hungry again.'

Sam squeezed through the hole he had made with the knife and stared at the egg in the middle.

'Skipper,' he called. 'Come here a minute. See what you think.'

Pushing the rucksacks ahead of her, Skipper crawled along until she reached the cell where Sam was sitting.

'What is it?' she asked.

'Look,' said Sam. He nodded towards the egg and Skipper saw that there was something wriggling inside it. 'I'd say it's about ready to hatch.'

'Oh *yuk*,' she said. 'Don't think I want that crawling out of my rucksack in the middle of the night. Let's leave it and go for the next one.'

Sam inched past on his hands and knees until he came to the far wall of the cell, where he proceeded to cut another hole before poking his head through into the next one.

'This one looks fine,' he said. He slid into the cell and used the knife again to free the egg from its base. Skipper pushed his rucksack through the hole and he quickly rolled the second egg into it, pulling the drawstrings tight around the top and tying it shut.

'Job done,' he said.

'Good,' said Skipper. 'Then let's get out of here.'

Sam was about to move when there was a tearing sound beneath him. Seeing the horrified look on Skipper's face, he looked down and saw a large crack opening up in the floor between his knees. It snaked across the base of the cell and as his hands scrabbled for grip on the smooth pulpy walls he heard Skipper shout 'Sam, watch out!' Then, with a loud ripping noise, the floor of the cell gave way and he crashed down into the queen's egg chamber below.

With a surprised yelp he lifted his head to find that he had landed on the edge of several open cells, each containing the soft, creamy white bodies of newly hatched hornet larvae. As he watched, their grotesque, shiny brown heads seemed to sense him, swivelling round to stare blindly in his direction.

As Sam shrank back in disgust he heard a scraping sound and spun round to see three giant hornets crouching by the wall on the far side of the chamber. Dark, shining eyes stared at him malevolently and as the sharp jaws grated together, Sam knew he was only moments away from a horrible death.

There was nothing for it; no escape. He would have to stand and fight. At least it might then give Skipper a chance to return to Aurobon with the eggs. Gripping the handle of the knife tightly in his right fist, he stared defiantly into the eyes of the hornets and slowly, very slowly, began to beckon to them with his left hand.

'All right then,' he said, 'let's see what you're made of.'

The middle hornet began to advance menacingly towards him across the floor of the chamber and immediately all Sam's initial bravado evaporated. The sheer size of the insect was terrifying, like standing directly in the path of some hideous alien aircraft. As it thrust its head forward and opened its terrible jaws there was a loud crash and in a powdery explosion of dust and debris, Skipper landed with a thump on the floor next to him. Instantly she was on her feet again, pushing him towards the far end of the chamber.

'Run, Sam!' she shouted. 'Run!'

But Sam stood his ground; he had no intention of leaving without her. Seeing the hornet turn towards her, he rushed forward in a final act of desperation and in the confusion that followed became dimly aware of Skipper throwing something to the ground. There was a brilliant, blinding flash, an ear-splitting bang and then suddenly the chamber was filled with a thick, grey smoke which swirled around hiding everything from view. Stunned, Sam fell to his knees as his senses were overwhelmed by the intense combination of light, sound and smoke.

Beyond the roaring in his ears, he heard the buzz and clatter of hornets as they scurried around in utter confusion. Then Skipper grabbed him by the hand, pulled him to his feet and dragged him back through the smoke.

'Can you hear me, Sam?'

'Yeah, just about,' Sam gasped, struggling to catch his breath. 'What just happened?'

'Flash-bang grenade,' said Skipper. 'Causes temporary confusion.'

'You can say that again,' said Sam.

'When the smoke clears,' Skipper went on, 'those hornets are going to go crazy. We need to get out of here right now.'

As the angry buzzing grew louder they ran through the smoke until they reached the far side of the chamber. Sam tried to punch a hole through the outer wall, but the paper was thicker and stronger than before and his fist just bounced off.

'Quick, bend over!' said Skipper.

'What?'

'We're going to have to cut our way back into the upper chambers,' said Skipper. 'I need you to be my ladder.'

Still reeling from the shock of the grenade, Sam put his hands on his knees and felt Skipper scramble onto his back. He slowly stood up again and held her feet firmly on his shoulders.

'OK?'

'Fine. Quick – pass up the knife.'

Sam shuddered at the thought of climbing through cells of hungry, wriggling larvae, but he supposed it was preferable to being attacked by angry hornets. Keeping one hand on Skipper's foot, he passed the knife up to her with the other and heard the now familiar sound of its serrated blade sawing through the paper. As he stared into the smoke to check for hornets, he noticed to his surprise that – far from disappearing – the smoke was becoming both thicker and blacker.

'Skipper – I thought you said the smoke was going to clear,' said Sam.

'Don't worry,' said Skipper. 'I'm nearly through. We'll be out before they spot us.'

'You don't understand,' said Sam urgently. 'The smoke is getting *thicker*.'

As Skipper jumped down from his shoulders to investigate, Sam heard a crackling in the air, felt the heat on his face and saw fingers of orange flame flicker across the roof of the chamber.

'The grenade!' he shouted. 'The nest is on fire!'

At that moment a hornet lumbered through the smoke just as a sheet of flame leapt from the smoke and transformed it into a living fireball. As the blackened hornet fell sideways and curled up like a leaf in a bonfire, Sam threw his arms up to shield his face from the intense heat.

'Look!' Skipper shouted. 'The wall!'

Through the smoke, Sam saw that a large hole had opened up in the side of the nest, growing wider with every second as the fire spread out from its centre. The breeze outside was fanning the flames through the hole and Sam realised the egg chamber was fast becoming one giant chimney, funnelling fire and smoke up through the nest with a thunderous roar.

'If we stay here we'll be burned alive!' Sam shouted above the noise of the firestorm. 'We have to get out of here now!'

Skipper looked at him and nodded.

'OK,' she said. 'Let's just give them something to keep them occupied.' Pulling the pin from a high explosive grenade, she lobbed it into the smoke and then they were racing through the flames, running past melting cells and burning hornets as the floor beneath them disintegrated and they jumped through the fiery hole into the cool, clean air.

As a loud explosion blew the nest apart behind them, Skipper's hand slipped from Sam's grasp and he noticed that his jacket was on fire. Tumbling through a kaleidoscope of leaves, sky and flames he called Skipper's name and then the world splintered into bubbles that hissed and split into silence. He looked up through the gloomy water to see a small, bright circle of light high above his head.

Then Skipper grabbed him and together they swam away from the darkness, back towards the life that had so nearly deserted them.

Eighteen

Sam sat on the edge of the hollow tree stump and stared out across the deep lake of rainwater that had collected in its middle. As he watched the sunlight sparkle across the surface, he thought how fortunate they had been to fall into the water. If they had landed on the forest floor, they would almost certainly have been killed.

Skipper interrupted his thoughts by pressing a soft, wet square of moss against his arm.

'Ow,' he said, wincing. 'That hurts!'

'Come on, you baby,' said Skipper. 'Just hold that against it for a few minutes. It'll take the heat out of it – stop it blistering.'

'Thank you, nurse,' said Sam. He pushed the spongy moss against his forearm and felt the cool water soothing his burns. 'We flew out of there like a couple of fireworks didn't we?'

'Could have been worse,' said Skipper, pointing towards the base of the tree where several dead hornets

lay smoking on the ground. 'I'd say their stinging days
were definitely over.'

Sam suddenly became agitated.

'The eggs!' he cried. 'What happened to the eggs?'

Skipper leaned forward to show Sam that she was still
wearing her rucksack on her back.

'*Voila*. Where's yours?'

Sam shot her a worried look. 'I think I must have left
it back in the nest.' He stared awkwardly at the reflection
of the trees in the water, embarrassed by his mistake.
'Sorry, Skipper.'

Skipper shrugged. 'Don't worry about it. You had
other things on your mind. Besides, one is all we need,
remember?'

'Yeah, but what if it's a dud?'

Skipper poked him in the ribs. 'What if the sun stops
shining? What if the stars fall from the sky?' She smiled
and patted his leg. 'Trust me, Sam. Everything'll be
fine.'

Sam nodded.

'I guess so.'

Skipper stood up and put her hands on her hips.

'Having said that . . . the next part's going to be a bit
tricky.'

Sam threw the piece of moss into the pool with a plop
and watched the rings spread out across the water.

'Can't be trickier than the last part, surely?'

Skipper sucked her teeth thoughtfully.

'Different kind of tricky.'

Sam followed her gaze past the smouldering remains of the nest to the branch where they had left the robber fly.

'Oh,' he said. 'I see what you mean.'

'I'll go, Sam. You stay here and get your strength back. I should easily make it before nightfall and then we can head back to the fabric gap.'

Sam was about to protest when he realised that there was absolutely no point; Skipper was a brilliant climber and he would only hold her up if he went with her.

'Well OK,' he said. 'If you're sure. But promise me you won't talk to any strange hornets.'

'I promise.'

Skipper carefully removed the coil of ropes, then placed the rucksack containing the egg on the ground next to Sam's feet.

'You can babysit Junior.'

As she slung the rope over her shoulder, Sam looked up at the tree that towered high above the forest floor and saw a cloud of hornets buzzing angrily around the place where their nest used to be.

'Be careful,' he said. 'Don't take any unnecessary risks.'

Skipper raised an eyebrow.

Sam looked at her and held up his hands.

'OK, OK. Take as many as you want.' He waved her away with the backs of his fingers. 'Go on, go. *Shoo*. Get out of here.'

Skipper smiled.

'See you later,' she said.

Sam watched the small figure set out across the forest and several times he almost went after her. But something made him stay, and before long she was lost from sight.

It was after he had been sitting quietly at the edge of the pool for about ten minutes that Sam noticed a flash of something moving at great speed across the water. Shielding his eyes from the sun he saw that there were three canoe-shaped black objects, floating some way off upon the surface of the water. One of them shot away again and then came to rest several hundred metres distant. The movement was so swift that there was no real sense of acceleration or braking. These things were either completely still or somewhere else.

As he looked more closely at the nearest one, Sam noticed that it had a pair of reddish eyes at the front. Clinging to the underside of its body was a silver bubble of oxygen and two huge legs stuck out from its middle like oars. Sam remembered once seeing something similar, skating across the surface of a pond and realised that he was looking at a water boatman. He shook his head in amazement. It had never occurred to him that some day he would come across one the size of a large speedboat. But it looked fairly harmless. Sam glanced back over his shoulder into the forest. With any luck, Skipper would have started climbing the tree by now. It would probably be several hours before she made it back again.

The midday sun was high above the trees and the

forest was heating up like an oven. Sam wiped the sweat from his brow as steam rose from the damp moss all around him. The thought of plunging headlong into the cool water was all at once irresistible. Pulling off his damp shirt and placing it over the rucksack, he crouched on the lip of the tree stump and dived neatly into the pool with a small splash.

Under normal circumstances, Sam's assumption that water boatmen are harmless to humans would have been quite correct. People are several thousand times bigger than water boatmen and so water boatmen do not attack them. But, unfortunately for Sam, scale was no longer on his side.

And so it was that, a few hundred metres away, the nearest water boatman froze as the tiny, sensitive hairs on its legs picked up a new and strange vibration in the water.

Like a shark, it was a voracious hunter. And it knew that vibrations in the water mean only one thing:

Food.

Swivelling around in the water, the creature pointed its sharp, beaky proboscis directly towards the source of the vibrations and zoomed in on the splashes with its dark-red eyes, moving its powerful legs forward with a sharp click.

Then, as Sam swam up and broke through the surface of the water again, it shot towards him like a speeding bullet.

In death, as in life, timing is everything.

If a large tadpole hadn't chosen that exact moment to

swim up and investigate Sam's arrival in the pool, he would never have known what hit him. As it was, he felt a rush of wind, heard a thud and a pop and then a huge wave swept over his head and smashed him hard against the side of the tree stump. Struggling to the surface again he saw a fat tadpole splashing and twitching next to him, a bloodstain spreading rapidly across the surface of the water. He looked up to find himself staring straight into the eyes of its killer. There was a squelch as the hideous bug thrust its jaws deeper into the dying creature and then with a splash of its legs, it swivelled around to face Sam.

Sam knew that he was next on the menu. He scrabbled frantically behind him for the lip of the tree stump, but his fingers slid uselessly against the wet, slippery moss and he was unable to find any grip.

As the last remnants of life ebbed away from the tadpole, it gave a final thrash of its tail and hit Sam squarely across the face. The force of the blow sent him reeling back beneath the surface and as he opened his eyes he saw the shimmering, silvery lines of air bubbles beneath the water boatman's body.

Sometimes, when people are in great peril – they discover that they are capable of doing the most extraordinary things. And so it was that, in those few terrifying seconds, Sam saw the tiniest of opportunities and went for it.

Diving down into the shadows, he picked up a rotting piece of wood from the bottom, arched his back and with a last desperate effort, thrust himself upwards.

There was a pop, a flash of silver and suddenly he was inside the oxygen bubble, floating like an astronaut in a space capsule.

Gulping down lungfuls of oxygen, he watched the tadpole's empty skin float past and guessed that the water boatman would soon be on the move again.

Taking a final breath, he punched his fist through the bubble wall and grabbed one of the creature's legs near the point where it joined its body. Clutching the piece of wood in his other hand, he quickly pulled himself onto its wet, slippery back and then inched his way forward on hands and knees. Reaching the centre, he sat down and considered his options. The edge of the tree stump was still within swimming distance, but Sam knew that, even with a dive, it would take him about ten seconds to reach it. Given the slipperiness of the stump, the odds were pretty much stacked against him. The water boatman would just turn around and bust him open like a balloon.

He looked out across the water and saw that the other boatmen were grouped together over on the other side. At least right now he only had one to contend with.

'All right,' he said softly, and stood up. 'Here we go.'

Then, picking up the soggy, dripping piece of wood, he flung it with all his might towards the centre of the water.

Sam's idea was that the boatman would head towards the splash, giving him a chance to swim to the side while it was distracted. But he hadn't been prepared for the speed with which everything happened. The moment the

wood hit the water, the boatman took off at such speed
that Sam felt as if a rug had been whipped out from
underneath him. Before he knew what was happening, his
feet were above his head and he was somersaulting backwards through the air. But a surge of adrenalin kept his
mind focused and immediately he hit the water, he flipped
over fast and struck out for the side. Seconds later his fingertips touched wood and he tried desperately to pull
himself up, but again the sides were too slippery and he
fell back, swallowing a mouthful of water in the process.

Coughing and spluttering his way to the surface, he
noticed some yellow fungus over to his left, jutting out
from the wood like giant dinner plates. Glancing over his
shoulder he saw the boatman scanning the surface, sensing new vibrations in the water. As it swivelled around to
face him, Sam knew that he had been seen and with a
whimper of fear he threw himself forward, feeling his
fingers sink into the firm, spongy flesh of the fungus.
Crying out as his muscles stretched to breaking point, he
jerked his legs clear just as the creature thundered into
the side like an express train and the water exploded
violently beneath him. With the last of his strength he
somehow managed to drag himself on the top of the
fungus where he collapsed with exhaustion, his heart
hammering like a fist against his chest.

A few minutes later, Sam regained enough breath to
make the final climb over the lip of the tree stump. Looking back, he saw that the water boatman was still scut-
tling around in circles trying to locate him. He bent

down, picked up a large stone and threw it as hard as he could at the creature's head.

'Yeah, get lost y'freak!' he shouted angrily as it took off at high speed across the water. 'Go home to mummy!'

He was practically dry by the time he reached the spot where he had left the rucksack, and after checking that the egg was still safely inside, he leaned down and placed it carefully at the base of the tree stump. Then he pulled on his shirt and trousers and stared up through the branches. He guessed that Skipper would probably be over halfway up by now. With any luck, she would be back before nightfall and they would be able to return the egg to Aurobon without any more hitches.

Exhausted, Sam stretched out on the edge of the tree stump and closed his eyes, lulled by the music of birdsong and the breeze that whispered softly through the leaves above him.

In his dreams, he heard voices calling to him. They were the voices of his mother and father, but as he stretched out his hands to them they grew fainter, until at last they faded away to nothing.

'Please,' he cried. 'Don't leave me.'

But the voices were lost and all that remained was the sound of the wind, moving across a dark and empty landscape.

He awoke with a start.

Dust blew into his eyes and a loud buzzing filled the air. Blinking and rubbing his eyes, Sam breathed a sigh of relief as he watched the robber fly land in front of him and realised that Skipper must have been successful.

Leaping down from the top of the tree stump, he ran excitedly towards the rope ladder that came tumbling from the fly's underbelly.

'Hey, Skipper!' he shouted as he reached the top of the ladder and clambered through the hatch. 'We did it! We did it!'

The heavy butt of the pistol struck him so hard across the back of his head that he was unconscious before he hit the floor.

'Congratulations, kid.'

The man stared down at Sam's crumpled body, and a smile spread slowly across his face.

'You don't wanna mess with ol' Norzun,' he said. 'Didn't no one ever tell you that?'

Nineteen

Alya was at the Vermian Military Airbase checking soldier ants for signs of parasites when the rumours started. Word spread like wildfire. People were saying they had caught Vermia's Enemy Number One and that they would be bringing him in tonight.

Intrigued, Alya made her way to Terminal One where her high-level security pass allowed her to slip through a ring of heavily armed guards and into the landing zone. A group of young soldiers were talking excitedly about their expected visitor, occasionally glancing in Alya's direction to see if she had noticed them. But she remained studiously aloof, her official badge a shield against unwanted attention.

It was nearly an hour later that the dark shape of a giant robber fly appeared beneath the storm clouds, circling once before touching down upon the snow-covered landing strip. For a moment, everything seemed calm and still, as if nothing out of the ordinary had happened. Flurries of snow continued to drift down from the plum-coloured sky and the soldiers stared through the glass doors, momentarily silenced by the fly's sudden appearance. Then, as the doors of the building slid open and a blast of cold wind awoke them from their reverie, they remembered what they were supposed to do and disappeared off across the airfield in a clatter of boots and rifles.

Alya watched a truck shunt some steps into place below the fly's wings and then a black uniformed pilot pushed someone roughly through the hatch in front of him.

Alya was puzzled. If this was Public Enemy Number One, then he was certainly a good deal smaller than she had expected.

As the figure reached the bottom of the steps the soldiers surged forward, swallowing him up in a blur of fists and boots. Alya bit her lip and turned away, suddenly very afraid of her fellow countrymen. No doubt the man was evil and posed a terrible threat to all of them. But to inflict unnecessary suffering on any living thing was alien to her and the scene made her feel sick.

The group approached the doors, dragging the prisoner along in their midst. His face was hidden from view, but she could tell by the way he stumbled that he was in a bad way.

The doors slid open and the soldiers thundered through, shouting and swearing as they manhandled their captive away for interrogation. As they passed, a gap momentarily opened up between two of the soldiers and Alya caught a brief glimpse of the notorious prisoner.

To her absolute amazement, it seemed that he was nothing but a young and terrified boy.

When at last they had gone, Alya stood shivering in the middle of the empty hall. Watching the snowflakes drift down from a sunless sky, she turned up her collar and wondered why it was that she suddenly felt so ashamed.

Alya spent the next few days searching through classified files stored on the Central Intelligence computer system. Although she knew it was strictly forbidden, her encounter with the boy at the airbase had merely added to her growing suspicion that the Ministry of Information and Culture was very selective about what it allowed the people of Vermia to know. Her history lessons at school had portrayed Vermian soldiers as brave heroes who would ensure the fulfilment of ancient prophecies. Earth people, on the other hand, were monstrous, evil creatures who would destroy both their own world and Aurobon unless they were eliminated.

But although Alya's quicksilver mind had led her to discover the keys to their ultimate destruction, it now made her question the morality of it. She wanted to be sure that it was as necessary as she had always been led to believe. So, using the high-level clearance that her newly found success had given her, she had started to comb through the powerful computer database, entering keywords like *Earth*, *human*, *war* and *culture* in an attempt to discover the truth.

And what she discovered was nothing short of a revelation to her.

Initially, she was reassured by the fact that there was plenty of evidence to back up the lessons that she had been taught. Time and again she found examples of pollution, violence, suffering and countless wars waged by humans on other humans. But gradually her careful research into the various human cultures that existed on Earth began to reveal that many of them were apparently peace-loving, responsible stewards of their world. And to her mounting horror and shame, she discovered that some of the most terrible, unspeakable acts of brutality were to be found not on Earth, but here in Aurobon. For the first time, Alya saw with her own eyes the carefully catalogued records of methodical cruelty, meted out to captives held behind the walls of Vermian prisons.

Clicking through sickening images of Vermian soldiers systematically destroying villages across Mazria, she suddenly awakened a memory in her own mind – a memory of her mother and father screaming at her to run as flames danced against a starlit sky and bullets kicked up dust all around her.

And as she sat alone at the computer watching images of ordinary people on Earth going about their daily business, Alya realised two things; firstly, that it had not been Vahlzian soldiers who had killed her family, and secondly, that she had been lied to all her life.

The inhabitants of Earth were not monsters; they were people, just like her.

The monsters, it seemed, were much closer to home.

In order to celebrate their latest achievements, General Martock and his inner circle had taken over the whole restaurant for the evening. Martock took another swig of expensive red wine and Alya felt her stomach heave as she saw how it glistened and shone on his greasy lips like freshly spilt blood. She stared queasily down at her exquisitely prepared plate of steamed vegetables and laid her fork to one side, unable to put from her mind the images that she had stumbled across the previous evening.

Sensing that she was being watched, she looked up to find the steely gaze of Major Krazni studying her intently from across the table.

'What's the matter, Miss Blin?' he asked. 'Lost your appetite?'

Alya shook her head. 'I'm sorry,' she said, 'I'm not very hungry.'

Krazni continued to stare at her suspiciously, but General Martock roared with laughter and thumped the table so that all the cutlery rattled.

'Of course she isn't hungry, Major!' he shouted. 'This is the greatest moment of her young life! She is far too excited to be hungry! Isn't that right, my dear?'

Alya smiled a sad smile. 'Yes, I expect that's it.'

Martock chuckled indulgently. 'Well, I suppose we can let you get away with not eating, but drinking is another matter. Come on, someone. Refresh the young lady's glass!'

A young waiter, impeccably dressed in freshly ironed black trousers and white linen jacket, hurriedly retrieved a bottle of wine from a bucket of crushed ice and filled Alya's glass up to the brim.

'So I should think!' exclaimed Martock. 'We can't have the poor girl dying of thirst! Now then, gentlemen. I think perhaps it is time for a little toast. Please be upstanding for the new young star who shines so brightly among us!'

There was a clink of cutlery on china as Alya's fellow diners set their knives and forks down upon their plates, reached for their glasses and stood up. Alya made to join them, but Doctor Jancy put a hand on her shoulder and gently pushed her back into her seat again.

'It's you, you fool,' he whispered, not unkindly. 'The General is talking about you.'

Alya blushed and remained seated, staring awkwardly down at the white cotton tablecloth as General Martock cleared his throat and a hush fell upon the assembled company.

'I know it is unusual for us to have female company on such an occasion,' he said, nodding in Alya's direction. 'Normally such a thing would be frowned upon. But in this instance the Emperor Odoursin has given his blessing. For this is no ordinary young woman. On the contrary, her achievements are quite extraordinary. She has accomplished something which many thought to be impossible. Almost single-handedly, she has discovered a way of influencing human behaviour. And by doing so, she has given us the tools with which to pursue our Empire's highest aim – the annihilation of human life on Earth. Once this has been achieved, there will be no one left to stand in our way and the rise of the Vermian Empire will be unstoppable. Gentleman, we are poised on the verge of greatness. And for that we all owe a debt of gratitude to the young woman who sits at our table this evening. So I ask you all to raise your glasses and drink a toast to the brightest new scientist of her generation. Gentlemen, I give you Alya Blin!'

'To Alya Blin!' cried the voices from around the table, and they were the voices of generals, scientists, politicians – the highest ranking officials in all of Vermia.

It should have been a moment of supreme triumph, for it was a moment that Alya had dreamed of many times throughout the lonely months of research.

She had finally made it.

But as she looked around the table, she could think of nothing but her dead family and the bruised, battered face of the young boy she had seen at the airbase, his frightened green eyes staring wildly into her own as he searched desperately for someone to rescue him from his nightmare.

Twenty

It was hard for Sam to know how long he had been in this place. Whenever they moved him for interrogation – which they did frequently – he was always blindfolded. All he knew was that his cell was in some kind of basement at the airbase. He knew this because when he first arrived they had taken him down several flights of steps. There were no windows, and the only light came from a bare bulb which burned constantly. He had no idea whether it was night or day.

The questions were always the same: 'What's your name? Where have you been hiding? Where is the girl? What is the location of the Resistance base?'

And Sam would always tell them the same thing: 'My name's Sam Palmer. I haven't been hiding. I lost my memory. What girl? What resistance?'

And then they would get angry and lay into him.

Now he sat in the corner of his cell, dipping a corner of his blanket into a mug of water and dabbing at his cut, swollen lips. His left eye had closed up completely, but out of his right eye he watched a spider scuttle across the floor and disappear off under the door of his cell. The fact that even such a small creature had made it to freedom lifted his spirits slightly.

'Good luck,' he whispered. 'Kill some flies for me.'

He thought about Skipper back in the forest and wondered: a) if she knew that he had been captured; b) whether she had found the rucksack with the hornet's egg in it and c) whether she had managed to make it back to Aurobon. The odds didn't look good. He'd heard Norzun contacting other fly squadrons with the coordinates of the hornets' nest; with the storm gone and no Vahlzian forces to slow them down, they would have been there within the hour. He supposed it all depended upon how quickly she'd been able to get out of there. But Sam knew what she was like. If she'd thought that there was any possibility he was still there, she'd have kept on looking for him, right up until the moment they found her . . .

Sam stiffened. There were voices in the corridor, which usually meant only one thing – they were coming back to interrogate him. His stomach churned and his hands began to shake. They had only just finished with him. He didn't know if he could face another session. But he knew he must avoid giving away the location of the airbase. If he revealed that, then everything would be lost. He *had* to hold out, at least until Skipper could get back and warn them.

Sam put down his blanket, waiting for his tormentors to kick the door open. But something was different this time. He listened. Usually there were a whole bunch of them, shouting and queuing up to take a pop at him. But this time there were only two voices. The first he recognised as belonging to the regular guard, but the second one was new. And it was female.

'Major Krazni sent me,' the woman was saying. 'He wants me to run a check on the prisoner's DNA. Here are my authorisation documents. I think you'll find them in order.'

There was a rustling of papers followed by the sound of footsteps approaching along the corridor. Sam stood up just as the door opened to reveal the smirking, sadistic face of the guard.

'Lady back here wants to check on your DNA, kid,' he sneered. 'The fun don't stop for you, do it?'

'It shouldn't take long,' said the woman's voice brusquely. 'However, there is a slight risk of infection and I wouldn't want to put you at any risk. So if you wouldn't mind . . . ?'

The guard frowned and his thick eyebrows met in the middle of his forehead.

'Oh . . . right. Infection you say? Well maybe I'll just wait down the hall.'

'I think it best. This'll only take about twenty minutes.'

The guard stepped back into the corridor to be replaced by a young, dark-haired woman in her early twenties. Sam was surprised to see that she had a fresh, open face, quite unlike any of the others. But, he reminded himself, appearances could be deceptive.

'I'll just be at the end of the block if you need me.'

'Fine. Thank you.'

The guard vanished into the shadows and the woman closed the cell door behind her.

Sam stared at her.

'Taking a bit of a risk aren't you? Shutting yourself in a cell with a dangerous criminal?'

The woman smiled.

'You don't strike me as the killing kind,' she said and Sam found himself unnerved by the apparent kindness in her eyes. He would definitely have to be careful with this one.

'If it's my blood you're after,' he told her, 'then maybe you should check out the interrogation room. They've been decorating the walls with it in there.'

The woman nodded gravely. 'I am sorry you have been treated so badly. But I want to help you.'

Sam gave a hollow laugh.

'Of course you do,' he said, his voice heavy with sarcasm. 'That must be why you work with all these nice people.'

'I was there at the airfield when they brought you in,' said the woman. 'I saw what they did to you, and I'm sorry. I don't want to be a part of that.'

'Well, you know what?' said Sam, 'from where I'm sitting, it looks pretty much like you already are.'

But as he spoke, Sam remembered catching sight of

her face as he was dragged through the terminal. He had seen something in her eyes then, a look which had reached out to him in his distress.

He nodded.

'I remember,' he said, more gently. 'Who are you?'

The woman looked over her shoulder as if to check that they were still alone.

'My name is Alya,' she said. 'And you're right. I do work for the government.'

Sam stared at her suspiciously.

'Then why would you want to help me?'

He noticed Alya glance at the cell door again and the fact that she seemed genuinely nervous reassured him a little.

'Look,' she said, 'we haven't got much time, but I think it's important that you know something about me. Then maybe you'll realise why I'm doing this. Why you can trust me.'

Sam shrugged.

'I'm listening,' he said.

'You need to understand,' Alya went on, 'that ever since I can remember, I wanted to be a scientist. I saw the world as this huge, complicated puzzle and felt that if I could only solve it, figure out what everything meant, then everything would be OK.'

Sam saw sadness in her eyes and asked: 'Did you succeed?'

'No,' replied Alya. 'The more I found out about the world, the more I found out how complex the puzzle really was. I soon realised that the most I could hope for was that I might solve the tiniest part of it. So I decided I would just concentrate on one small part of the puzzle and become an expert in that field. I thought that by becoming the best, I would finally *be* someone. I believed that through hard work and achievement, I would be happy.'

A silence fell between them for a while and Sam stared at the young woman with a growing sense of fascination. It was as if in telling him these deeply personal thoughts, she was hearing them herself for the first time. From the look in her eyes he felt certain that she had never spoken of these things before – perhaps had never even acknowledged them in her own mind until now. But why was she telling *him*?

'Did it make you happy?' he asked.

'No,' said Alya. 'For years I convinced myself that everything was OK, but underneath it all I was beginning to have serious doubts about the work I was doing. I sensed that I was shutting my eyes to some unpleasant truths. The past few days have finally opened my eyes.'

'What do you mean?'

'I realised that all the things I worked so hard to achieve were not solving the puzzle at all – instead they were helping to destroy an irreplaceable part of it.'

Somewhere outside in the corridor, Sam heard the guard clear his throat and spit.

'What's all this got to do with me?' he asked.

'While I was waiting for them to bring you in the

other day, I was expecting to see a monster. But when I looked into your eyes, I saw something quite different – something I haven't seen in a long time.'

'What was that?' asked Sam.

Alya smiled sadly. 'It was goodness,' she said. 'The moment I saw you I knew that you could never have done any of the terrible things they were accusing you of.'

Sam looked closely at the young woman standing opposite him in the stark light of a single bulb and wondered at this strange turn of events. Although still unsure whether he should trust her, he was finding it increasingly difficult not to. Could she be his guiding light, the one who would lead him out of the darkness? It was almost too much to hope for.

Alya reached out and touched his arm. 'I mean it,' she said 'You are a good person, Sam. And I realised last night that if I want anything at all in this life, it's to be a good person too.'

'But what happened to make you so sure about all of this?'

Alya quickly checked the door again before continuing.

'Two days ago, I learned how to read the minds of parasitic worms,' she said. 'I learned how to understand their language. And now I can make them do whatever I want them to do.'

'What?' said Sam. 'You've lost me completely.'

'Forget the details,' said Alya. 'The important thing is that – because of what I've done – the Vermian Empire can now influence human behaviour in a way that will probably lead to their extinction. And knowing what I know now, I don't want that to happen.'

'Sounds as though you've left it a bit late,' said Sam.

'There's still time,' replied Alya. 'But not much. That's where you come in. I need your help.'

'I thought you were here to help *me*,' said Sam sceptically.

'I am,' said Alya. 'But in order to help you, I need you to help me first.'

'Look at me,' said Sam. 'Just look at me for a minute. I've got one eye closed and I can hardly stand up. How can I possibly be of any help to you?'

'Simple,' said Alya, 'just tell me where the Resistance base is. Tell me where your friends are hiding out.'

Sam smiled, a bitter, joyless smile.

'I don't know what you're talking about,' he said coldly.

When Alya spoke again, there was a new urgency in her voice.

'Please,' she said. 'Think about it for a minute. Vermian forces are only weeks – maybe days – away from destroying every human being on Earth. There's no way I can possibly stop them on my own. But if I can get in touch with your friends I can give them information which might help them disrupt any attack on Earth, or at least delay it for a while. But I need you to tell me where I can find them.'

Sam shook his head.

'But if I tell you and you're lying, then my friends will die.'

Alya nodded. 'I know, Sam. But if you don't, then millions will die. You *have* to tell me.'

Sam was silent for a long while. He knew there was a very real possibility that this woman had been sent to trick him, but there was something about her that seemed genuine. Either she was extremely clever, or she was telling the truth. It was a terrible decision to make, but Sam knew that, one way or the other, he had to make it. Very slowly, he put a hand on the back of Alya's head and pulled her face close so that her cheek was touching his own. 'All right,' he whispered, 'I'll tell you. But if anything happens to them, I swear I'll come looking for you. Do you understand me?'

'Yes,' said Alya, her serious brown eyes fixed for a moment upon his own. 'I understand.'

Twenty-one

Joey Pestralis had been running his pest control business for less than eighteen months, but already his annual turnover was close to a hundred thousand dollars. In fact he'd had to take on Bobby Morgan simply to cope with the demand. Sure, he paid the kid one fifty a week, but when you were making eight grand a month it was peanuts.

'Hear that buzzing sound, Bobby?' he'd say as they unpacked their gear beneath a nest of angry yellow-jackets. 'That's the sound of dollar bills, flying into our pockets.'

Bobby would laugh that goofy laugh of his and then the two of them would get on with the job of spraying their way to another few hundred bucks.

Joey's mum had been heartbroken when he dropped out of school two years ago. She said she'd wasted all her money paying for a college education. But she changed her tune soon enough when he turned up with a brand new fridge and plasma TV screen.

'I'm so proud of you, Joey,' she said, holding his face

and kissing him on both cheeks. 'Making your way in this world all by yourself.' He'd stuck the screen on the wall and she'd curled up happily on the couch with her fist in a bucket of popcorn, watching her favourite soaps.

'What'd I tell you, Ma?' he said. 'Your Joey's going places.'

And he certainly was. In fact, the place he was going this afternoon was a big step in the right direction. A *leap* in the right direction, actually. If this contract came off, he could take a fortnight's vacation in Hawaii.

Joey pulled the truck into a dusty lay-by and turned to look at Bobby who was staring at the map.

'Are you sure this is right, Bobby? I can't see nothin' but dirt and telegraph poles.'

Bobby shrugged and handed him the map.

'Take a look for yourself. Far as I can see, this is the only road coming off the main one. And look. There's the quarry. See?'

Joey peered out of his side window and looked at the two hundred metre drop down to the stones below. He took the map and smoothed it across his knee, paying particular attention to the part with the red circle drawn around it. *U.S. Government Facility* it said. *Restricted Access.* Bobby was right. The map showed it at the end of a dirt track with a quarry marked over on the left-hand side.

'Hell, Bobby,' he said. 'We're in the back end of beyond. Guess it keeps their army boys out of trouble, though. Nearest bar must be miles away.'

Ten minutes later, the truck rumbled to a halt outside a three-metre-high fence with razor wire strung across the top. A soldier in combat fatigues strolled out from his guard post, a rifle slung over one shoulder and a clipboard in his hand.

'Can I help you, sir?' he asked, crouching down level with Joey's open window.

Joey smiled. 'Reckon it might be the other way round,' he said, winking at Bobby. 'I'm here to solve your little insect problem.'

The man nodded and checked the sheet on his clipboard. Joey noticed that his face was covered in angry red bites.

'You Pestralis Pest Control?'

Joey jerked a thumb backwards.

'You'd better believe it. Leastways, that's what it says on the truck.'

The soldier glanced at the side panel where a cartoon picture showed a fly with its tongue hanging out, being struck over the head by a mallet. Above it were the letters: PPC and beneath it the words: *Bug-free Zone.*

'Got any ID?'

Joey fished out the authorisation letter from his top pocket and handed it through the window.

'OK.' The soldier pointed beyond the barrier to a cluster of buildings in the distance. 'See where those cars are parked? Report to the CO there. He'll bring you up to speed on the situation.'

Joey nodded and slotted the gear lever into first,

waiting for the barrier to rise.

'Between you and me, Buddy,' said the soldier as the barrier slowly jerked into life, 'I'd say you're gonna have your work cut out here today.'

'Well, Buddy,' grinned Joey, rubbing his finger and thumb together, 'between you and me, that's just the way I like it.'

Joey had once considered joining the military himself, but getting up early had never really been his thing. His first thought, upon meeting the Commanding Officer, was that he looked as though he could use a couple more hours sleep himself. Looking at the bites on his face and neck, Joey decided that the guy could do with a decent bug screen too. Maybe he'd flog him a set or two before the day was out.

'Glad you could make it,' said the CO, extending a hand towards him. 'My name's Colonel Jackson.'

'Joey Pestralis,' said Joey, shaking his hand. 'And this here's Bobby Morgan.' He smiled and then added: 'My second-in-command.'

'Good to meet you,' said the Colonel. 'Please. Take a seat.' He took off his cap, threw it on the desk and began to scratch at a red lump on the side of his head. 'As you can see, we're having a bit of a problem with insects here at the moment.'

'Well, that's what we're here for, Colonel.' Joey leaned back and folded his arms. 'Can I ask what kind of problem?'

'Flies,' said the Colonel. 'Hundreds of the darn things. Thousands, actually.'

'Inside you mean?'

'Some. But no – outside, mainly.'

Joey shrugged. 'Well it *is* summer, I guess.' He didn't want to do himself out of a job, but there wasn't a whole lot he could do about flies buzzing around in the great outdoors.

'Yeah, but you see, this isn't *normal*. Take a look at this.'

The Colonel unbuttoned his cuffs and pushed up his sleeves to reveal a mass of red lumps which extended from his wrists to his elbows.

'Let me see those.'

Joey leaned forward and took a closer look.

'Wow,' he said. 'Insects did that?'

The Colonel nodded and buttoned his cuffs again. 'Now you can see what we're up against. These things just come out of nowhere. Whole swarms of 'em biting chunks out of us. We're getting pretty sick of it, I can tell you. Do you think you can help?'

Joey thumbed his nose. 'Yeah, I'm sure we can do something. But tell me, how big are these flies?'

The Colonel frowned. 'Well, let me see. They're not tiny, that's for sure.' He held up his finger and thumb and framed a couple of centimetres between them. 'I'd say they were about . . . so big. Vicious little critters they are, too.'

Joey nodded thoughtfully.

'Colour?'

'Not sure exactly. Black, maybe, or brown?'

'OK. We'll check 'em out later. But we're probably looking at some kind of horsefly. The American possibly, or maybe the three-spot.'

'Horseflies. Really?'

'That'd be my guess at this stage, Colonel. Aggressive attacks and vicious bites are all characteristic of that particular insect.'

'But I don't get it. We've been on this base for years and never had this problem before. What do you think's causing it?'

Joey shrugged. 'Could be any number of things. Maybe some local farmer's moved his cattle out and left the flies without their usual food source. Or maybe it's just down to climate change. Impossible to say, really. But I've got something in the truck which will help you keep their numbers down. What do you say we go set it up?'

'Sure,' said the Colonel. 'Set up a million if they'll get rid of the damn things.'

Half an hour later, the Colonel stood in the middle of the compound looking at one of the strangest contraptions he had ever seen. Four plastic legs supported what appeared to be a medium-sized shiny black football. Fixed above the football was a pyramid of netting leading up to the neck of a large plastic bottle.

'What the hell is that?' he asked.

'It's a horsefly trap,' replied Joey proudly. 'What do you think? I designed it myself.'

The Colonel walked around it, examining it carefully.

'Well, I guess you boys know what you're doing. How does it work?'

'Simple really. Horseflies are attracted by shape, temperature and dark colours. So when the black ball heats up in the sun, the horsefly sees a warm head above four legs and thinks: 'Horse'. So it flies over, lands on the ball and climbs up looking for a place to bite. But when it gets to the top, it realises it's made a mistake. Then, attracted by the light, it flies up into the bottle where the heat of the sun kills it.'

The Colonel nodded approvingly. 'Very clever,' he said. 'But does it work?'

'Are you kidding? I'm telling you, Colonel, I've been to farms in high summer where they're catching sixty or seventy flies a day.'

'Sounds good to me,' said the Colonel. 'It's about time we evened up the score. You boys fancy a beer while you're waiting?'

'You bet,' said Bobby who generally let Joey do the talking, but knew that important matters demanded an individual response. 'Got any potato chips?'

The sun was fierce as the three of them stood around the trap in the heat of the afternoon, watching two large black flies buzzing around in the bottle. A third fly was busy crawling over the surface of the ball, making its way to the top.

'There you go,' said Joey. 'That's your problem right

there. Three-spot horse flies. See those white patches on their backs? That's where they get their name from.'

The Colonel bent down and peered into the bottle. Then he turned to Joey and shook his head.

'That ain't them,' he said.

'What?' said Joey. 'Are you sure?'

The Colonel crouched down and took a closer look.

'No,' he said. 'These are too big. Now I come to think about it, the ones we had were smaller and lighter coloured. More brown than black.'

Joey looked at the Colonel doubtfully. To most people, a fly was just a fly. But to Joey it was the enemy and so he had made it his business to find out everything about them. As far as he could tell, the only kind of fly that fitted the bill in this case was the one buzzing around in the bottle, right there in front of him. But Joey decided to be patient. After all, time was money and he happened to know that money was something the US Government had in plentiful supply. It didn't take a genius to work out that the longer this job took, the more of it would end up in his pocket.

'Hmm,' he said, scratching his head. 'OK, Colonel. In that case I think perhaps we'd better stick around for a while. See what else we can find.'

'Well, Bob,' said Joey as they sat out on the steps of the CO's office, sipping cold beer and watching the sun go down. 'I don't know about you, but I reckon I could get used to this.' He grinned, clinked his bottle against

Bobby's and took another swig. 'Sure as hell beats working for a living.'

Bobby grinned and nodded. 'Don't it ever,' he said.

Suddenly, his hand twitched and he dropped the bottle with a cry of pain.

'Ow!' he shouted. 'God-*dammit*!'

'What is it, Bobby?' asked Joey. 'What's up?'

Bobby rubbed his hand furiously.

'Something just bit me,' he said. Then he yelped, slapped his neck and swore. 'Hey! What the hell's going on?'

'Here,' said Joey. 'Let me take a look.'

He was just reaching out for Bobby's hand when there was a loud buzz in his ear followed by a sharp, stinging sensation on his cheek. As he reached up to touch it, a cloud of flies suddenly descended upon them in a thick swarm. Bobby screamed and Joey felt himself being bitten viciously on his neck, face and arms.

'Get inside, Bobby!' he shouted, crouching down and slapping at the flies as they dived aggressively again and again to deliver their painful bites. 'Get inside now!'

As Bobby ran for cover, Joey gritted his teeth and slammed the flat of his hand down on one of the yellowy-brown flies that had latched itself onto his forearm. Then, squeezing it tightly as though his life depended upon it, he put his head down, let out an anguished cry like a warrior going into battle and ran quickly up the steps toward the shelter of the building.

'See?' said the Colonel, 'what'd I tell you? It's brown.'

'More like yellow,' said Bobby, rubbing at the bites on his face that had swollen into angry red weals. 'Did you see those little devils? They jus' went ape-crazy for us.'

Joey leaned forward and stared at the squashed, mis-shapen fly that he had deposited on the smooth surface of the Colonel's desk. Although he had pretty well flattened it, the sharp blood-sucking mouthparts were easily identifiable.

'You want to know the weirdest thing?' asked the Colonel. 'There were fifteen or twenty men around when you were attacked just now. But this time, not a single one of them was bitten. It was as though the flies were just after you two.'

'That certainly is unusual,' said Joey. 'No doubt about it. But then again, maybe your guys just had the good sense to wear some industrial strength insect-repellent.'

'Well,' said Bobby. 'I'm definitely gettin' me some of that before I walk out through those doors again.'

'I wouldn't bother,' said the Colonel, peering out through the window. 'There's no sign of them now. They've completely disappeared.'

Joey was thoughtful as he gunned the motor back along the dirt track. He watched the clouds of dust kicking up in his rear-view mirror and ran his mind over the day's events once more. Whatever those insects were, they didn't resemble any biting fly he'd ever come across before. Glancing over at Bobby, he saw that he still held the glass sample tube with the dead insect safely wedged inside.

'You take good care of that little critter now, Bobby,' he said. 'Don't you lose him. When we get back we're gonna find out exactly what he is. And then we're gonna go back up there and give all his little friends the good news with a few hundred gallons of bug juice.'

He scratched irritably at the bites on his arm and spun the steering wheel around to bring the truck parallel to the edge of the quarry.

'I'm telling you, Bobby. There ain't no insect on the planet who's going to get the better of Joey Pestralis.'

Unfortunately for Joey Pestralis, however, this was some way short of the truth. Because at that moment, the thick carpet of flies which had lain hidden beneath the seats of the truck rose into the air with a fearful buzzing and descended upon the terrified men like a plague from hell. And as Joey screamed and clawed at his eyes, the truck skidded off the road in a screech of tyre rubber and crashed over the precipice, its wheels spinning wildly in the air.

The only small consolation – if it could be described as such – was that, as they plunged towards the quarry floor two hundred metres below, the two men remained unaware of the sharp rocks that were rushing up to meet them. Unaware, that is, until they tore through the windshield and smashed their world into a million pieces, puncturing the fuel tank and turning the truck into a white hot fireball of smoke and flame.

Twenty-two

As the explosion filled the screen, a huge cheer went up among the assembled members of Vermian Strategic Command.

'Well done, everyone,' said Field Marshal Stanzun into his headset microphone. 'Excellent job.'

He smiled and took off his headset. With the war against the Resistance in Aurobon progressing so effectively, Stanzun had found himself spending increasing amounts of his time overseeing these Earth-based operations. Since taking on this job, he had realised that the Earth campaign gave him much greater freedom to make his own decisions. In the war against Vahlzi, every movement of troops or insect squadrons had to be sanctioned by Odoursin. But as far as Earth was concerned, all Odoursin cared about was the annihilation of the human race and didn't concern himself too much with the detail. As long as Stanzun could show that progress was being made, he was more or less free to make whatever strategic decisions he thought necessary. And that was something which suited Stanzun just fine.

Glancing across at General Martock, he was pleased to note that his senior officer was clearly delighted with the success of the operation.

'Brilliant work, Field Marshal,' he was saying, clapping his hands together in a show of enthusiastic appreciation. 'Quite, quite brilliant.'

'Thank you, General,' said Stanzun, acknowledging this rare morsel of praise with a slight bow of the head. 'We've got a great team of pilots working on this one.' He flicked one of the many switches on the control desk in front of him and the image on screen changed to a close-up of the smoking wreckage.

'What are we looking at now?' asked Martock.

'This is one of our search and rescue teams,' replied Stanzun. 'They're going in to retrieve the pilots.'

'Ah yes, the ant squadrons,' said Martock. 'Tell me, have we solved the problems with the parasites now?'

'Oh, absolutely,' replied Stanzun. 'Largely thanks to your Miss Blin, General. She's turning out to be quite a find, I believe.'

Martock smiled. 'Indeed she is, Field Marshal. But according to Major Krazni, she is also, perhaps, someone to be watched.'

Stanzun raised an eyebrow in surprise. He had always assumed that the young scientist had a bright, successful future mapped out ahead of her. But if Krazni had sniffed out some hint of misconduct on her part –

whether real or imagined – then her days were almost certainly numbered. It was, thought Stanzun, rather a shame. He had been quite taken with her.

'So tell me, Field Marshal,' said Martock, changing the subject. 'Where are we with current operations?'

'Well, General. As you saw a moment ago, we identified and eliminated two extra targets who were threatening to disrupt our work at the nuclear facility in North Dakota.'

'Disrupt? How?'

'We were concerned that if they identified the type of fly we are using, it might have sparked off some kind of investigation. Rather than complicate matters, it seemed easier just to eliminate them both.'

Martock nodded. 'Of course. What about infection levels?'

'It's early days, obviously, but we're seeing something approaching a 95 per cent success rate on hitting selected targets.'

'How many targets are left to hit?' asked Martock.

Stanzun turned to face a row of computer terminals behind him and called to a blond-haired man seated at a desk in the centre.

'Lieutenant Milsech, can you spare us a moment?'

Milsech tapped a couple more numbers into his keyboard and then made his way over to them.

'Sir?'

'Lieutenant, can you give the General a rundown of targets hit so far and an overall picture of what remains to be done?'

'Certainly, sir.' He turned to face Martock and saluted smartly.

'At ease, Lieutenant. Tell us what you know.'

'Well, sir. Once the research labs had supplied our people with the bio-information on toxoplasma parasites, we were able to adapt our tsetse fly squadrons very quickly. The flies have proved extremely successful in delivering toxoplasma to humans through multiple bite wounds. Infection of all targets has now been completed at the North Dakota base – the one you just saw up there on the screen.'

'Anywhere else?'

'Yes, sir. In the past few hours we've received positive reports confirming infection of key personnel at bases in Nebraska, Phoenix, Washington, Virginia and Hawaii. But as I'm sure you can appreciate, General, our tsetse fly squadrons have been operating at full stretch for the past couple of days and we're seeing a lot of exhausted pilots arriving back at the base. So if it's all right with you, sir, we're going to stand them down for a day or two before we hit the final targets.'

Martock frowned. 'How will that affect the timescale?'

'Not at all, General. Although the parasites should reach the brains of their human hosts within the next ten days, they have all been engineered to remain inactive until the next cycle of the moon begins. When that happens, the bio-rhythms produced in the brain will trigger the parasites into action. By which time, all targets should have been successfully infected.'

'You say the parasites will become active during the next lunar cycle. When is that exactly?'

'In twenty-one days' time,' replied Milsech. 'Three weeks from today.'

Stanzun looked at Martock nervously. 'I know this is not happening as quickly as the Emperor Odoursin would like it,' he said. 'But we want to make sure that we get it right this time.'

'I'm sure you do,' said Martock. 'And,' he added pointedly, 'I'm sure you will.'

'You can count on us, sir,' said Milsech, who was hoping for a promotion at his end of year review.

Martock recognised the young officer's ambition and smiled. 'I'm glad to hear it, Lieutenant. Well, gentlemen, much as I would like to stay, I am afraid I must leave you to your own devices. You see, there is a small matter that Major Krazni and myself must attend to rather urgently.'

'Of course, General,' Stanzun replied, and saluted.

As he watched him leave, Stanzun remembered what Martock had said about the young scientist, Miss Blin. He imagined the girl's frightened eyes as she heard whatever accusations Krazni would level against her and – just for a moment – he felt a pang of regret.

She had seemed so very promising.

It was strange, he thought, how quickly in life triumph can turn itself into disaster.

It was past midnight when the cab delivered Alya to the steps of her apartment building. The wind had dropped and she noticed that the blanket of snow which had lain across the city for so long was gradually turning to slush. Paying the driver with the last of her change, she made her way wearily up to the third floor. The last few days had been exhausting and she was looking forward to a hot bath and a good night's sleep. Yawning, she pushed her key into the lock and let herself into her flat.

But as she closed the door behind her, she sensed that something was wrong. Something, was different. With the hairs prickling on the back of her neck, she reached anxiously for the light switch, but found to her dismay that it was no longer working. She was about to make her way across to the kitchen when suddenly the table lamp came on with a click and – unable to help herself – she let out a cry of shock and surprise. For there, sitting alone in her comfortable blue armchair, was Major Krazni.

'Hello, Miss Blin,' he said. 'Welcome home.'

And in the soft glow of the lamplight, she saw the silver glint of a long and very sharp knife.

Twenty-three

By tipping his head back slightly and peering down through the bottom of his blindfold, Sam could just make out the black, polished boots of his captors. When he had attempted this in the early days, the guards had quickly worked out what he was doing and rewarded him with a beating. But he had since learned to be more subtle about it, tilting his head so slowly that the movement was virtually indiscernible. Not that it achieved anything very much, but Sam had discovered that when your freedom has been taken from you, even the smallest of victories becomes important.

There were three of them and they were doing their old routine of leaving him to sweat in silent suspense. Over the past few weeks, the lack of food and sleep together with the constant interrogation sessions had weakened Sam to the point where sometimes he found it was all he could do just to stand up.

But something had changed.

In spite of their constant efforts to wear him down, he found that – mentally – he was actually becoming stronger. A week ago he had been close to breaking point; one more night without sleep, he thought, one more night at the hands of these thugs and he would probably have told them anything. But then, just when it seemed that the darkness would finally engulf him, a young woman had emerged from the shadows. Her name was Alya Blin and she had promised to help him. She had brought him a piece of chocolate one night, which he had hurriedly crammed into his mouth while the guard was busy having a smoke at the far end of the corridor. Days later, the rich sweet taste still swirled around in his memory like a dark, milky blanket. But Alya had brought something else too, something he had thought was gone for ever.

She had brought him a spark of hope.

And now, even as he fell to the floor and the boots of the men tried to stamp and smother it, he curled himself around it and felt its warmth burning inside of him. *This will end* it whispered, *this will end, this will end, this will end . . .*

Somewhere far away, a voice said, 'Enough. Pick him up.'

Hands seized him roughly under the arms and lifted him up onto the chair again. He slouched forward, but a pair of hands gripped him tightly by the shoulders and pulled him upright. As the blindfold was pulled from his eyes, the world swam back into focus and he became aware of a new figure in the room. Cold green eyes stared at him through horn-rimmed spectacles and Sam knew immediately that his life was of no consequence to this man; it was merely a commodity that he would dispose of when it suited him.

'Ah, Sam Palmer, isn't it? So nice of you to drop by and see us.'

Sam said nothing.

'Oh, I'm sorry,' said the man, extending a hand in greeting. 'How rude of me. Major Krazni, Head of Intelligence.' He looked down at Sam's handcuffs as if seeing them for the first time, and then retracted his hand again.

'Oh. Oh, dear. Well – never mind.'

From the corner of his eye, Sam noticed the guards grinning nastily at the Major's little joke. This was obviously as good as it got for them.

'The thing is, Sam, I am responsible for identifying and removing threats to national security. In your case, that would appear to be fairly straightforward. Here you are, we've identified you and so now it just remains for us to remove you, doesn't it?'

'Kill me, you mean,' said Sam.

Krazni smiled. 'We don't like to use such vulgar terms here,' he said. 'I like to think of it more as letting nature take its course. After all, those marsh dogs do get so terribly hungry – and who am I to deny them a little treat now and again?'

Sam stared at Krazni with a mixture of fear and contempt.

'You're sick,' he said. 'You're all sick.'

Krazni's lips tightened into a thin, angry line and he stepped forward so that his face was inches away from Sam's.

'If we are,' he said, 'then it is because we are infected by people like you. But the good news is, I think we may have found the cure.'

Sam looked Krazni in the eye and managed a weak smile.

'You think you know everything,' he said, 'but you're wrong.'

This time it was Krazni's turn to smile.

'Perhaps,' he said, 'but I bet I know what *you're* thinking. Shall I tell you?'

Sam made no answer.

'All right, then. It goes something like this: you're thinking about how you've held out from telling us where your friends are hiding so that they can attack us. And you think that, perhaps, somebody has told your friends where you are and maybe – just maybe – they will come and rescue you.'

Krazni paused and raised his eyebrows. 'How am I doing so far?'

Sam said nothing, but inside he was worried; Krazni's assessment was pretty close to the mark.

'Now I know the truth is important to you, Sam. And I would hate to think of you misleading yourself in any way, believing things to be true when they're not. So I thought to myself, how can I help the poor, misguided boy? And then it came to me.'

He nodded to one of the guards who opened the cell door and shouted down the corridor. There was the sound of footsteps approaching and then two soldiers entered the cell dragging a thin, dishevelled figure between them. Although his face was bruised and swollen, Sam thought there was something about the man that he recognised. The soldiers relinquished their grip and the man fell in an untidy heap against the wall. Slowly, he raised his head and stared at Sam as though he had seen a ghost.

'Sam,' he said at last. 'Sam . . . is it really you?'

And when he heard the familiar voice and looked again into the man's troubled eyes, the tears he had managed to hold back for so long ran down his cheeks as he whispered, 'Yes, Commander. Yes. It's me.'

Sam gazed at the shabby figure of the man who had once led the Vahlzian forces to victory during the first war, and when he saw what they had done to him he felt as though his heart would break. But Firebrand was shaking his head and staring hard into Sam's eyes, and Sam saw a flash of the old spirit once more.

'Keep the faith, Sam,' he said, 'it's not over yet.'

'How touching,' said Krazni, turning to Sam. 'He's right of course. I mean, as long as there are people whom you can trust, people you can put your faith in, then that's what matters isn't it, Sam?'

Sam glared at him. 'What would you know about faith?'

Krazni smiled. 'Enough to know that it is the talisman of fools.'

'At least I believe in something,' said Sam. 'And nothing you say or do can ever change that.'

'Well, I'm delighted to hear it,' replied Krazni. He began to walk towards the door and then turned back. 'Oh I nearly forgot. There's someone else who would like to see you.'

He nodded to one of the guards who disappeared out into the corridor. Sam felt his stomach churn and he shot Firebrand a frightened look. Then the door opened and a young woman walked in.

It was Alya.

'Well, well,' said Krazni with a smile, 'look who it is. Miss Blin, let me introduce you to Sam Palmer. Although – forgive me – I believe you two may already have met.'

'Yes,' she replied, 'that's right. We have.'

And when Sam looked at Alya and saw how she was unable to meet his eye, he knew that he had been betrayed.

'And tell me Miss Blin. What did you talk about?'

'We talked about the location and layout of the Resistance base. He told me that the only way to get into the secure underground storage section was via fingerprint and eye recognition. He told me that his details are now stored in the central system and that he is able to gain access by this method.'

'She's lying!' shouted Sam, leaping to his feet. 'She's making it all up!'

Strong hands pulled him back into his chair and held him firm.

'On the contrary,' replied Krazni calmly, 'I think we both know that Miss Blin is telling the truth. And by your reaction, I can see that it is so.'

He turned to Miss Blin and put a hand on her shoulder.

'You see, Sam, Miss Blin works for us. Your precious notions of faith and trust are nothing but illusions, by-products of weak and wishful thinking. They are mirages in the desert, nothing more. Strength is what matters, Sam. Strength and power. And that is why your people will be destroyed and forgotten, and the Vermian Empire will rule for ever.'

Krazni walked across to the door and opened it.

'So tell me, Sam. Where is your precious faith now?'

But Sam had no answer. And as they dragged him from the room, he stared at the woman who had betrayed him, thought of all those who would die because of it and his mouth fell open in a soundless scream of despair.

Twenty-four

The robber fly had been set up almost exactly like a small passenger jet. Rows of comfortable seats were arranged in groups of three on either side of a central aisle stretching from the rear of the fly to the cockpit door at the front. Small oval windows had been fitted at intervals along each side of the abdomen and through one of them Sam could see the snow-covered mountains a thousand metres below. He looked down at the plasticuffs that bound his hands tightly together and then glanced around to establish the whereabouts of the guards. The one next to him on the aisle side was engrossed in a glossy magazine about guns and explosives. A couple more guards talked quietly in the row behind and two others sat directly in front, discussing the relative merits of wearing a second pair of gloves during winter operations.

Craning his neck, Sam could see that Firebrand was similarly hemmed in over on the opposite side, while

Krazni sat next to Alya Blin at the front of the plane, poring over various maps and documents which they had spread out on a table in front of them. Sam felt his lip curl in disgust, unable to conceal his hatred of the young woman who had taken him into her confidence and then betrayed him without a second thought.

Perhaps Krazni was right. Maybe strength was all that mattered. In which case, he would use whatever he had left of it to try to save his friends.

Sam slowly raised the handcuffs up to his mouth and pulled at them with his teeth, partly to relieve the pressure on his wrists, and partly to see if there was any way of freeing himself before they reached the base. But an elbow in the ribs from the guard next to him suggested that it would not be easy.

'Do that again and I'll blow your head off,' he snarled. Then he returned to reading about which gun would be best for the job.

Sam lowered his hands and looked out of the window again. The squadron of robber flies was flying in formation and he counted nineteen of them alongside, flying so close that their wingtips were almost touching. Several of them had been converted into transport aircraft and he could see the hard faces of Vermian special forces troops, staring at the clouds from behind rows of tiny glass windows. Sam glanced at the windows across the aisle and saw a similar number of flies on the other side of the aircraft, making about forty in total.

He knew that you didn't put a force like this together

unless you really meant business. There was no doubt about it – Krazni was intent on locating the airbase and destroying it. Once that objective was achieved, he planned to use Sam and Firebrand to gain access to the high security areas so that he could destroy them too.

Well, when it came to it, they would have to kill him, because there was no way he was going to co-operate. He knew that Firebrand would feel the same way. If only he could figure out a way to cause some kind of disruption, to at least give the people on the ground a chance . . .

The fly banked left and Sam's attention was caught by a flash of colour from somewhere down below. He pressed his face against the window and his eyes were drawn to a patch of yellow, shining brightly against the snow. As the fly began to lose height, Sam suddenly realised what he was looking at. A squadron of thirty or forty wasps was laid out on the mountain in neat rows, polished and gleaming in the winter sunlight. Sam's heart sank as, for the first time, he took in the geography of the area and realised that they had finally arrived in the skies above the base. They were actually flying over the very last wasp squadron in existence. And instead of being protected by their high security shelters, the wasps were laid out like ducks at a shooting gallery, defenceless against the killers whose dark shadows passed over them like clouds across the sun.

As Krazni pulled Alya to her feet and pointed down through the window, Sam buried his head in his hands. What were they thinking of? They must have been about to launch an attack of their own. And now they were all as good as dead.

The other robber flies began to peel off now, breaking formation and streaking out of the sky at great speed towards the ranks of yellow and black insects below. Sam could see a few tiny figures running for cover as the first flies struck, slamming into the wasps with such ferocity that many of them simply disintegrated upon impact, fragments of legs and wings tumbling down the mountainside in an avalanche of destruction. One by one, the wasps were torn apart until the whole area was littered with the wreckage of their broken bodies.

Sam viewed the scene of devastation in utter despair. They had spent so long protecting their precious wasps and now they had lost them all without bringing down a single robber fly. They hadn't even managed to get airborne. How could they have been so stupid?

As the robber fly touched down on the mountaintop, Sam was pulled from his seat by the guard who pushed him roughly towards the door. Sam looked down at Krazni who was already descending the ladder and then turned back to the guard and raised his hands in the air.

'I can't climb down with these things on,' he said, nodding at the handcuffs. 'What do you want me to do?'

The guard glared at him.

'Maybe I'll just push you out,' he said. But Sam could tell by the way he looked around for someone in authority that he was unsure of what to do next.

'Look, why don't you just cut the cuffs off and let me

climb down. I mean, we're stuck up a mountain surrounded by a whole bunch of robber flies. I'm not exactly
going anywhere, am I?'

'Well, OK,' said the man, frowning uncertainly. 'But
if you try anything . . .'

'You'll shoot me,' Sam interrupted. 'Yeah, I know. You
said.'

A look of anger crossed the man's face and he grabbed
Sam's cuffs, pulling him forward so that they cut into his
wrists and made him cry out.

'Don't get smart with me, kid,' he hissed, and pulled
a knife from his belt.

Before Sam could say anything, the man sliced neatly
through the plasticuffs and pushed Sam away again. 'Go
on,' he said, 'get going.'

Sam quickly scrambled down the ladder and found
himself standing next to Firebrand, who had also had his
cuffs removed and was rubbing at the sores on his wrists.
Most of the robber flies had now landed on the mountaintop and were crowded so closely together that they
formed a canopy of wings over the whole area. The
wreckage of broken wasps was strewn all around them
and heavily armed special forces were now fanning out in
a wide circle, securing the landing zone.

'You OK, Commander?' Sam asked quietly.

Firebrand nodded. 'Yes. You?'

'I guess so. What now?' He glanced over at Krazni
who was pointing to the stretch of rock which concealed
the entrance to the base. 'Do you think we can take him?'

'Not yet,' said Firebrand. 'Wait until they stick a gun to my head, then make a break for it. Run as fast as you can and don't look back. Go down the side of the mountain.'

Sam shook his head. 'I'm not going anywhere. I'm staying with you.'

Firebrand turned to him. 'They're going to kill us, Sam. You know that don't you?'

Sam put a hand on his shoulder.

'Keep the faith, Commander.'

There was a click and Sam felt something cold on the back of his neck.

'You must have some kind of death wish, kid,' said the guard behind him, pushing the gun barrel further into Sam's flesh. 'Now get away from him.'

Sam moved back a few paces as Krazni turned and looked in their direction. 'We've located the entrance,' he shouted. 'Bring the boy over here.'

'What about the other one?' the guard called back.

Krazni paused for a moment as though considering his options. Then he seemed suddenly to reach a decision.

'Miss Blin,' he said curtly. 'Follow me.'

Sam watched the two of them pick their way between the shattered remains of the wasps until they stood facing Firebrand.

'I want you to take a good look around you, Commander,' said Krazni. 'This is what happens to those who stand in our way. You and your people are history now. Do you understand? It is over for them.'

He pulled a pistol from the holster on his belt and snapped off the safety catch.

'And now, Commander, it is over for you also. On your knees.'

Firebrand remained standing, staring defiantly into Krazni's eyes until two soldiers seized him by the arms and forced him to the ground.

As Krazni pointed the pistol down at the top of his head, Sam shouted 'No!' and tried to run at Krazni but he was pulled back by the guard who pointed his own gun at Sam's temple.

'Go on,' he said when Sam continued to struggle. 'Make me shoot you.' As he put a thick arm around Sam's neck and held him fast, Sam saw Krazni turn to Alya and smile.

'I've got a better idea,' he said and handed the pistol to her. 'You do it.'

Alya's face was white now; as white as the snow that lay across the mountaintop.

'I – I can't,' she stammered.

'You can,' said Krazni, 'and you will. Let us see where your loyalties really lie, shall we, Miss Blin?'

'Please,' pleaded Alya, 'don't make me do it.'

'Take it,' hissed Krazni, thrusting the pistol into her hand. Sam watched Alya take the gun and, with her hand trembling, point it at Firebrand's head.

'Miss Blin,' said Krazni, 'I am ordering you to shoot him. So do it. Do it *now*.'

Sam saw the fear in Alya's eyes, watched her finger

tighten around the trigger and then suddenly she pointed the gun straight up into the air and fired it three times in quick succession. As the sound of the shots echoed around the mountaintops, Alya turned and flung the gun into Krazni's face, knocking him backwards into the snow.

Krazni put a hand to his mouth and stared at the ground as droplets of blood fell from his lips, staining the snow a deep crimson.

'So,' he said, 'that's how it is.'

He got to his feet, picked up the gun and aimed it at Alya. But then, suddenly, he stopped and began pointing at something on the edge of the mountain. His expression quickly changed to one of extreme terror and he began gesticulating frantically to the other soldiers, shouting and screaming to them at the top of his voice. But his words were abruptly lost in a roar of beating wings and as Sam turned to see where the sound was coming from, a hundred giant hornets rose up from the side of the mountain and descended upon the Vermian forces like a host of avenging angels.

In the confusion, Sam felt the guard's grip loosen and he slammed his elbow back into the man's stomach. As the man stumbled backwards, Sam managed to run a few metres but was quickly blown over as the wind from the wings of the attacking hornets swirled around the mountaintop. The sudden blizzard of snow made it virtually impossible to see and all around was the deafening buzz of hornet wings and the crunch of their jaws as they tore the robber flies into a thousand pieces. Sam staggered blindly through the snow for a short distance, but every few seconds a powerful gust of wind caught him and flung him to the ground again. He lay in the snow and listened to the crackle of machine guns spitting flame and hot lead into the air. Bullets whined overhead and he heard the shouts and screams of a fierce, hard-fought battle. Explosions reverberated loudly around the mountains, but in spite of the danger and destruction that surrounded him, Sam pressed his face into the cold snow and smiled.

She had done it. Skipper had made it back with the hornet eggs. Maybe now, at last, the tide was turning . . .

And then, as suddenly as the battle had started, it stopped. Where seconds before the air had been filled with the chatter of bullets and the roar of wings, now there was only the sporadic shouts of officers barking orders at their men. As the smoke cleared, Sam was astounded to discover that not a single robber fly was left standing. In all directions, huge hornets crouched above the smoking remains of robber flies which had obviously been no match for their powerful jaws and fearsome stings. Mixed up with the debris was the tangled wreckage of Brindle's wasp squadron which had been destroyed during the first assault, and scattered all around were tiny fragments of the robber flies' compound eyes that had exploded from shattered cockpits. As the sunlight caught them, they flashed and glittered like diamonds and Sam found it strangely uplifting to find beauty in such an unexpected place.

From somewhere nearby, a frightened cry cut through the air. Sam jumped to his feet and saw a woman calling to him from the wreckage of a robber fly. The fly's eye-screen had been blown out by an explosion, pinning her to the ground beneath its heavy, reinforced metal frame. Now smoke billowed from a hole in the fly's thorax and the woman was trapped behind a wall of orange flame.

'Help me,' she cried. 'Please, help me!'

'Hang on!' Sam shouted. He sprinted across the snow as fast as he could, ducking down beneath the fly's shattered wing until he was standing only a few metres away from where she lay. The heat from the flames was so intense that he had to shield his face with his arms. But as he peered frantically through them in an effort to find a way through, he suddenly caught sight of the woman's frightened face.

It was Alya.

Alya Blin.

Sam stopped and took a step backwards.

This was the woman who had betrayed him. The woman who had cared nothing for the lives of him or his friends.

Why should he risk his life to save her now?

'Please!' The voice was desperate now.

Staring into the flames, Sam saw her terrified, pleading eyes and knew in his heart that he could not leave her to die.

Cupping his hands, he scooped up some snow and rubbed it over his hair and face. Ignoring the freezing water that trickled down his back, he pulled his tunic over his head and ran forwards into the flames. There was a scorching roar of heat all around him and then seconds later he was stumbling out beyond the fire.

'My legs,' whimpered Alya, 'they're trapped.'

Sam noticed that her hair was beginning to smoke and, tearing off his damp tunic, he threw it over her head.

'Put that over your face,' he urged. 'It'll protect you from the flames.'

Feeling the heat searing the back of his neck, Sam grasped the solid frame with both hands and pulled. As his muscles strained against the weight and the hot metal burned into his palms he cried out in pain and frustration, but it was no good. The screen was too heavy. He had barely moved it a centimetre.

'All right, listen to me,' he said. 'I'm going to try and lift this thing up again, OK? And when I do, you've got to swing your legs out of there first chance you get. Because I don't think we're going to get two goes at this. All right? You ready?'

Alya wrapped the now steaming tunic around her face so that only her eyes were showing and then nodded.

'OK. Here we go.'

Spitting on his hands, Sam thrust them beneath the frame again and heard the sizzle of hot metal on flesh. He screwed up his eyes and directed all his strength away from the pain and into his arms. With an anguished cry he pushed with all his might, but despite his best efforts it still wouldn't move. Suddenly he became aware of someone standing next to him. There was a loud creak and Sam felt the metal frame move upwards. Alya swung her legs free, staggered to her feet and gave him a look of utter relief and gratitude.

'Run!' he shouted, and as she disappeared through the flames, he dropped the frame with a loud crash.

'Careful,' said a small voice beside him, 'that nearly landed on my foot.'

Sam turned to find a small blonde girl standing next to him, wiping her hands on the front of her jacket. She grinned. 'Looked as though you were struggling a bit. Thought I'd come and give you a hand.'

Sam stared at her with delight and amazement.

'Skipper!' he cried, throwing his arms around her. 'You're safe!'

Skipper peered over his shoulder at the fire that raged all around them and raised an eyebrow.

'Is that what you call it?' she said.

And then, as she stepped back, she noticed the bruises on his face for the first time.

'Oh, Sam,' she whispered, stroking his cheek with the backs of her fingers. 'Look what they did to you.'

She leaned forward and, just for a moment, rested her forehead against his.

Then she took him by the hand and together they ran through the flames.

Sam pressed a handful of snow against the burns on his neck and stared at the lines of Vermian prisoners, cuffed and lined up against the rocks ready to be taken down to the secure areas below ground. He estimated there were at least two hundred of them, possibly more. There was no sign of Krazni, however, and Sam guessed he was probably among the fallen; grey blankets covered the silent forms of those for whom this battlefield would be a final resting place.

He was heartened to see that Firebrand was already taking control of the situation, barking orders and organising everyone as if he had never been away. Six hornets patrolled the skies overhead while the others returned to their underground hangars for repairs and refuelling.

'Are you all right?' Skipper asked, brushing the top of Sam's head with her hand. 'Your hair looks a bit singed.' She took a step backward and put her head on one side. 'It quite suits you, actually. Gives you a sort of . . . rugged look.'

'Well, you know. Some of us have it . . .' He squinted over at the line of prisoners and noticed Alya on the end of it. She had taken the tunic from around her face, her wrists were cuffed, and she was shivering. Immediately, Sam's tone changed.

'If that one had her way, we'd all be dead. You know that, don't you? Maybe I should have just left her to it.'

'Who?' asked Skipper.

'Her,' said Sam. 'Over there.'

Skipper followed Sam's gaze and stared at Alya for a few seconds before suddenly letting out a loud squeal.

Then, to Sam's amazement, she ran across to where Alya was standing and proceeded to fling her arms around her. Sam could hear the sound of their happy, excited voices floating back to him through the cold air and he watched in stunned silence as Skipper pulled out her knife and cut through Alya's plasticuffs. Then, arm in arm, they walked back across the melting snow towards him.

As he watched them approach, Sam's anger intensified with every step that they took until, when they were only a short way off, he could contain himself no longer.

'Skipper!' he shouted. 'What do you think you're doing? Do you have any idea who that is?'

'Yes, of course,' replied Skipper evenly. 'It's Alya.'

'That's right,' said Sam, staring angrily at the two of them. 'It's *Alya*. The one who betrayed me. The one who tried to kill us all!'

Skipper shook her head. 'No, Sam,' she said gently, 'don't you see? It was Alya who saved you.'

Twenty-five

After a short debriefing session with Vahlzian Intelligence officers, where he told them everything he could remember about the layout of the Vermian Military Airbase, Sam made his way past lines of prisoners to the officers' mess where he found Skipper and Alya sitting at a table, sipping from mugs of steaming hot chocolate. While Skipper went to fetch him a cup, Sam stared at Alya in disbelief.

'I know what you're thinking,' she said after a while. 'But you know, things aren't always as they seem.'

'I just don't get it,' he said. 'If you were trying to help us, then why did you tell Krazni the location of the Resistance base?'

Alya sighed and as she pushed back her hair with one hand, Sam noticed how the ends had shrivelled in the heat of the fire.

'Believe me, Sam, that was never the original plan.'

'So what happened?'

'Well . . . once you'd told me where the airbase was, I flew out to Vahlzi on the pretext of checking over the ant squadrons. I knew some of them were still infected so it was the perfect cover, no questions asked. Once I got to Vahlzi, I was able to make contact with the Resistance people and tell them what I knew. They were suspicious at first, but once I told them all about you and showed them that I knew the exact co-ordinates of the airbase, they began to take me seriously. Next thing I knew, they had bundled me into the back of a stolen beetle and brought me here.'

'And that's how we first met,' said Skipper as she sat down again and passed Sam a mug of hot chocolate. 'But let's just go back a bit. After I left you in the forest, I saw the robber fly arrive and guessed it had probably come looking for us. But as I was halfway up the tree, there wasn't much I could do about it. When I got back and found you gone, I realised they must have taken you away. But I knew you would have tried to leave the egg, so I searched around and found it pretty quickly. My main priority was then to get it back here so that the engineers could develop the hornets as fast as possible. The idea was that if we could get them quickly enough, we might be able to stage a surprise raid on the prison and get you out of there. But then Alya turned up.'

'Yes, and by the time I got here, the hornets were almost ready,' Alya went on. 'The engineers had used a new heating process to speed up the hornets' development and the results were incredible. As soon as I saw them I thought they had an excellent chance of pulling off a successful raid. I knew the layout of the prison and I was able to give Skipper and the others a detailed plan of where they were keeping you and Commander Firebrand. It was all looking very promising.'

'Problem was,' said Skipper, 'one of our operatives from Vahlzi then turned up with news of some radio transmissions they had intercepted. Apparently Alya had been seen "talking to known Vahlzian sympathisers" and was now officially reported as missing. We realised then that her cover was blown. We knew that if she returned to Vermia, Krazni's secret police would be on to her.'

Sam turned to Alya. 'So why did you go back?'

'I knew it was risky,' said Alya, 'but when I actually thought about it logically, I realised it was our best chance of success.'

'How come?'

'I guessed Krazni would be waiting for me, so with Skipper's help I took pictures of the area surrounding the airbase. Then when I got back, I was able to tell Krazni that I had tricked you into telling me the location of the airbase and that I had gone to check that the information was correct before bothering anyone with it. I was then able to show him the photographs. But I knew he was still suspicious, so then I had to play my trump card.'

'Which was?' asked Sam.

'To make Krazni believe that I had betrayed you. Unfortunately, in order for it to appear convincing, I had to make you believe it too. I'm sorry about that, Sam. If it's any consolation, I felt dreadful about it.'

'I still don't understand why you had to come back,' said Sam.

Alya shrugged. 'Two reasons, really: one, to set the trap; two, to get you and the Commander out. You see, I knew that once they had swallowed the other stuff, it would be relatively easy to convince them that they needed your eye and fingerprint scan to get into the secure areas. And knowing Krazni as I do, I knew he wouldn't be able to resist bringing Firebrand along and showing him what he assumed would be the final destruction of his forces.'

'So the trap was set,' said Skipper. 'Before Alya left, we agreed that she would try and persuade the Vermian Council to put together a large force of robber flies to attack the base. For our part, we arranged to put our wasp squadron out on the mountaintop in order to lure as many robber flies down as we could. And then, when they had all landed, we unleashed the hornets.' She grinned. 'It worked like a charm!'

'So there you have it,' said Alya. 'The story so far.'

'How we stuck it to Mad Major Krazni,' added Skipper helpfully, 'by Alya Blin.'

Alya smiled and held her hand up in the air for Skipper to smack. 'Read it and weep, Major,' she said. 'Read it and weep.'

'I don't know what to say,' said Sam. 'I'm so sorry, Alya.'

Alya looked at him in surprise.

'Whatever for, Sam?'

'You know. For not believing in you. For thinking you were betraying me, when you were saving my life.'

'No, Sam,' said Alya, suddenly serious again. 'I'm the one who should apologise. That was a horrible thing that I had to do. And anyway,' she added, 'despite everything you've been through, you still managed to save me from a fire this afternoon. So I guess that pretty much makes us even, doesn't it?'

Sam rested his chin on his hand and wondered at the courage of this brave young woman who had risked her life to save them all.

'Yeah,' he said with a smile, 'I guess it does.'

He lifted his mug of hot chocolate and held it up above the table. Skipper clinked her own mug against it. 'Here's to sticking it to the rest of 'em,' she said. Then they all clinked their mugs together and Alya beamed happily.

'I'll drink to that,' she said.

'Hey, get off me,' said Sergeant Brindle, unable to keep the smile from his lips – lips that were not generally accustomed to such undisciplined shows of emotion. 'You don't know where I've been.'

'Oh, but I do,' said Skipper, releasing the burly sergeant from an enthusiastic hug. 'You've been hiking through blizzards haven't you?'

'Blizzards?' said Brindle dismissively, a small pool of

melting snow forming around his boots. 'Couple of flurries maybe. Nothing to write home about.'

Firebrand, who had now resumed overall command of operations, stared doubtfully at Brindle's soaking wet clothes and glacier-blue face.

'Maybe you should go and warm up, get yourself something to eat,' he suggested.

'Maybe later, sir. First I would like to acquaint myself with the current situation if that's all right, sir. And may I also say, sir, that is good to see you again.'

Firebrand smiled. 'Likewise, Sergeant. Likewise.'

Sam couldn't help but be impressed. He had last seen Brindle bailing out of his wasp into a frozen wilderness. Now here he was several weeks later, having trekked several hundred miles in sub-zero temperatures, refusing all offers of comfort in his impatience to get on with the next phase of the operation. Sam was reminded of an experiment he had once carried out in science where you had to sort materials in order of their hardness. Chalk, sandstone, granite, diamond . . . Brindle.

He would have topped the list every time.

They took their seats in the small Operations Meeting Room and Firebrand stood up at the front to address them. Although he looked older and thinner than he had done during the last campaign, there was no doubt that the Commander had got his old fire back again. Sam could see it in his eyes; the passion and determination were clear for all to see as he paced the room, listening intently to Alya's report on the latest developments in Vermia.

'Tell us about these worms,' he said, 'how do they kill people on Earth?'

'They don't,' said Alya. 'Not directly, anyway. The plan is, the worms – or *flukes* to be completely accurate – will affect the behaviour of certain people in such a way that they will then kill everyone themselves.'

'I don't understand,' said Firebrand, impatient to find out what he was dealing with. 'Explain?'

'Well, research revealed that a certain species of parasitic worm – *toxoplasma gondii* – was infecting millions of people on Earth as part of a natural cycle that already existed. It was able to affect people's behaviour by finding its way into their brains and influencing their thought patterns. Then I noticed that worms and humans had the same impulse translators.'

Firebrand frowned. 'They had what?'

'The impulse translator. It's a tiny piece of neurological material that allows a worm to transfer its own desires to the brain of its host. It's a bit like downloading a program into a computer. Once it's in there, the computer can do different things. Same thing with people. All we had to do was write a program compatible with the worm's neurological structure and then the worm would go off and "download" it into whoever we chose. And then, effectively, we could make people do whatever we wanted them to do.'

'And it works?' asked Firebrand incredulously.

'Oh, it works all right,' said Alya. 'And that's the reason we haven't got much time.'

'But how does Odoursin plan to infect every single human with these worms?' interrupted Skipper. 'Surely that's impossible, isn't it?'

'Ah, but he doesn't need to,' explained Alya. 'If you target the right people, then you can just stand back and let them do the rest. And that's exactly what the Vermian Strategic Command are doing.'

Firebrand was looking more and more worried by the minute. 'So who exactly are they targeting?'

'Defence staff working at nuclear weapon sites across the United States,' said Alya. 'Plus key personnel in the command and control structure. The plan is to use parasites to trick these personnel into believing that they are under attack from nuclear weapons. They will believe that the only course of action left open to them is to launch a massive retaliatory strike against the countries responsible. Which, in turn, will trigger a huge nuclear response from *those* countries. Billions of people will die, and those who survive will have little fight left in them. Stage two of Odoursin's plan is then to effectively enslave survivors by gradually and methodically infecting them with more parasites. These parasites will be programmed to create various other desires in people – desires which will be useful to the Vermian regime.'

'What sort of desires?' asked Sam.

'Oh I don't know – decontaminating areas hit by nuclear weapons, cleaning up other sources of pollution on the planet, that sort of thing. But ultimately, people will be programmed to hunt each other down. It's horrific when you think about it. Odoursin intends to use any survivors first as slaves, and then as executioners.'

'How are they getting these programmed parasites into humans?' asked Skipper.

'InRaD came up with the tsetse fly as a solution,' explained Alya. 'They'd already been working on a prototype which was fast, manoeuvrable and already equipped to carry similar parasites.'

'Why didn't they use mosquitoes again?' Sam asked.

'Not compatible with these particular parasites,' replied Alya. 'Same with horseflies. Whereas the tsetse fly was ready almost straight out of the crate. It only needed minimal re-engineering to its salivary glands and then it was good to go.'

'All right,' said Firebrand. 'Like you say, we haven't got much time. My guess is that Odoursin will already be planning a retaliatory strike against us, so I've got a squadron of hornets on standby, ready to intercept it when it comes. In the meantime I suggest we mobilise another full squadron as soon as possible, attack the hangars where the tsetse flies are kept and then take out the parasite labs. Can you draw up a plan for us, Alya?'

Alya shook her head. 'I'm afraid it's too late for that,' she said. 'Tsetse flies started hitting their targets weeks ago. Chances are they'll all be infected by now. The parasites will have been programmed to lie dormant in the brains of their hosts until the next cycle of the moon. The change in biorhythms will then trigger them all into action at the same time. They will start transferring their thought patterns into their human hosts and that will be all it takes to start a nuclear war.'

Firebrand looked at her in horror.

'But the next cycle of the moon is tomorrow night!' he cried. 'Surely there must be something we can do?'

Alya nodded. 'There is, but it's a bit of a long shot.'

'Let's hear it,' said Firebrand.

'OK,' said Alya. 'The thing is, there's a set procedure that has to be followed before any weapons can be launched. Understandably, the possibility of some nut-case deciding to crack off a few nuclear bombs is one that governments are fairly keen to avoid.'

'Understandably,' said Skipper. 'Sorry, go on.'

'So the procedure goes something like this: a defence system identifies a threat, the threat is checked with other defence systems and, if it is confirmed, then the nuclear weapons facilities are put on red alert. In other words, they start preparing for a retaliatory strike. But they can't carry out any strike until it has been autho-rised by their Commander-in-Chief, the President of the United States.

'Now I happen to know that they've been having big problems infecting the President. The guy wears thick suits, hates insects and has bug screens on all his windows. He's the only one with the launch codes, and if they don't infect him then there's no nuclear war. If we can fly a bunch of hornets there soon enough, we might have a chance of taking out the tsetses before they can get to him. Like I said, it's a long shot, but it's all we've got.'

'I'm in,' said Skipper, 'definitely.'

She thought for a moment and then said, 'But what if they've already infected him? What then?'

Alya stared at the floor and then shut her eyes, as if the enormity of what she had helped to cause was too much for her to bear.

'Odoursin will have won,' she said at last, 'and it will be the end of everything.'

Twenty-six

It was five in the morning and Martock could sense the tension among the assembled Council members as they stood around the long, rectangular table, awaiting Odoursin's arrival. They all knew that, in the years since his accident, Odoursin had found it difficult to sleep due to the pain from his burns. It was likely, therefore, that his personal physician would have given him a sleeping draught only hours before.

Given his increasing unpredictability, waking him was certainly not a decision to be taken lightly. On this occasion, however, the Council had come to the conclusion that it could not be avoided.

The news, it seemed, was spectacularly bad.

An attempt to destroy the Vahlzian Resistance base had ended in complete disaster, with two squadrons of robber flies wiped out and enemy hornets now controlling the skies over Vahlzi.

Reports were coming in that organised groups of

Resistance fighters had already overrun several positions on the eastern side of the city.

It didn't take a genius to work out that unless Odoursin gave his permission to postpone the attack on Earth and divert all forces back to the west, there was a very real danger that Vahlzi would be retaken by enemy forces.

And if that happened, Vermia would be next on their list.

But would Odoursin listen? Martock knew that he was obsessed with the destruction of human life on Earth, and anything that stood in the way of that was unlikely to go down well. Add to this the fact that Odoursin would have had very little sleep, and the prospect of a positive meeting was not looking good.

A hush fell upon the Council as the door of the bunker swung open and Odoursin strode to the head of the table, fury simmering just beneath the surface of his blanched, twisted features. As his eyes narrowed into fiery slits of rage, he stared around the room and hissed, 'Who is responsible for waking me at this hour?'

When it became obvious that no one was going to answer, Martock cleared his throat and said, 'I am sorry, Your Excellency. But the Council felt that you should be informed of the latest developments.'

'I see,' said Odoursin icily, 'so you are saying that everyone is to blame.' He glared angrily at Martock until he dropped his gaze and then said, 'Well? What is this important news that could not wait?'

Realising that by breaking the silence he had unwittingly elected himself as spokesman, Martock swallowed nervously and turned to address the Emperor once more.

'The attack on the Resistance base has ended in failure, Your Excellency,' he said. 'The enemy has developed a new insect – a giant hornet – which is far superior to our robber flies. A squadron of them was used against us in the attack on the enemy base and these hornets now control much of the airspace around Vahlzi.'

Odoursin made no immediate reply, but Martock could see the anger building in his eyes as he digested this piece of news. After a few more seconds of uncomfortable silence, Odoursin's gaze alighted on Field Marshal Stanzun.

'So Field Marshal,' he said coldly, 'are we to put this down to your incompetence?'

Martock saw Stanzun blink twice as all attention in the room was suddenly focused upon him. But Stanzun was a brave man who was used to staying calm in a crisis, and when he spoke his voice betrayed no obvious signs of nervousness.

'It would have been impossible for us to predict such a turn of events, Your Excellency,' he replied. 'If our sources are to be believed, then the enemy's discovery of this rare insect was purely accidental – it was just bad luck on our part.'

'There is no such thing as luck!' spat Odoursin angrily. 'Only poor planning and preparation!'

At this point, Lieutenant Reisner – Leader of the Ant Squadrons – raised his hand and began to speak. Most of the Council were unable to hide their surprise, knowing it to be an unwritten law that junior members of the Council do not address the Emperor unless invited to do so. But a brief conversation with the young officer before the meeting had led Martock to expect the interruption, even though he had tried to dissuade him from it.

'Forgive me, Your Excellency,' said Reisner, 'but I think it would be prudent for us to pull all our resources back from Earth immediately. That way we can hit Vahlzi with everything we've got before they have the time to consolidate their positions.'

Odoursin slowly turned his head to face the young officer.

'Really? Is that what you think?'

'Yes,' said Reisner. 'I think, quite frankly, that anything else would be madness.'

'I see,' said Odoursin. 'Thank you, Lieutenant, it is always important to speak one's mind on such matters.'

Martock saw Reisner smile nervously and felt sad at the young man's innocence.

'Come here, Lieutenant.'

Reisner looked at Odoursin quizzically.

'Come here,' Odoursin repeated, 'I have something for you.'

Reisner left his place at the table and walked slowly towards Odoursin. If he suspected anything, he didn't show it.

Odoursin smiled.

'Shut your eyes,' he said.

Martock turned away just as the sound of the gunshot split the air, echoing loudly around the chamber. When he looked back, Reisner lay untidily against the wall. His eyes had fallen open one last time and in death they displayed a look of utter surprise.

Odoursin calmly replaced the pistol in his holster and stared defiantly around the room.

'Tell me,' he said, 'does anyone else want to make a suggestion?'

As evening fell, Martock stood at the edge of the airfield and watched the pilots sprint eagerly across the tarmac toward their waiting insects. Odoursin's view had prevailed as he had guessed it would, and the Earth mission was going ahead as planned. Above him, the air was thick with the squadrons of tsetse flies and robber flies, sweeping up through the darkening sky toward the fabric gap which would lead them towards their ultimate goal: the destruction of human life on Earth.

In spite of his excitement, however, Martock felt an underlying anxiety that was hard to ignore.

Odoursin's brutal treatment of Reisner this morning had clearly demonstrated that he was not a man to be reasoned with. But Reisner was right: in his obsession with ridding the Earth of its human parasites, Odoursin had failed to see the wider picture which was developing in Aurobon.

Martock knew that unless the Earth mission was completed quickly, then Odoursin's regime was in grave danger. It was essential that they hit their final target quickly and returned all their forces to Aurobon for a last, decisive attack on Vahlzi.

It could be done, Martock was sure of it. And if they were successful, then their hold on power in both worlds would be virtually unassailable.

But Martock knew it would be a close run thing. And as he watched the swarms of flies silhouetted against the coloured moons that rose over Vermia, he thought sadly of the words that the young lieutenant had spoken to him that morning before the meeting began.

'I will have to tell Odoursin the truth as I see it,' Reisner had said. 'I will have to tell him the truth because he is my Emperor, and I love him.'

Twenty-seven

'These are really comfortable,' said Sam, sinking back into the black leather seat of the hornet and feeling it mould itself around his body. 'You could go to sleep in them.'

'Probably best not to,' said Skipper, leaning down into the cockpit through a hole in the top of the head, 'seeing as how you're supposed to be flying it.'

'Aren't you coming? I thought you were flying with me.'

'Not this time, Sam. There aren't enough pilots to go round, so we're flying solo this mission.' She paused. 'Are you OK with that?'

'I s'pose so,' said Sam, feeling butterflies fluttering around his stomach. 'But I've never flown one of these before. What are they like?'

'Same as a wasp really,' Skipper reassured him. 'Except they're ten times as powerful, so you might want to keep an eye on your air speed indicator. Things come at you much faster in one of these.'

Sam smiled and patted the instrument panel. 'I like it already,' he said.

'Where is he then?' called a voice from somewhere outside. Sam heard the sound of feet climbing up the metal ladder and then a beaming face appeared at the hole in the top of the cockpit.

'Mump!' said Sam, extending his arm up to shake his hand. 'How are you doing?'

'Hi, Sammy,' said Mump, squeezing Sam's hand enthusiastically. 'I'm doing great, thanks! Hey – I heard you were here for the big scrap earlier on!'

'Absolutely,' replied Sam. 'Wouldn't have missed it.'

'Me neither,' agreed Mump. 'It's always a pleasure to see those Vermian boys getting a taste of their own medicine.'

'Or, in this case, drinking the whole bottle,' said Sam with a grin. 'Swallow it down, fellas!' He smacked Mump's hand as he raised it up. 'Swallow it *down*!'

As Mump chuckled happily, Sam thought for a moment and then asked: 'Hey Mump – are you and Zip flying this next mission?'

'But of course,' said Mump airily, 'when things get hot, they always call on the Dream Team to put out the fire.'

'Oh please,' said Skipper, catching Sam's eye, 'spare us.'

'Where's Zip now?' Sam asked.

'Just climbing out of the shower I expect,' said Mump. 'Again.'

'Ah,' said Skipper with a mischievous look in her eye. 'That wouldn't have anything to do with the arrival of Alya, of course.'

'No, of course not,' said Mump, grinning.

'Well,' said Sam, 'I'd love to sit here gossiping all day, but don't you think we should get going?'

'Better had,' said Skipper. 'Oh – thanks for the explosives, by the way. Hope you saved some for yourself.'

'Don't worry,' said Mump, 'I've got plenty.'

'Explosives?' said Sam, alarmed. 'What are they for?'

'For making big bangs,' explained Mump helpfully.

'Yes, thank you, Mump. I know what explosives do. But what do we need them *for*?'

'Just in case,' said Mump. 'I find they often come in handy.'

'Well, be careful,' said Sam. 'I know what you're like. Can't have you wiping out the White House.'

'Samuel,' said Mump, pretending to be offended, 'safety is my watchword. Rest assured that proper procedures will be followed at all times.'

Skipper giggled. 'Tell me, Mump. What *are* proper procedures exactly?'

'Simple,' said Mump. 'One: cause maximum chaos in the shortest possible time. Two: try not to get your head blown off.'

'Sounds good,' said Sam. 'I'm all for that.'

'OK, my lovelies,' said Mump, climbing back down the ladder. 'See you for tea at the White House.'

'Two sugars in mine, please,' said Sam.

Hornet

'Right, Sam,' said Skipper, 'we're leaving in about five minutes. Do you have all your flight co-ordinates?'

'Yup. Flight engineers loaded them this morning.'

'We should be flying in tight formation most of the way out, so you probably won't need them, but if you get lost for any reason then they'll guide you onto your target.'

Sam watched the wall in front of them suddenly dissolve in a flash of blue. A shaft of bright sunlight lit up the inside of the cockpit.

'Time to go,' said Skipper.

'Weather's improved,' said Sam. 'That's a good sign, isn't it?'

'It'll be spring-time before we know it,' said Skipper. 'When all this is over, Zip says he's going to take us fishing. Fancy it?'

Sam imagined himself in the mountains with his friends, breathing the clear air and sitting by the cool waters of a mountain stream.

'I would love to,' he said. 'Let's definitely do it. When we get back.'

The words felt like a talisman; *we will come back*, they said. *When this is over, we will come back and our lives will be better . . .*

'But first, we've got to catch some flies, eh?' said Skipper, touching him lightly on the shoulder.

Then she was gone.

And as Sam closed the hatch and started up the engines, he put a hand to his shoulder and wondered when, if ever, he would see her again.

Colonel Jackson made his way across the compound to the Weapons Control section where he knew that Sergeants Ryan Hanson and Scott Mercer would be starting their shift. It was 90 degrees in the shade and part of him envied the two men their comfortable, air-conditioned bunker. At least the plague of troublesome flies seemed to have disappeared, which was some consolation. Whatever they had paid those pest control boys, it had been worth every cent.

He stopped for a moment beneath the shade of the water tower and massaged his eyes with a finger and thumb. Wiping a sleeve across his forehead he watched a patch of warm air shimmer above the hot tarmac. He couldn't remember a time when he'd suffered such a bad headache. The pills hardly seemed to touch it. Every now and then he would get a blinding flash of red that sent fingers of pain searing through his skull and a vivid image of heat and fire would burst into his mind.

Colonel Jackson was a brave man, but this was something new that he had never experienced before.

It *unnerved* him.

Perhaps it was time he started drinking two litres of water a day, just like the Doc recommended.

Trouble was, it didn't taste nearly as good as a cold one straight from the fridge.

'You OK, Ryan? You're not looking so good.'

Sergeant Scott Mercer had worked this shift with

Ryan Hanson for nearly eighteen months and they had got to know one another pretty well. You didn't spend six hours a day holed up with someone and not get to find out a fair bit about them. So Mercer knew all about Hanson's likes and dislikes, he knew how his kids were doing in school and he knew when he was feeling out of sorts. And tonight, he was definitely out of sorts.

'Yeah, I guess I'm OK.' said Hanson. 'It's just my head, y'know? It's all right for a while and then all of a sudden it feels as though it's gonna explode. You ever had anything like that?'

Mercer scratched at the insect bites on his arm and nodded. 'Funny you should say that, but just before I came in this afternoon I had a real blinder. In fact, it was so bad I had to go and lie down for a while.'

'Maybe we've been staring at these screens for too long,' suggested Hanson, rubbing his temples with the tips of his fingers. 'Do you ever wonder what the point of it all is?'

'How d'you mean?'

'Well, thirty years ago everyone was terrified the Russians were going to turn round and nuke us at any second. But no one really thinks that's going to happen any more, do they?'

Mercer shrugged. 'Maybe not. But perhaps that's because there's people like us, sitting in little bunkers with their finger on the button.'

Hanson nodded. 'Yeah, I guess so. Hey, what's up, Scott?'

Scott Mercer put his head down on the desk and pressed the heels of his palms against his eyes. The pain was intense, unbearable. It was like staring into the mouth of a volcano, staring until the molten rock exploded and the red hot lava poured through every alleyway of your brain. There was nowhere to hide . . .

When he opened his eyes again, he noticed that Hanson was staring at his computer screen with a look of utter horror on his face.

Turning to look at his own screen, he saw that it was covered in red dots.

Each dot was moving slowly towards the centre.

Each dot was blinking.

Each dot was a nuclear missile, twelve minutes away from striking the United States of America.

Twelve minutes and counting.

Twenty-eight

The hornet squadron broke through the clouds in formation and turned north-west along the Potomac River towards the centre of Washington. Sam could see the moon rising over the city and he watched the night vision display at the bottom of his screen blink into life. The streets below were fairly well lit, but it was reassuring to know that it was there. A red arrow on the navigation display rotated a few degrees towards a flashing green circle and Sam looked up to see a brightly illuminated white building just a few miles to his right. He banked the hornet round and saw the others do the same, holding formation as they turned and dropped towards the target.

'There it is,' said Sergeant Brindle calmly over the radio. 'The White House.'

Zip's voice came crackling in over the airwaves. 'Do we definitely know he's there?' he asked. 'Be a bit of a bummer if he was away on holiday.'

'He's there all right,' replied Brindle. 'We just got confirmation from an ant patrol in the Oval Office. He's just eaten a sandwich, apparently.'

'What sort?' asked Mump. 'I'm starving.'

'You'll see for yourself in a minute,' said Brindle. 'All right, remember. Soon as we're on target, we split up and look for open windows. We'll do an internal sweep to hunt for flies and then regroup and secure the perimeter. Skipper, you take your section to the left, my section, we're going right. You copy?'

'Roger that,' said Skipper and Sam watched Brindle's section peel off towards the right hand side of the building.

'OK, pair up folks,' said Skipper. 'Stay with your wing man and let's hit 'em hard!'

Sam followed Skipper's hornet down as it dropped suddenly and fell away towards the smooth green lines of the floodlit lawn that lay like an emerald in front of the White House.

The President's face was ashen as he listened to the news that he had always hoped would never come.

'How can you be certain?' he asked, speaking into the phone while looking around at the grim-faced defence staff who had suddenly seemed to materialise from nowhere. 'Could it be a system error?'

'No, Mr President. We have confirmation from five separate units. This is no error, sir. It's the real thing. The Vice President is already on his way to the Presidential Command Bunker.'

The President replaced the receiver and screwed his eyes shut for a few moments in an effort to dampen the fires that burned inside his head. *I must be coming down with a fever* he thought. *Bad timing.*

Defence Secretary Dan Steele interpreted the President's expression as a possible sign of indecision and decided to try to move things along.

'The computer link is fully operational, Mr President. You'll be able to see the status of the incoming missiles for yourself. You might want to check it, sir. It's on the desk.'

The President glared at him. 'I know where it is, Dan,' he said.

Steele cleared his throat awkwardly as his Commander-in-Chief snapped open the lid of the laptop and stared at the screen.

'I can't see anything,' he said. He'd been through this scenario countless times as part of his induction to the top job, and the training had left him in no doubt that – in the event of an enemy attack – the computer screen would be blinking with red dots charting the progress of the missiles. But this time the screen was blank.

'There's nothing there,' he said. 'Look – come and see for yourself.'

His aides quickly gathered around the desk and began pointing at the screen.

'But, Mr President sir,' insisted Defence Secretary Steele. 'There's dozens of them. What are we going to do?'

The President gasped and closed his eyes as something erupted in his brain, an explosion of red heat that burned into his mind. He was falling through bright tunnels that swirled and pulsated all around him; then his eyes were open again and he was looking at the screen and the screen was covered in red dots.

'How can this be possible?' he breathed. 'China *and* North Korea?'

'We think they must be operating together,' said Steele. 'It's the only explanation.'

'Get me the hotline,' said the President, his voice shaking. 'Now.'

'We are unable to establish a connection at this time, Mr President,' said General Miller nervously. Miller had recently been promoted to Head of Internal Security and was beginning to wish someone else had got the job.

'What the *hell* do you mean?' snapped the President.

'We've tried everything,' replied Miller. 'I'm sorry.'

'All right,' said the President grimly. 'Get me the Briefcase.'

The Briefcase was the name for the Mobile Command Centre which was never more than ten metres away from the President at any time. Special Agent Griffin was one of the three agents on duty who knew the combination of the case and he had never dreamed that the day would come when he would actually have to open it. His hands trembling, he placed it on the desk, punched in the numbers and snapped open the catches.

The President lifted the lid and took a key from his pocket.

'Give me the other one,' he said.

Griffin took the second activation key from his jacket and placed it into a slot in the briefcase. He waited until the President had inserted his own key and then twisted it a quarter turn to the right. The screen lit up dark blue. Across it in red were the words:

CONTROLLED ACCESS
FINGERPRINT IDENTIFICATION REQUIRED

The President placed his thumb on a small glass panel and as a white light began to flicker the words on the screen changed again.

READING . . . VERIFIED . . . CONFIRMED
ENTER SECONDARY VERIFICATION:
RETINAL SCAN

Leaning forward, the President placed his left eye above the panel and the light flickered again.

READING . . . VERIFIED . . . CONFIRMED
ENTER ACCESS CODES
0 0 0 0 0 0 0 0

The room was silent except for the tapping of the President's finger on the number keys. Then with a beep, a new screen appeared.

COMMAND ORDERS

ALERT STATUS
MISSILE STATUS
LAUNCH ORDERS
ABORT

Running his tongue over dry lips, the President scrolled the cursor down to **LAUNCH ORDERS** and then paused to look up at the grim faces surrounding him.

'Gentlemen,' he said. 'May God be with us.'

Then he pressed 'ENTER'.

As Sam followed Skipper's hornet low across the lawn towards the leaded, rectangular windows he saw what appeared to be a layer of smoke drifting from the roof of the White House.

'Hey, Skipper,' he said into the intercom. 'Looks like there might be a fire on the roof.'

Suddenly Skipper's hornet pulled up hard and went vertical, shooting up into the sky at great speed.

'Stay with me, Sam!' she shouted and Sam pulled the joystick back as hard as he could, slamming back into his seat as the wings roared and he rocketed after her.

'What's going on?' he shouted, keeping his eyes fixed on the orange and black body of Skipper's hornet as it powered upwards in front of him.

'That's no fire, Sam,' replied Skipper as she levelled out above the White House and began to circle. 'Take another look.'

Sam looked down and the first thing he noticed was that the smoke was curling down from the roof and spreading out across the lawn. The second thing he noticed was that the smoke wasn't actually smoke at all, but a huge swarm of flies.

'Hell's teeth!' exclaimed Sam as he recognised the hideous insects. 'Robber flies. Hundreds of 'em.' Noticing that one group of flies had formed into a writhing mass on the lawn he pressed the zoom facility on his display screen and was immediately confronted with a close-up showing the flies wrapping themselves around one of the hornets. By sheer weight of numbers they had managed to smother it and bring it crashing to the ground.

'They've got one of Brindle's crew,' said Skipper. 'Damn it! They must have been expecting us.'

Sam watched as groups of flies began to systematically pick off the other hornets, clustering around them in bundles and forcing them out of the sky. Sam heard the helpless cries of hornet pilots echoing across the airwaves as Brindle's voice screamed at them to take evasive action.

'They're killing us down there, Skipper,' shouted Sam. 'What are we going to do?'

'Get on my wing,' said Skipper.

'What?' asked Sam, unable to tear his gaze away from the frightening scenes unfolding on the White House lawn below.

'Get on to my wing,' repeated Skipper. 'I've got an idea.'

Sam pulled back on the throttle, gradually increasing his speed until he was flying right next to Skipper's hornet. Glancing through the side screen he could see Skipper giving him the thumbs up. She was so close he felt he could almost reach out and touch her.

'OK, Sam, here's what we're going to do. In a moment I want you to fly underneath me and keep your engine speed steady.'

Sam frowned. 'What for?'

'Trust me, OK?'

Sam pushed the joystick forward slightly and felt the nose tilt. The hornet dropped several metres and he carefully moved the stick sideways, easing the aircraft beneath Skipper's. There was a slight bump as the other insect's legs brushed the top of his cockpit and then he was directly below it. He could hear the other hornet's wings humming just above his own and he chewed his lip anxiously. The tiniest mistake could mean a mid-air collision that would probably kill them both.

'That's good, Sam. Right, brace yourself – I'm coming in.'

There followed a noise like the bristles of a giant scrubbing brush banging against a window and six thick, black legs suddenly clamped themselves around the outside of Sam's hornet. It began to sway violently from side to side and Sam wrestled frantically with the controls.

'Skipper!' he yelled. 'What are you doing?'

'Cut your engines, Sam!' Skipper yelled back. 'Now!'

Sam twisted the ignition off and the hornet began to lose height rapidly. Above him, the engines of Skipper's hornet rose to a howl, straining to take the weight of his aircraft as they levelled out once more.

'Skipper!' shouted Sam angrily at the intercom. 'What's going on?'

'I'm not going to lie to you, Sam,' said Skipper, her voice sounding strained. 'What I'm going to ask you to do next is extremely dangerous. If I could do it myself I would, but I need to keep us both flying. If you don't want to do it, I'll understand. But I think it may be our only chance.'

Sam felt fear and adrenalin pump through his veins. If Skipper thought it was dangerous then there was a strong possibility it could kill him. But then this whole operation was life-threatening. And if they failed, billions would die.

He remembered what Firebrand had said:

Keep the faith.

'Go ahead, Skipper,' he said. 'Whatever it is, I'll do it.'

'OK,' came the reply. 'Keep your COMs headset on and climb into the back of the hornet. You'll find some wooden crates which you'll need to open.'

Sam clambered between the seats and made his way over to a small stack of crates. Prising the lid off the nearest one he found that it was full of a grey putty-like substance.

'What's this stuff?' he asked into his headset microphone.

'High explosive,' replied Skipper. 'Courtesy of Mump, remember? Now I need you to make six little balls of it. About the size of your fist.'

Sam dug his fingers into the explosive and found that it was pliable, like plasticine. Working quickly, he used the palms of his hands to roll up six balls which he stuffed into the pockets of his flying jacket.

'OK. Now what?'

'See the little blue box on the floor over to the right? Take out six of the radio detonators.'

Sam knelt down and opened the smaller box. Inside were rows of black, pencil-sized sticks. Each one had a metallic red tag attached to the end and a small, three-way switch numbered 1 to 3. He counted out six detonators and put them into his pocket with the explosives.

'These aren't going to go off are they?' he asked nervously.

'I certainly hope so,' said Skipper. 'But not yet. They're perfectly safe until you pull the tags off. But make sure all the switches are in position one.'

Sam hurriedly retrieved the detonators from his pocket to check that they all still had their tags and that the switches were set on 1. Satisfied that they were all intact, he put them back in his pocket.

'All right, Sam. Have you got your CRB?'

'Got it.'

'Right, this is the tricky part. I need you to climb on top of your hornet and attach the explosives to the middle segments of my hornet's legs. One lump and one detonator per leg.'

Sam swallowed nervously and felt his heart beat faster. What was she planning?

'I'm on my way,' he said.

Unclipping a small silver torch-like object from his belt, he pointed it at the roof of the hornet and pressed the button on the side. There was a blue flash and as the wind roared through the hole that suddenly appeared, Sam could see the orange underbelly of Skipper's hornet a metre or so above his head.

Climbing on the boxes, Sam placed his hands on either side of the hole and pulled himself into the howling gale that swept between the two hornets. Screwing up his eyes, he grabbed at the middle leg of Skipper's hornet and wedged the first lump of explosive into a small gap in the knee joint. Then he pushed a detonator into its soft centre and pulled out the red tag which flew off into the wind. A red light began to wink on the side of the detonator, indicating that it was now armed.

One down, thought Sam as he shakily lowered himself flat against his own hornet once more.

One down and five to go.

All eyes were on the Briefcase.

There was a heady, dream-like quality about the room now, a feeling of inevitability as the realisation dawned on everyone present that the last minutes of their lives were ticking away. The world in general was about to change for ever. Their own worlds in particular were about to be obliterated.

They stood and stared at the screen in hypnotic silence, transfixed by the flashing words which read:

ENTER LAUNCH CODES
0 0 0 0 0 0 0 0

'Done it,' said Sam, collapsing back into his seat. Breathing heavily, he stared down at the White House lawn, its elegant fountains foaming above neat, symmetrical ponds far below him. His legs and arms had suddenly turned to jelly.

'Fantastic work, Sam,' said Skipper. 'Now it's my turn. I'd strap yourself in if I were you.'

Sam quickly snapped his buckle together, pulled the strap tight and winced.

'Be gentle with me,' he said.

There was a roar from Skipper's engines, the horizon slid upwards and then they were plummeting down towards the cloud of robber flies that drifted like black smoke across the White House lawn. As they approached, Sam saw the swarm part in the middle, curl at the edges and rise up to meet them.

'They're coming straight at us,' he said.

'I know,' said Skipper calmly, maintaining a straight course. 'That's the idea.'

Seconds later they entered the swarm and the screen went black. Sam heard the thud-thud-thud of robber flies slamming into the top of Skipper's hornet and the moan of the engines as they strained beneath the extra weight. Then the sound of the engines stopped altogether and his body felt weightless as the hornet dropped from the sky like a stone.

'Skipper!' he cried, but there was no reply.

Struggling against the constraints of his safety harness, Sam reached desperately for the ignition key. If he could only start his engines again, maybe he could somehow stop them from crashing . . .

Then, in a roar of wind, something thudded hard into the seat next to him and a hand grabbed his arm.

'Not yet, Sam. Give it a few seconds.'

As the wind swirled through the hole she had made, Skipper pulled a small black box from her pocket and threw it into his lap. Stunned, Sam picked it up and saw a little red light blinking on the top. A small dial was set to 1 and in the centre of it was a red button.

'When I say now,' said Skipper, strapping herself into the co-pilot's seat and pointing her CRB up at the hole in the roof to close it again, 'press that button, OK?'

'OK,' said Sam, still in shock.

'But hold on tight,' she added, ''cos I'm driving now.'

She leaned forward and twisted the ignition key. As the engines growled back into life she rammed the joystick sideways and Sam felt the blood rush to his head as the hornet flipped over onto its back.

'Now!' she shouted. 'Now!'

Sam jabbed at the button, there was a series of loud thumps as the explosives blew the legs off the other hornet and then Skipper pulled full throttle and they scorched up into the sky, leaving the ball of robber flies tumbling away below them.

'Now turn the dial to two,' said Skipper.

Sam clicked the dial round to the next number and felt his head spin as Skipper flipped the hornet back onto its front again.

'Look down there,' she said. 'They're all piling in.'

Sam saw that the entire swarm of robber flies seemed to have converged on Skipper's hornet, forming a dark ball all around it. He looked back at Skipper and was surprised to see that she was smiling.

'Press it again,' she said.

Sam glanced down at the box in his hand. He looked at the squirming ball of robber flies falling through the air.

Then he pressed the button.

There was a brilliant, blinding flash and a bright circle of light sliced through the darkness like a silver saucer, followed almost immediately by a loud explosion and a ball of orange flame.

'Wow,' said Sam, impressed. 'That was one heck of a firework.'

'It's nothing to what's coming if we don't pull this thing off,' said Skipper as the shattered remnants of flies fluttered like soot from the sky. She pushed the joystick forward and accelerated down towards the White House.

'OK.' she said. 'Let's go and see the President.'

The hornet plunged down the chimney and emerged through the fireplace in an upstairs room. It flew quickly through the open door, buzzing loudly above the heads of startled security personnel as it headed down the red carpeted staircase and along the marble hallway hung with cut-glass chandeliers.

'Come on,' muttered Skipper to herself as she pulled the throttle back as far as it would go. 'Come on!'

They flew on through the West Wing, past the executive offices and Cabinet Rooms until at last, at the very end of the corridor, they came to the door of the Oval Office.

It was shut.

'Damn and double damn!' shouted Skipper. She landed the hornet on the door handle and slammed her fist down on the control panel. 'We have to get in there!'

'What about the keyhole?' suggested Sam.

'Looks too tight,' said Skipper. 'But it's got to be worth a try.' She walked the hornet across the handle and the cockpit darkened as she thrust its head into the narrow tunnel. Beyond the circle of light up ahead, Sam could clearly see the President seated at his desk, surrounded by six or seven others. A couple of security men were staring anxiously out of the window, trying to locate the source of the recent explosion.

There was a thud and a grating sound as Skipper tried to move the hornet further into the keyhole.

'It's no good,' she said. 'We're too big. If we go any further we'll never get out again.'

'Let's take a look,' said Sam. 'See what they're up to.' He activated the zoom facility and they stared at a close-up of the President's grim, lined face concentrating on something in front of him.

'Look,' said Skipper. 'There on his neck!'

Sam looked at where she was pointing and saw the two angry red insect bites just beneath his ear.

'Zoom out a bit,' said Skipper.

Sam took the magnification down a couple of notches to reveal a laptop and an open metal briefcase sitting on top of the ornate wooden desk.

'That's it,' whispered Skipper. 'It's the Mobile Command Centre.'

'Then we're too late,' said Sam. 'They've already got to him.'

The President turned to Defence Secretary Steele and pointed to the door.

'Get over to the Presidential Command Bunker, Dan. The Vice President's going to need your help.'

Steele shook his head.

'I'm staying here with you, sir.'

The President glared at him with fire in his eyes.

'Defence Secretary Steele, that's an order.'

Steele stood to attention. He figured he had less than seven minutes to get to the bunker which lay a mile deep beneath the surface of Washington DC. He knew he probably wouldn't make it. But an order was an order. And at least he would get to see the trees and the sky one last time.

'Yes, Mr President,' he said quietly. Then he turned on his heel and made for the door.

The President of the United States turned back to the keyboard and began to type in the launch codes.

$$3 - 7 - 4 \dots$$

As the Defence Secretary approached the door, Skipper thrust the hornet into reverse and flew back into the air just as the door swung open.

'Go!' shouted Sam as he was flung violently against his seat belt. 'Go!'

$$4 - 0 \dots$$

The hornet's motors roared and as they flew at break-neck speed past the white fireplace, the flags and the paintings of rural Texas, Skipper turned and shouted: 'Think of a number!'

'What?' Sam yelled back over the howling engines.
'THINK OF A NUMBER!'

$$\dots 3 - 9 \dots$$

'Six!' screamed Sam as they accelerated over the President's shoulder. 'Six!'

Skipper pushed the joystick forward and the hornet slammed headfirst into number six on the keyboard.

$$\dots 6$$

'What the—' exclaimed the President.

Special Agent Griffin swatted the hornet away with the back of his hand, smashing it back against the long sash windows behind the President's desk.

INCORRECT CODE

read the display.

Inside the hornet, Sam groggily lifted his head from the control panel, wiped the blood from his lips and peered through the screen. He turned to Skipper who was holding her wrist.

'I think we did it,' he said. 'I think we stopped him.'

Skipper shook her head and stared out into the room. 'No,' she said. 'Look.'

Sam looked again.

RE-ENTER LAUNCH CODES
0 0 0 0 0 0 0 0

'What?' he shouted. 'No!' He pulled back on the throttle once more, but there was no response and he knew then that the engines must have stalled on impact. They watched in horrified fascination as the President retyped the codes

$$3 - 7 - 4 - 4 - 0 - 3 - 9 - 5$$

and a new screen appeared.

LAUNCH COMMAND

SILOS: 16 84312 – B 14 73642 – F
CO-ORDINATES: N26 – 48 E 21 – 42   N32 –27 E38 – 36

ORDER CONFIRMED

ABORT   SEND

'I can't start the engines!' shouted Sam, desperately twisting the ignition key. 'They won't fire!'

Defence Secretary Dan Steele looked at the time displayed on his mobile phone and knew that he was not going to make it. He stood alone on the lawn, looking up at the stars and listening to the fountains pattering across the surface of the pond. As he thought of his wife and children asleep somewhere in the suburbs – at peace beneath the glittering sky – he hesitated, and then put the phone back in his pocket. They didn't know of the horror that was about to descend upon them and – much as he longed to – he decided it was better not to wake them.

The President moved the cursor above the SEND command. He was about to click on the mouse when he heard a cry of pain and looked up to see that the other members of his team were holding their heads. He paused, confused. Then suddenly he was holding his own head and it seemed to him that his brain was on fire, consumed by blue flames which raced down the crimson corridors of his mind and burned away all fear and confusion, cleansing his thoughts and leaving him breathless and gasping like a man who has awoken from a nightmare.

He looked at the missile tracking system and saw that all the red dots had vanished from the screen.

Turning back to the Briefcase, he moved the cursor to the left and clicked ABORT.

Then he looked at General Miller who, along with everyone else, was staring at the blank screen in disbelief.

'What the hell just happened here, General?' he asked quietly.

General Miller shook his head. 'I don't know, Mr President,' he said. 'But whatever it was, I don't think it's happening any more. Everything looks completely clear.'

At that moment the phone rang and the President snatched the receiver off the hook.

'Are you sure?' he asked after a while.

He listened some more and then nodded. 'OK,' he said. 'That's what we've got too.'

Slowly and carefully, he replaced the receiver and turned to General Miller.

'General,' he said. 'I want you to get everyone together immediately. I want to know exactly how this happened and I want to know today.'

'Yes, Mr President,' said General Miller. 'I'll get right onto it.'

He turned to go, but the President put a hand on his shoulder and stopped him. 'There's one more thing,' he added, looking around at the men who had gathered in his office to witness the end of the world. 'This must never, ever get out.'

He paused and stared out of the window at the flood-lit rose garden.

'As far as the rest of the world is concerned, this never happened.'

So it has all been for this, thought Steele.

All the struggle, the love and the passion was to end in a fireball that would turn everything to meaningless dust.

Steele searched the sky and wondered if he would see the missiles approaching in the last seconds before his life was over.

Would he know the moment of his death?

A ringing sound.

Steele thrust his hand into his pocket and flipped open the cover of his phone.

'Yes?' he said. He nodded, listening and saying nothing. 'Thank God,' he said at last. 'Thank God.'

Standing alone on the White House lawn trying to make sense of it all, he was startled to see what appeared to be a large hornet flying over his head before disappearing off into the darkness.

It had, he thought, been a day for surprises.

Suddenly – like a wave rolling in to the shore – a feeling of relief swept over him and he fell to his knees, resting his face against the soft, cool grass. Then Defence Secretary Steele began to weep as he hadn't wept since he was a child, and his tears soaked into the dark, sweet earth like rain.

'For a second there I thought we'd had it,' said Sam. 'How come he never pressed the button?'

'I don't know,' said Skipper as they flew up above the White House. 'I don't understand it. Maybe something went wrong with the parasites. Or maybe,' she added with a smile, 'we just got lucky at last.'

But sitting alone in his apartment and watching the dawn break over Vermia, Doctor Janik Jancy knew it had nothing to do with luck. Staring out of the window at the empty streets, he remembered how he had discovered Alya in the laboratories late one night before she disappeared, trying desperately to alter the codes that were to be programmed into the parasites.

'Miss Blin!' he had hissed at her in the half-light. 'What are you doing? Do you want to get yourself killed?'

She had told him everything then, about the cruelty of the camps and the atrocities that the Vermian Empire was committing in the name of freedom. 'And look,' she had said, showing him the pictures from Earth. 'These are not monsters we are about to kill. They are people. Don't you see? They are people, just like us.'

But Jancy had pulled her out of the room and sent her home. 'It is not our concern!' he had told her angrily. 'We are scientists, not politicians! If you lose sight of that, then you will lose your life too. Now go home!'

And Alya, with tears pouring down her cheeks had cried bitterly, 'Life is a wonderful thing, Doctor Jancy. But surely it is not to be had at any cost?'

He had been unable to sleep that night, thinking about what she had said. The next day he had tried to contact her. But she was nowhere to be found, and no one could say where she had gone. He guessed that Krazni had got wise to her plans and arranged her 'disappearance' as they liked to call it. But in the days that followed, he realised two things: firstly, that he cared for her a good deal more than he had ever cared for anyone, and secondly, that he would never see her again.

All of which had led him to do what he recognised now as probably the one decent thing he had ever done in his life. He carefully and painstakingly programmed the parasites to self-destruct seven minutes after they were first activated. He had figured that this would give enough time to abort the launch of the missiles while still giving the people on Earth enough of a scare to ensure that they completely reviewed their safety procedures.

Odoursin wouldn't be able to try the same thing again any time soon.

Outside, Jancy heard the sound of car doors slamming. Looking down into the street he saw the soldiers running up the steps of his apartment building and knew what they had come for.

He had, after all, been expecting them.

For as Alya had said: life was a wonderful thing, but it was not to be had at any cost.

Twenty-nine

'This is Hornet Seven calling all units,' said Skipper into the intercom. 'Mission is accomplished. I repeat: mission is accomplished. All units return to base immediately.'

'Hello, Hornet Seven. This is Hornet Four.'

Zip, thought Sam, relieved.

'Nice work, you two. Take it easy and I'll see you back at the ranch.'

'Thanks, Hornet Four. Any sign of Hornet Five?'

'Yeah, no worries. Mump downed a couple of hundred flies and now he's on his way home.'

'Good news. What about the others?'

'Don't know. I saw at least five brought down. Search and rescue teams are going in now, so fingers crossed we haven't lost any.'

'Here's hoping. All right, Hornet Four. Stay safe.'

'You too. See you back there.'

As they circled the White House, Sam spotted another hornet skimming across the lawn below.

'Look,' he said. 'Down there. Who's that, do you think?'

'Don't know,' said Skipper. 'Brindle maybe?'

Selecting the all-channels frequency, she pressed transmit.

'Hi,' she said. 'We're currently above the White House and we can see one of you guys down there by the fountain. You want to check in with us – let us know you're OK?'

There was no reply. Sam watched as the hornet turned suddenly and started to climb.

Skipper frowned.

'Strange,' she said as it accelerated up through the sky towards them. She leaned forward and spoke into the intercom again.

'This is Hornet Seven. Pilot, please identify yourself.'

The radio remained silent as the hornet continued on its upward path, getting closer with every passing second.

'I don't like this,' said Skipper. 'It doesn't feel right.'

'Your Excellency,' said Krazni, staring at his target through the screen. 'I have located our friends. Shall I bring them into the parlour for supper?'

There was a moment's pause and then the cracked, painful whisper of his Emperor breathed like a ghost across the airwaves.

'Thank you, Major,' he said. 'I shall look forward to it.'

'What's he *doing*?' asked Sam as the hornet approached them at high speed.

'I don't know,' said Skipper. 'But I don't think I'll stick around to find out.'

She reached forward and cut the motors, folding the hornet's wings so that they spun into freefall just as the other hornet roared into the airspace they had occupied a split second before.

For a few moments there was silence except for the swoosh of air outside the cockpit. Then Skipper fired up the engines again, flipping the hornet onto its back and executing a 360-degree turn that drained the blood from Sam's face.

'Awww, Skipper!' he protested. 'I think I'm gonna be sick.'

'Shut up, you wuss,' said Skipper, banking the hornet round hard to the right. 'Have a look out of your side a minute. Is he still with us?'

Sam swallowed the bile in his throat and looked back through the side of the cockpit.

'No,' he said. 'I think we lost him.' He swallowed again. 'Could we fly straight now?'

Krazni was directly beneath them now, flying in their blind spot.

He knew they couldn't see him.

It had taken him years of planning and hard work to get this far. His careful, patient strategy had paid off; by ruthlessly eliminating those who crossed him, he had quickly risen to become one of the most powerful men in Vermia. Vahlzi was defeated and the human plague was about to be eliminated. And with Martock interested only in an easy life, Krazni knew it wouldn't take much for him to become Odoursin's number one.

Up until now, everything had gone according to plan.

But all of a sudden, things had started to go wrong. First there was the screw-up at the Vahlzian Resistance base.

And now this.

Hearing the girl's voice on the radio he remembered how – as he had escaped from the mountain in the stolen hornet – he had caught sight of her, arm in arm with the boy.

He had no doubt that the pair of them were behind all of this, just as they had been before.

But this time they were going to pay for it with their lives.

And he knew someone very special who was ready and waiting to help them do it.

His face white with fury, he red-lined the wing motors until they screamed into the wind and executed a sharp, fast turn which brought his cockpit level with the rear of their hornet. Then he opened the jaws of his hornet as wide as they would go, pulled full throttle and slammed hard into the back of them.

There was a pop as the sharp jaws punctured the insect's body, followed by a loud crunch as the tail section crumpled like a paper bag.

Skipper squeaked with fright.

'Pull away!' shouted Sam. 'Pull away!'

'I can't!' Skipper shouted back. 'The engines aren't responding!'

Krazni smiled to himself and pushed the stick forward so that the nose tilted downwards at 45 degrees. He throttled up to maximum power and the two hornets went into a steep dive, accelerating towards the ground at lightning speed. He leaned forward and pressed *transmit* on the intercom.

'Hello, my friends,' he said, as the engines whined and the wind roared outside the cockpit. 'This is Major Krazni checking in, as requested. Whereas you, of course, are about to check out. *Permanently.*' He chuckled unpleasantly, pleased with his little joke. Then his voice changed suddenly; became hard and bitter.

'This is where it ends!' he spat. 'So much for your faith, Sam Palmer. So much for your wretched faith!'

Sam gripped the arms of his seat as the ground rushed up to meet them.

He heard Skipper whisper, *'No. Not like this.'*

Shutting his eyes, he waited for the smash as they ploughed into the hard earth.

Somewhere above them, Krazni's engines roared and faded into the distance.

Then, suddenly, they stopped in mid-air.

Everything was eerily silent.

The cockpit began to rock gently back and forth and it reminded Sam of being at a fairground, sitting at the top of a Ferris wheel with the seat swaying in the breeze. It felt incredibly peaceful and for a few moments, he wondered if he was dead. Turning to look at Skipper, he noticed that her face was white.

He reached out and gently touched her arm.

'Hey,' he said, 'it's all right, Skipper. We made it. We survived.'

But Skipper continued to stare straight ahead as though transfixed by what she saw.

'No,' she said quietly. 'It isn't all right, Sam. It isn't all right at all.'

Sam was puzzled.

'What do you mean?'

But Skipper made no reply. Instead she raised her hand and pointed up ahead through the hornet's eyes.

Sam looked up and gasped. The outside of the cockpit appeared to be covered with silver cables that criss-crossed the screen in a glittering net of breath-taking beauty. The cables – although strong – were obviously quite flexible, stretching and wobbling as the hornet continued to sway gently against them.

'What the heck is that?' he asked.

'It's a web,' whispered Skipper, as though she was frightened to speak too loudly for fear of being heard. 'We're caught in a spider's web.'

Sam's heart beat faster as he realised that Krazni must have released his grip at the last moment, hurling them headfirst into the web before flying his hornet clear. As he stared at the sparkling grid that lay like frosted ropes across the screen, Sam became aware of a strange vibration in the cockpit, a faint sound which reminded him of electricity humming along a telegraph wire. He looked at Skipper, and as they listened the hornet began to quiver all over, like a steel track awaiting the arrival of a distant train.

'It's coming,' said Skipper. 'The spider is coming for us.'

Using a secret fabric gap known only to himself, Odoursin had taken the spider deep beneath the city of Vermia and emerged next to a tree on the White House lawn. Against the advice of his generals, he had been determined to oversee the operation himself, to watch the final minutes of humanity tick away here on Earth before retreating back into the darkness as the missiles found their target.

But the operation had failed – only temporarily according to Major Krazni – but still it had left him incandescent with rage. How much longer would he have to wait before this plague of humanity was expunged from the face of the Earth for ever? Gradually, from the mist of confusion, the truth had begun to emerge. It appeared his ambition had been frustrated once again by the same two people who had sabotaged his previous plans: the wretched girl pilot and her friend Sam.

But then came the news he had longed for:

Krazni had found them.

Odoursin peered down through the spider's eyes at the hornet trapped in his web.

At last he could do what no one else seemed capable of doing: he would destroy the pair of them. He remembered the words of the prophecy from the Book of Incantations: *The Great One shall come and Earth shall be saved . . .* When the two of them were gone, nothing would stand between him and the bright new world he had dreamed of throughout the long and desperate years.

The vision would, at last, become reality.

His mind racing at a thousand miles an hour, Sam released his harness and searched for a possible means of escape.

'Give me your CRB!' he shouted in a sudden flash of inspiration. 'Quickly!'

'What? Oh . . .'

Skipper fumbled in her pocket and pulled out the small silver torch, throwing it to him just as the humming stopped and the whole cockpit turned upside down. Sam caught the CRB in mid air and then crashed down heavily onto the control panel. He saw Skipper dangling from her seat above him and then the whole cockpit rolled again and he tumbled around like a doll in a tumble drier, bumping from floor to ceiling to seat and back to floor again.

Moving the levers skilfully with his bony white hands, Odoursin used the spider's front legs to turn the hornet over in the web again and again until its legs and wings were bound fast by the sticky white threads. It gave him a warm feeling to imagine the pair of them in there, consumed by fear. Let them suffer a while longer, he thought. Let them pay for all the years of frustration they had caused him. There was no hurry.

He would kill them when he was good and ready.

And he would do it slowly . . .

Lifting his head from the floor where he lay, Sam saw that the hornet's eyes were now completely covered by the web and the interior of the hornet was gloomy, like the inside of a car when its windscreen is covered in snow.

Skipper released her buckle and dropped down next to him.

They looked at each other as something scraped against the top of the hornet.

'That didn't sound good,' said Skipper.

Seconds later – with a noise like knives ripping through leather – two massive fangs plunged into the cockpit, shattering the control panel and embedding themselves deep in the padded seats. With a cry of alarm, Sam leapt backwards and found himself next to Skipper in the rear of the hornet. As they lay in the semi-darkness there was a sound like water gurgling through pipes and then, with a loud whoosh, a green viscous liquid came gushing out of the hollow fangs, splattering over the seats and control panel before cascading down onto the floor. Immediately the fabric of the seats began to blister and smoke, filling the cockpit with thick, noxious fumes.

As the juices began to gather into a pool and spread towards them like an olive-coloured tide, Skipper grabbed Sam by the arm and pulled him further into the back of the hornet.

'Don't let it touch you!' she shouted at him through the smoke. 'It's digestive fluid – it'll eat away your skin!'

They huddled together against the crates at the back of the hornet and as the spider continued to pump in the vile, putrid-smelling liquid, Sam pulled out the CRB, pointed it in front of him and pressed the button. In a flash of blue, a hole opened up in the floor and the soupy fluids poured through it like floodwater down a drain. He turned round to find that Skipper had pulled the lid off one of the crates and was clutching a small detonator in her left hand.

'I swear,' she said grimly, 'that if we make it out of here, Mump will never want for a drink again in his life.'

Then she snatched the CRB from Sam's hand, opened up a new hole in the floor and pulled a knife from inside her jacket. 'OK,' she said, 'here's what we're gonna do.'

Noticing that green liquid was pouring from the base of the hornet, Odoursin angrily turned off the pumps and clamped the spider's front legs tightly around his prey.

So that was how they wanted to play it . . .

They wanted to prolong the agony.

Well that was fine.

If he couldn't kill them with the poison, he would simply open up the hornet like a tin can and slice them into tiny pieces.

Pulling back on the central lever, Odoursin waited until the spider had reared up on its hind legs as far as it would go, then he switched it into attack mode. Powering forward and down with the whole weight of the spider behind them, the sharp fangs tore into the centre of the hornet and split it down the middle like a ripe peapod.

'Go!' shouted Skipper as the roof ripped open and the spider's poison-coated fangs sliced through the air on either side of them. For a brief second, Sam was unable to move, transfixed by the sight of the white-faced Odoursin clearly visible behind the gleaming eyes of the monstrous spider.

He saw the look of hatred on his face, a look of such bitterness and loathing that he knew he had glimpsed a place of unending horror, a place where love had been extinguished for ever.

Then they pulled the tabs from the detonators, threw their arms around one another and jumped through the hole in the base of the hornet.

It seemed to Sam as though they would fall for ever, the cool air rushing past them and the smell of damp

earth rising up from below. But then, just as it seemed
that they would hit the ground, the strand of web that
Skipper had wrapped around her waist reached the end
of its length and pulled them up with a jolt, leaving them
bouncing gently a couple of metres from the ground.

'OK?' said Skipper.

'OK,' said Sam.

Pulling out her knife, Skipper sliced through the silvery
strand above her head and they fell to the ground with a
thump that knocked the wind out of them. Rolling over
onto his back, Sam saw the spider in the centre of the web
was attacking the hornet with a new ferocity.

Any second now . . .

Using the spider's razor-sharp fangs, Odoursin slashed
the hornet wide open.

*Where had they gone to? He had seen the boy's terrified
eyes, knew he was hiding here somewhere . . . they both were
. . . there was nowhere for them to run to now . . . no escape
. . . yes, oh yes, he would kill them, tear their hearts out,
make them finally see that he was the One, the saviour of
everything, and they would know in their agony that his was
the only way, the only way, the only way . . .*

The detonator's red light blinked faster, faster, faster,
and then went out.

. . . the only way . . .

Sam covered his face as the massive explosion tore
through the hornet and ripped the spider apart in a

maelstrom of smoke and flame, hurling tiny fragments high into the night air.

Something crashed, exploding behind him.

Odoursin's mouth opened in a scream of terror as the explosion howled crimson fury, splitting and vaporising him into a billion flaming atoms.

ahhhhhhh . . .
> *bright bright bright*
>> *so bright*
>>> *so bright*
>>>> *so bright . . .*

Embers fell to the ground like stars from another world, settling and cooling on the dew-covered grass, their fires going out one by one, crumbling, becoming dust . . .

As Sam lowered his hands and felt the warm wind on his face, he saw the flames spread from the heart of the spider's web and watched its delicate strands curl and crumble in the fierce heat. Smoke drifted across the wet grass and the light from the moon momentarily disappeared behind its dark veil.

He felt a small arm slip inside his own and felt Skipper's cheek resting against his shoulder.

'Is that it?' she whispered, as the smoke swirled around them in thick clouds. 'Do you think it's finally over?'

But before he could answer, there was a loud buzzing

of insect wings overhead and as he watched the shape of a huge hornet land on the grass in front of them Sam knew that it would soon be over for ever.

Krazni had finally caught up with them.

Exhausted to the point of near collapse, he summoned the last of his strength and stepped in front of Skipper, spreading his arms wide to protect her.

'Run,' he whispered. 'Run away and don't look back.'

But Skipper just stepped right up beside him and shook her head.

'No,' she said. 'Never.'

And then as they stood together, shoulder to shoulder, waiting for their world to end, the smoke cleared and there – standing beneath the hornet in full uniform – was Commander Firebrand.

Sam stared in awe at the man who had struggled through Vahlzi's darkest hours to come to their aid and said:

'We thought you were Krazni!'

The Commander smiled then, and shook his head.

'No,' he answered. 'Krazni is dead. I have come to take you home.'

Turning slowly, Sam looked over his shoulder and through the gloom he could just make out the charred wreckage of Krazni's hornet smouldering behind him.

Then, as Firebrand walked through the smoke and Skipper ran and flung her arms around him, Sam saw at once that this was a new beginning, and that everything would be different from now on.

Thirty

Seizing the advantage of their air superiority, the Vahlzian hornet squadrons were quick to inflict heavy losses on the enemy robber flies over Vahlzi, and soon the fields and woods around the city were littered with the wreckage of insects that had been torn from the skies.

Once the threat of robber flies had been removed, the hornets moved swiftly to attack Vermian supply lines, leaving its soldiers cut off and surrounded by an army of well-organised Resistance fighters.

Thousands of leaflets were dropped over the city, informing Vermian soldiers of the death of their Emperor and encouraging them to surrender. The leaflets assured them that if they laid down their weapons and gave themselves up, they would be well treated and reunited with their families once the war was over.

Weakened by lack of food and constant air attacks, many soldiers surrendered almost immediately. A handful of troops from the Vermian Special Forces continued to fight fiercely among the ruins for several weeks, but in the end even they were defeated by the newly formed Flea Battalion which, in a daring attack, leapt through the ruins at dawn and blew apart the last of their defences.

For the people of Vahlzi it was a time of renewal; a time for slowly rebuilding the homes and lives that the war had torn apart. The cruel years of Vermian rule had taken their toll, but for the most part their spirits had been bruised, not broken. Like children shut indoors on a summer's day, they had caught glimpses of sunshine and longed for its warmth; now, at last, they were able to walk from the shadows and out into the bright lanes of freedom. Although war against the last remnants of Odoursin's regime still continued to be waged in the streets and underground tunnels of Vermia, the hornets had control of the skies and – with Odoursin gone and the Vermian leadership in disarray – the end was now in sight.

The winter snow was melting, and as the first green shoots pushed their way up through the earth, so a new energy began to stir in the streets and alleyways of Vahlzi. From their shattered houses, their brick-built hovels and their underground shelters, the people came together, a community of survivors working to raise a new city from the dust. Together they shared a vision of a future without tyranny or oppression; a vision of a life where, at last, they could be free.

The Vahlzian airbase which had been destroyed early on in the war was rebuilt upon the site of the original, reconstructed using materials salvaged from the ruins and rubble of the old one. It was designed not only as a home for the hornet squadrons, but also as a centre of excellence where the best young pilots would come and train to be the air aces of the future. When the war ended they would ensure that the people's hard-won freedom would not be easily relinquished.

Standing at the window of her room in the plush, newly built officers' quarters, Skipper looked out at the lights of the city, twinkling in the distance. She watched a large transporter moth take off from the landing zone, bound for the airfields of Vermia which had recently been secured by Vahlzian Special Forces. There was no doubt about it; since they had started using the hornet squadrons to attack Vermian positions in the city, the enemy's resistance had quickly crumbled. They simply had no weapons that could match the overwhelming superiority of the hornets.

And so, generally, life was good and getting better. The feeling was that if things went according to plan, the war would soon be over and an air of optimism now permeated the whole of Vahlzia, a belief that it was safe to look beyond tomorrow, to plan for a future built on the firm foundations of hope and faith.

But Skipper was uneasy. She knew that Sam was unhappy, and she knew why. He had told her yesterday as they sat beneath one of the hornets, drinking coffee and watching the spring sunshine burn off the skirts of mist that covered the lower slopes of the mountains.

'I know we succeeded,' he said. 'We fought for what we believed in and against all the odds, we won. We actually did all the things we set out to do.'

'So . . . that's good then, isn't it?' Skipper had asked. 'We did it, Sam. We made things better. Doesn't that make you happy?'

'Yes, it does,' replied Sam. 'Of course it does. But still . . . I just can't get away from the fact that I've left something behind. That somehow I've let people down. That I've let down the people who need me.'

'You'd never do that, Sam,' said Skipper. 'You'd never let anyone down.'

'Last time I was here,' Sam continued, 'I got back didn't I? I went home to my life on Earth, to my family. But now – now it doesn't feel like it did before. I can't see them. I can't even picture their faces any more. Something's different, and I feel so sad about it. It feels as though something's changed for ever. Skipper, do you think I'll ever get back?'

'I don't know,' she said. 'But maybe something has changed. Perhaps you don't belong there any more, Sam. Perhaps this is your home now.'

'But it doesn't feel like it,' Sam replied. 'It doesn't feel right. I feel like I need to go back and find them, to help them somehow.'

He stared at the distant mountains and Skipper saw that there were tears in his eyes.

'But I don't know how to, Skipper. I don't know how.'

Skipper had said nothing then, partly because she knew that silence was sometimes the only answer, and partly because she did not want to say goodbye.

But now, as she looked at the three coloured moons rising over Vahlzi, she felt a great sadness in her heart, as though she had lost something important too.

Somewhere, far away, something was calling to her.

And so, without quite knowing why, she made her way silently down to the runway where the moonlight threw strange, secret shadows beneath her waiting moth.

It had been a long time, but she remembered the route as though it were yesterday. She flew east for several hours, crossing the open plains and the marshlands of Mazria before turning north-east over Vermia. Several times she was approached by hornet night patrols operating a no-fly zone in the area, but her identification beacon quickly provided the authorisation needed and she was allowed to continue her journey unhindered.

Morning was just breaking as she finally located the fabric gap and flew up into the bright folded clouds, aided by the air currents that rose from the sun-warmed slopes of the eastern mountains. She rode the turbulent air through mysterious corridors woven with streams of silver light until at length she was caught in an irresistible force that sucked her away into a different sky. Pulling back hard on the joystick, she spiralled down from the fabric gap before levelling out once more above the valleys and farms of an English countryside. The sun was rising above the hedgerows and the music of bird-song filled Skipper's ears as she flew the moth along the quiet lanes of the small village, fluttering past field mice and early morning rabbits until at last she came to a large, redbrick Edwardian house.

Sam's house.

In truth, now that she was here she could not remember exactly why she had come, but as she flew across the overgrown garden and saw the little blue slide and the rusted swing, a feeling of longing grew within her that she did not understand.

A 'For Sale' sign stood at an angle in the middle of the lawn, with the word 'Sold' plastered diagonally across it.

Skipper landed on the top of the sign and remembered the first time she had seen Sam here all those years ago, kicking a tennis ball against the garden wall while his mother potted up seedlings and his father dug over the vegetable patch. Unknown to him, she had been piloting a wasp, circling high above as part of a mission to protect him from Vermian forces that were trying to kidnap him. Despite their best efforts, however, the Vermian Empire had succeeded and brought Sam to Aurobon. But then at the end of it all he had returned to Earth again; back to his family and his other life.

So why not this time?

Why was he still in Aurobon?

Determined to find some answers, Skipper flew around the house to try to find another way in, an open window perhaps, or a gap under a door. Finding neither, she searched around for another route and her eyes fell upon the chimney pots at the top of the house. Of course! Pulling back on the joystick she lifted the moth up over the tiles and then as she approached the chimney pot at the far end of the house she put the wings into reverse thrust, hovered briefly, and then dropped down into it.

Applying the air brakes to slow her rate of descent, Skipper kept her eyes fixed on the square of light below her until, a short while later, she emerged into the brightness of a small bedroom.

She flew one circuit of the room to check that all systems were still functioning properly and then brought the moth smoothly in to land on the wooden bedpost. Looking around, she saw that all the bedclothes had been stripped off the bed and the room itself was empty save for several large cardboard boxes, most of which had been sealed up with brown parcel tape.

Staring out through the moth's eyes, she noticed that one of the packing cases was still open on the far side of the room, and lying on the top of it were what appeared to be a handful of photographs. Intrigued, Skipper took off again and flew across the room, skilfully manoeuvring the moth so that it fluttered and hovered just a little way above the box.

Tilting the head of the moth forward, she leaned across the instrument panel and peered out. There in the very middle of the box was a photograph of Sam, smiling and waving at the camera.

There were other photographs too. Sam's mother and father, hand in hand, holding up a fork and a spade and laughing, Sam on his bike and his father standing next to him with a spanner.

She looked down at the other pictures: Sam on a skateboard (she smiled at this), Sam's mother, sitting on a tartan rug in summer, cuddling a small baby, Sam . . . Skipper was surprised by the sudden ache that she felt in her heart as she looked back at the picture of Sam's mother holding the baby.

What was it about this particular picture that affected her so?

She looked across at another photograph – half hidden beneath a flap of cardboard – and saw that it was of a little blonde-haired girl aged about three or four. She was smiling shyly, standing next to a snowman and her coat was buttoned up to her chin.

She was wearing bright yellow mittens and on her feet were a pair of shiny red shoes.

Then Skipper remembered.

'No!' she cried, 'no, no, no, no, no!' And she lifted the moth away out through the chimney pot and up into the blue, blue sky, high above the fields and the valleys and the little farms with their tiny sheep and horses until finally, when the tears blurred her vision and she could no longer see, she came to rest in the long grass that grew tall beside the old stone church.

Stumbling from the moth out into the morning sunshine, she leant against the stalk of a primrose, buried her face in her hands and cried as she had never cried before.

After a time, she became aware that she was not alone. Wiping the tears from her eyes, she looked up and saw that a man was standing a little way away from her, leaning against the churchyard wall that towered high above them both. He seemed to be gazing at something in the distance.

As Skipper watched, he turned to look at her and she saw that it was Salus, Guardian of Worlds. She remembered the last time that she had seen him, and how they had walked together by Lake Orceia.

'Hello, Skipper,' he said.

'Hello,' said Skipper quietly. She wiped her eyes again and realised that the tears were still falling and she could not stop them. 'I'm sorry about this,' she whispered. 'I'm not sure why I *am* crying exactly. Only . . . there was something about those pictures . . . that little girl in the photograph. Who was she?'

'Come with me,' replied Salus, 'and I will try to explain something to you.'

They made their way between the tall stalks of grass until presently they came to a large expanse of white rocks. Skipper sat on one with a flat top and saw how it was embedded with tiny crystals which shone in the sunshine.

'Four years ago, when Sam first walked in Aurobon, his body still lived on Earth. You helped him to find his way home again. In doing so, you bravely sacrificed your own life in Aurobon. But at the moment you were lost, so were you found.'

'Found?' asked Skipper. 'What do you mean?'

'Although she did not know it, Sam's mother had been searching for you for many years. You were the child that she longed for and at that time great forces were at work. After your selfless sacrifice, you were reborn as her child on Earth. So you see, the little girl in the photograph is you.'

'But I don't understand,' said Skipper. 'If I lived on Earth, why didn't I remember until now? Why does Sam remember his life here so much better than I do?'

'Because,' Salus replied, 'he had been a child of Earth for much longer. When you are born, it takes many years to grow and become one with a new world. In many ways you were still closer to the life you had left behind in Aurobon. That is why you came back to it more easily when the Earthstone called to you.'

'What happened?' asked Skipper. 'Please tell me. I need to know.'

'The Vermian Empire cast its shadow across Aurobon,' said Salus. 'Vahlzi lay in ruins and the Foundation Stone was shattered. In his despair, Commander Firebrand took the Earthstone and flung it into Lake Orceia. And as it sank into those deep waters, the Earthstone called across the worlds to those it knew could save it.'

'You mean us?' asked Skipper.

'Yes,' said Salus.

And it was then that she remembered what had happened.

The light failing on a winter's afternoon. She was four
years old, dressed in a warm coat and yellow mittens.
She ran down the winding path through the trees and
watched her little red shoes make tiny footprints in the
snow.

'Not too far, sweetheart,' her mother called behind
her.

A blue butterfly, beautiful and strange in the cold, still
air. Leaving the path, she followed it down through the
bushes and out across the silver, ice-covered lake where
the snow swirled and danced all around her.

She knelt down and reached out her hand. Behind
her, footsteps on the ice, people calling to her. Her mother and father and her brother. She looked up and waved
to them, not understanding the fear on their faces.

'Look!' she cried. 'See!'

But just as they reached her, the ice cracked and the
butterfly flew away.

She was falling, falling down into the cold, endless
blackness and away for ever from the light that was fading somewhere far above her.

Skipper felt the tears welling up in her eyes.

'I had a mother and father,' she whispered. 'I was part
of a family.' She swallowed and her throat was swollen
with sorrow. 'It was my fault they died, wasn't it? They
all died because of me.'

'No,' said Salus and he took her by the hand. 'It was

time, that is all. They loved you very much,' he added.

'What does it matter?' sobbed Skipper. 'None of it matters any more. Not love, not anything. Everything is lost.'

'No, child,' said Salus gently. 'Just because something changes, it does not mean that it is lost. Like melting snow, it simply becomes something else.'

'But I am so sad,' said Skipper. 'I do not know if I can bear it any more.'

'Sometimes,' said Salus. 'we must shed our skin in order to grow. It is always painful.'

Skipper looked up from where she sat and noticed for the first time that beyond the white rocks that surrounded them was an enormous grey stone that towered high into the air above them. She stared at the huge letters that had been carved into it, stared at them for a long time until the tears ran down her face and she could no longer read the words.

She turned to Salus and said, 'Please – will you help me forget?'

Salus put his hands upon the top of her head and said, 'Little one, although you are stronger and wiser than most, you will forget this time, just as you have forgotten others before it. But know this: that love cannot be destroyed. The things that matter will stay with you always.'

As Skipper flew away across the fields, the sun broke through the clouds and bathed the land in a warm, yellow light. Here and there, clumps of snowdrops hung their heads while yellow crocus buds pushed their way up through the earth to greet the spring.

In a corner of the churchyard, a new headstone stood above a rectangle of white stones, as yet untarnished by the elements or the passing of time. It read:

Jack Palmer
1968–2005

Sally Palmer
1970–2005

Samuel Palmer
1991–2005

Poppy Palmer
2001–2005

fell through the ice
31st December 2005

Suffer little children to come unto me

Beyond the wall, Skipper flew away across the fields into clouds that drew her in and enfolded her, and carried her away from the world for ever.

Thirty-one

Sam dreamed of falling through water. He saw his mother and father fighting for breath below him, struggling to reach the circle of light that grew pale and dim above. But they were too far away, too deep for him to reach and soon he lost sight of them in the darkness. A red shoe floated past him and in the dim light he could make out a smaller figure, silently stretching out its hands towards him.

In desperation, Sam kicked his legs and dived deeper, deeper until at last he found her, still and unmoving in the freezing waters. Grabbing her hand, he looked around but could no longer see the surface. Then he saw a blue light shining above him and pulled his little sister towards it. The light grew and spread and suddenly he burst through the surface and found himself in a lake, surrounded by mountains. Gasping for breath, he dragged her towards a pool beneath a waterfall. Then everything went black.

In his dream, when he opened his eyes again, he saw ice crystals frozen on a pebble; clouds heavy with snow hung from a winter sky above him and he noticed a fire burning further along the shore. Shivering, he began to walk towards it.

As he drew nearer to the fire, he noticed a man dressed in a thick woollen robe standing next to it. His long, dark hair was woven with coloured threads and Sam recognised him as Salus.

'I remember you,' said Sam. 'You were here with me before. You were here at the beginning.'

'Yes,' said Salus.

Sam looked at the empty shoreline.

'Where are they?' he asked. 'What happened to my family?'

Salus was silent for a while. Then he said: 'Look around you, Sam. What do you see?'

Sam looked around and saw snow on the mountains, and trees, and the shining lake.

'I see water, mountains and trees,' he answered. 'And I see snow.'

Salus nodded. 'The snow is already melting, I think. One day soon it will all be gone. And in years to come, the trees too will have disappeared. They will lie buried and forgotten in the darkness beneath the earth. The days of sunlight in which they grew will have passed from all memory. Do you see?'

'Yes,' said Sam. 'But I don't know what it has to do with me.'

Salus reached into his robe and took out a shiny black object which he held up in the firelight. 'Do you know what this is?' he asked.

Sam stared at it for a moment.

'It's coal,' he said.

'You are right, Sam. It is a lump of coal. At least, that is what we call it now. But it is also what the trees became. The trees that grew here millions of years ago.'

He tossed it to Sam who caught it in one hand.

'Look at it. A piece of inert rock, buried beneath the ground and forgotten. Until one day, someone came and dug it up again. Brought it out of the darkness and into the light.'

Salus pushed another piece of wood into the fire and then turned back to look at Sam. 'Close your eyes for a minute, Sam,' he said, 'and think of a summer's day.'

Sam shut his eyes. He felt the warmth of the fire and imagined the sun shining down upon him.

'Millions of years ago there would have been just such a summer's day,' Salus went on. 'The sunshine warmed the earth and the leaves on the trees. But then the sun set and the day was finally over. Lost for ever, one might think.'

Sam opened his eyes as Salus threw the lump of coal into the fire. He watched as a bright yellow flame leapt from its heart and began to burn fiercely, rising and dancing in the centre of the fire.

Salus turned to him and smiled.

'Look,' he said, 'the sunshine is back.'

Sam gazed out across the water and saw the sky's reflection, and the trees and mountains locked beneath its steely surface. It was like staring through a window at a world that could never be reached.

'I'm not going back am I?' he asked.

'No, my child,' said Salus. 'Not this time.'

And as Sam wept, Salus put his arms around him and said, 'But you saved the one who once gave her life to save yours. And in time, your mother and father will find their way to different shores.'

Later, as they walked together beside the lake, Sam said, 'You were here with me at the beginning of things, and now you are here at the end of them.'

And Salus said simply, 'But the end is also the beginning.'

Thirty-two

With a whole fortnight's leave stretching ahead of them, Sam and Skipper had set off the previous day on the first leg of their camping trip, pitching the tent on the side of the mountain and falling asleep to the sound of the wind in the pines. Now it was early morning and the inside of the tent was already baking; Sam could feel the sunlight warm on his face as it filtered through the brown canvas. Outside, Skipper was bustling about and he could hear the sound of wood crackling on a fire. Crawling from his sleeping bag, he stumbled out into the sunshine and watched her pour a pan of boiling water into two enamel mugs.

'Smells interesting,' he said. 'Bit like old socks.'

'Don't knock it 'til you've tried it, Samuel,' said Skipper. 'It's acorn coffee – one of my specialities.'

'Yum,' said Sam without enthusiasm. 'Can't wait.'

'Trust me. You'll love it.'

Skipper had used a thin layer of coal as a base and then

constructed a neat pyramid of wooden sticks above it. Flames licked around the wood and the coals glowed red beneath, providing a steady heat with which to boil the water.

Skipper handed him a mug and sat down next to him. She flicked a small stone and Sam watched it bounce a couple of times on the rocks before disappearing over the edge of the mountain. He thought of all the dark times in the past when he had dreamed of this fishing trip, of how it had all seemed so distant and unattainable back then.

Now, in just a few hours' time, they would meet the others at Lake Orceia and the dream would become real.

'Quite a view isn't it?'

Sam looked at the distant towers of Vahlzi rising up through strands of early morning mist and, beyond the plains, the vast green forests of the south stretching away as far as the eye could see.

'It's beautiful,' he said. 'You know, I feel as though I've never really looked before. As though I'm seeing it all for the first time.'

Skipper sipped her coffee thoughtfully.

'You seem different,' she said after a while.

Sam frowned. 'Different? How?'

'You seem happier,' said Skipper. She put her hand on his arm. 'I'm really glad, Sam. You deserve to be happy. After all, we made it back, didn't we? We did what we had to do and we made it home again.'

Sam thought of his dream then, of the cold lake and

the mountains, and although he could no longer remember it clearly, he knew that Skipper was right.

This was where he belonged.

This was his home.

'Do you ever wonder what happened to us in those four years, Skipper?' he asked as they watched the sun burn away the morning mist, leaving little wisps of white cloud drifting high above the plains.

'I used to,' said Skipper, whose memory of her time on Earth had already faded. 'I used to think perhaps it was the Olumnus using their ancient powers to keep us safe somewhere until Aurobon needed us. But the truth is, I just don't know.'

'Does it ever bother you?'

Skipper shook her head.

'Not any more. I've come to the conclusion that the world has far more magic in it than we realise. But most of the time it's just disguised as every day things, hidden away beneath the surface, and there's not much point looking for it. The way I see it, you've just got to live the best way you can, and one day, when you least expect it, the magic will find you.'

Sam watched a yellow flame leap up from a piece of coal, dancing into the heart of the fire. He thought of the ancient sunshine, locked away in its dark heart until the fire set it free again.

He looked at Skipper and smiled.

'I think it's found me already,' he said.

As they climbed up the stony path and disappeared into the trees, the place where they had been was silent once more; silent except for the sound of water trickling over the stones as the last of the snow melted and ran down the steep mountainside into the valley.

Here the water joined with other streams and tributaries, all of them merging and coming together until at last they were a single shining river, moving slowly across the plains toward the sea which lay hidden and endless, somewhere beyond the horizon.

Acknowledgements

Love & thanks to Tory, Tim & Daisy, my editor Julia
Wells, my agent Ed Jaspers, all the good people of Faber
and the Conville & Walsh Massive.

Steve Voake